The
Alchemy
of
Time

The Alchemy of Time

of

SALLY GALLOT-REEVES

Behind the Open Door: The Alchemy of Time
Copyright @ 2025 Sally Gallot- Reeves

Interior Image Credit:
Ian Gonzales
gonzalesian50@gmail.com

ISBN: 979-8-89694-325-9 - Paperback
ISBN: 979-8-89694-324-2 - Ebook

Contents

To the Angels and Guides
surrounding me in love,
And all those who come
as spiritual companions
uplifting me, especially
in the vessel of a dog.

Thank You,
I am forever grateful…

CHAPTER 1

Closing Up for Winter

"But why do we need to do it?" Cassie asked her father as they walked across the yard to the potting shed.

"It's December now, Cassie, and snow's coming," Daddy said as he continued to walk. "We have to get ready."

"But why? The potting shed won't fall down."

"Yes, the shed won't fall down. But the snow will block the gate and doors."

"I can help shovel it open," Cassie said as she looked at the ornate iron fence and gate that surrounded the shed.

"That's a great offer, Sunshine, but the snow can get very deep. The potting shed will be here in the spring for you to play in again."

Cassie watched her father open the latch on the gate by lifting the gardening trowel from behind the small metal hand rake. "Ladies first."

Cassie entered and sat on the ground beside the flower garden that she and Nanny Phe had planted last summer. "Hello fairies," she said as she took off her shoes and socks.

"See how all the plants have died off, Cassie? They are ready to sleep through winter so they can grow again. The potting shed needs to rest too."

"The fairies have gone inside. The roots protect them."

"It's winter. Put your shoes and socks back on," Daddy said.

"I will. Just a minute. I have to stand up and feel the earth."

"Really quickly," Daddy said, turning towards the stone shed.

"But where can Poppy and I play school, Daddy? We need to be out here to help Patrik too."

"Be that as it may, Cassie, it's too cold and snowy to be out here in the winter."

"We could build a fire in the fireplace. That would keep us warm."

"No fires. You are not old enough for fires."

"But how will Patrik and I get to the magic tree?"

Daddy turned and smiled at Cassie. "I am very sure that Patrik, your imaginary dog friend, has the ability to go anywhere he wants to. I don't want you down by the tree in winter. It's too icy and dangerous."

Cassie stood a moment, her eyes welling up with tears. "Patrik is real, Daddy! Can we go say goodbye to the tree then?"

Daddy took a deep breath as he leaned down and faced her. "Yes. Reluctantly, yes, we can go say goodbye to the tree."

Cassie nodded. "Patrik says to tell you he likes that idea."

"And I'm delighted that he does," Daddy said as he shook his head. "As always, things go easier with Patrik's approval. Come on, let's go over and open up the potting shed doors."

Cassie walked over to the shed and knelt down in front of two carved statues that stood on the granite steps. She patted their heads and touched the objects they held in their hands.

"Maybe we should put these inside the shed for the winter," Daddy said as he picked up one of the gnome statues and began thoroughly looking it over.

"They need to be out in the sun to use my crystals," Cassie said. "We have to leave them outside."

"But you won't be coming over here after today, Cassie."

"I still have the crystals from the river in the elemental kingdom," she said, placing one between the petals of the flower in one of the gnome's hands. "They send energy."

"Oh, does Patrik tell you that too?"

3

"No Daddy, remember? Archangel Uriel told me. The crystals send energy to Akaleia."

"And who was she again? I forget sometimes."

"Akaleia is the High Priestess of Lemuria," Cassie said. "Queen Epona lives in the Elemental Kingdom with Archangel Uriel. She is the Queen of all the fairies and all those in our garden."

"Yes, I remember that story now." Daddy chuckled as he turned the knob on the right-hand door and slowly opened it. He then lifted one of the gnome statues and positioned it against the door so that it couldn't close. "I remember this door too, Cassie. Whooshing wind. Tricky doors."

The afternoon sun filtered through the side windows and dimly lit the room. A wooden table and two chairs were neatly placed inside with some paper, pencils, and chalk. The small stone fireplace in the back corner provided a solid support for the roof and the eaves that encircled the entire room.

"Remember this, Cassie? When I climbed up on the table and found that old leather satchel behind the fireplace?"

"It has my light language in it, my letters."

"I know. That's what you told us."

"Can I have it back now? Is it still in your office?"

"Ah, yeah, somewhere," Daddy said, turning his head away.

"No Daddy, I need to see them. I am supposed to use them to help others."

"How are you going to use them? They are squiggles and marks, not letters."

"I know what they mean. I know what they are supposed to be used for. I am supposed to help Patrik build a bridge."

"Where is the bridge?"

"It's from the elemental kingdom to Lemuria. But then I think there's another bridge too."

"Cassie, you've told me this before, and it makes no sense to me. Until we know more about those papers and Dr. Blake's work, I'm not comfortable having you, or anyone, look more at them."

"Dr. Blake lived here with Patrik. Patrik knows too."

"If that's true Cassie, that was a very, very long time ago. Right now, let's walk down to say goodbye to that tree." Daddy moved towards the back of the room and the small door that led to the woods.

Cassie reached out and gently touched the handle on the little back door. "Hello fairies," she said, rubbing her hand up and down along the metal.

"I still think they are just irregular bumps. I don't see anything."

"They are smaller now, Daddy. Like the fairies in the garden. They have to go under too."

"Under what? Wait, never mind. I won't understand anyway."

Daddy turned the wooden handle and swung the half door to the right, lifting the rod hanging on the wall to secure it open. "I think we're good now. Ladies first. Wait up top for me."

Cassie giggled at being called a lady as she easily walked through the opening and waited for her father to come through.

Daddy groaned as he bent down on one knee, twisted at his waist, and maneuvered his head through the opening. "This isn't getting any easier, Cassie. Ask Patrik to make the door bigger will you?"

"Patrik's not here right now, Daddy. He's very busy with his work."

"But doesn't he talk to you when he's not here?"

"Yes." Cassie nodded.

"Well of course he does! Grab my hand, the stairs are a little icy in spots."

Cassie took her father's hand, and they began to slowly descend the granite stairs to the forest floor.

"I can see it!" Cassie exclaimed as she hurried down the rest of the way by herself.

"Be careful!" Daddy warned as he stepped sideways to avoid clumps of ice.

Cassie stood at the bottom of the stairs and looked up, trying to see to the top of the tree before her. "Magic Tree," she said out loud.

"Take a minute to say goodbye, and we'll go back up. It's getting darker with the sun lowering."

Cassie walked over to the tree and moved her hands across the bark. "This is where the opening is to the magic cave."

"Uh, yeah. What was that crazy chant you told us Patrik said to open the door?"

Cassie turned and smiled at her father, then began to run around the trunk of the tree. "Tree of Life, Worlds Unite!"

"Cassie, stop! Don't run down here."

"Tree of Life, Worlds Unite! Tree of Life, Worlds Unite!" she shouted as she stood in one place.

"I'm not going to say it. You remember what happened to Uncle Peter."

"I already said it, Daddy. It knows."

Daddy's face stiffened. "Let's go back up now, Cassie. Let's go."

"I need to say one more thing," pleaded Cassie.

"Make it quick. The tree will still be here in the spring."

Cassie closed her eyes and began her mind wishes. *Please protect Patrik. Please always be open so we can travel together and come back."*

When Cassie opened her eyes, Daddy had already moved towards the stairs.

"Done?" he asked. "Let's go up."

The sun was already setting behind the magic tree and shadowing the stairs as they climbed.

"Want my hand?" Daddy offered as Cassie tiptoed in front of him.

"I'm good, Daddy. They're helping me."

"Patrik's here?"

"No Daddy, remember? Patrik's working. The fairies are helping."

"I thought you said they went under."

"They can be under on any level they want to," Cassie said. "The sky says we are under."

"Are you telling me we are also under because the sky is above us?"

"Yes. We are under some things, and over others."

"I don't get it. Let's get going. It's going to be dark soon."

6

At the top of the stairs Cassie turned one last time towards the magic tree. "Goodbye for winter magic tree. I'll miss you."

"And that's a wrap. In you go."

Cassie walked through the open door as Daddy bent down again and followed behind her.

"I can lift the rod up," Cassie offered as she moved over to one side.

"Cassie, wait! Don't do that yet."

"It's okay. It won't whoosh."

"How do you know that?"

"It only whooshes when you don't believe."

Daddy inched his way through the door, stood up straight, and stretched his arms. "Not as young as I used to be."

Cassie handed the rod over to her dad who closed the little door, turned the knob, and carefully placed the rod across the door and handle to lock it tight.

"One down," he said as he walked back across the room to the table. "Cassie, do you want to bring these inside the house?" He pointed to the paper and pencils.

"Can I put them in my room? Poppy and I could play school in my room."

"Sure, we can do that. I don't think Mommy will mind. What about the chalkboard Nanny Phe gave you? Do you want to bring that in?"

Cassie stood in front of the chalkboard, "No, I want to write on it."

"Hurry up, please."

Cassie picked up a piece of chalk and began to write slowly and carefully across the board.

"Is that the Light Language letters again?"

"Yes."

Daddy sighed as he looked at the squiggly lines on the board, "Okay, I'll buy in. What does it say?"

Cassie's eyes glistened. "It says talk to me. It means I still hear you."

"Come on outside. Let's lock up the doors."

Once outside, Daddy reached into his back pocket and pulled out two bungee cords. "I am going to tie these around the doorknobs so when the storms come, and the winds blow, the doors won't be jarred open."

"Patrik can open them."

He lifted the gnome statues, carefully placing them in their spots on the granite step in front of the doors. "Tell Patrik he better not open them."

"Okay, Daddy. I will," Cassie said as she pranced out ahead of him singing, "Out through the doors, out through the garden, sleep well little fairies. Bye for now."

Daddy followed Cassie and secured the iron gate, taking a final look at the shed. "Have a good winter," he said under his breath, "no shenanigans out here."

"C'mon, Daddy," Cassie yelled. "The horses are out!"

Daddy turned to see Cassie climbing their next-door neighbor's fence to get closer to their palomino horses, Luna and Kai.

"Hey Jack," Millie greeted him from the paddock, "How are things going?"

"Good!" Jack said reaching out to pat Kai's nose. "Cassie and I just finished closing up the potting shed for winter."

"It is that time of year, for sure. Mike and I have one more chore to do to finish up the projects in the barn. We are hoping to get them done by this weekend, because you know, at some point it's going to snow."

"Poppy and I can't go out there anymore," Cassie sighed hanging her head.

"Not until spring," Daddy replied. "Come spring when the snow melts and it's warmer, you can go back out to the shed."

"It's hard to make changes for winter, isn't it, Cassie?" Millie asked. "Most days I won't be able to ride Luna or Kai."

"Does is get too cold for them?" Jack asked. "It gets below freezing fairly often."

"Yes, although if they are out here in the paddock, I can put a blanket on them. It's mostly the ice on the roads, and the snow on the trails gets too deep."

"I have to be really careful with Ned, too," Daddy said. "We don't get much walking done in the winter."

"How is that beautiful old black lab?" Mille asked. "I haven't seen him out for a while."

"He's a little slow getting up, actually."

"He likes to lick my face!" Cassie beamed. "And play with Patrik."

"Ah, yes. Patrik. We all like to play with Patrik!" Millie laughed. "Oh, sorry, Jack, I can get carried away. I just think he's really cute."

"You don't have to live with him."

"Very true, very true. I see Twirla put lights and a wreath out today," Millie added as she looked across the street to their neighbor's house. "Mike and I want to get some decorations up this weekend on our house too. We already got both businesses done."

"I saw that driving through town on my way home from work. Your veterinarian office and Mike's hardware store are both very festive."

"Mike has all the holiday decorating stuff in his outdoor gardening section. You should stop in."

"It's on my list. Cassie, maybe you would like to come with me Saturday and get some wreaths and garland for the porch."

"Can we go after dance class?" Cassie asked. "Can Poppy come too?"

"I forgot about dance class, but yes, we can go after that. We'll ask Mom and Twirla."

Millie turned to face her horses. "Nice to see you guys," she said. "I need to get this pair in the barn and fed before dark."

"C'mon, Cassie," Daddy exclaimed reaching his hand out to her. "Goodnight, Millie. Tell Mike I said hello."

"Will do. Let's get together sometime over the holidays, too."

"Where have you two been?" Mommy asked as they came through the back door and into the kitchen.

"Catching up with Millie after we finished closing up the shed for winter."

"And I patted Luna and Kai!" Cassie said, smiling.

"How's supper coming, do you want any help, Connie?"

"It's a beef stew, and we're almost done," Mommy answered, stirring the pot. "Ivy and Jim brought over some Christmas greenery today from their gardens. They're so sweet. Some boxwood and holly. It's on the front porch. It looks so green and bright!"

"That's really nice of them. We're so lucky to have such nice neighbors," Daddy said. "I want to make a plan for the weekend so I can finish the outside decorating. I'd like to get a Christmas tree, too."

"Daddy said Poppy and I could go with him to get decorations at Mr. Mike's store." Cassie beamed. "After dance class."

"Well good for him!" Mommy answered with a smile. "And that will give me some free time for some shopping on my own."

"Yeah, we need to finalize the gift plan. I have another idea I've been working on, too."

"Great," Mommy said. "And your mom called with some ideas."

"Hey, Cassie," Daddy said turning towards her, "go on up and tell Mandy dinner's almost ready, will you?"

"Okay Daddy," Cassie said, skipping towards the stairs. "I will."

"So, what are you thinking, Jack?" Mommy asked while Cassie lingered in the hallway. "Cassie has already asked Santa for a bike like Poppy. That's a big gift."

"Buttoning up the shed for winter was hard for Cassie. She's been stalling for a few weeks now before we could finally do it. She even had us go down to the magic tree to say goodbye to it for the winter."

"Don't be ridiculous. That's ridiculous."

"It is what it is. I'm making Cassie something she can play with over the winter. We can get some dolls, small dolls, and a dog for it. You know, a Patrik."

Mommy groaned. "I sort of like the idea, and maybe it will stop her from whining all the time to go out to the potting shed."

"Yes, my thoughts exactly! I started building it out in my work shed before Thanksgiving. My Dad and Mike are going to help me with the finishing touches."

"Okay, that sounds good, but time is ticking to Christmas. So, Cassie's all set. Mandy wants clothes and a new cell phone."

"A new phone? Ah, nix that. She has restricted use of her phone now, and until she gets that failing grade in math to come up, there's no new phone."

"She's trying, Jack. And she already got that warning from the school that clearly made her take notice. She's afraid she'll get kicked off the cheering squad."

"And she might!" Daddy said. "They are very strict about that."

"Do you think she needs a tutor?"

"Maybe. I don't know. She needs to get her homework done, I can tell you that, and study for tests."

"We already limited her phone and social media time."

"And I am hopeful," Daddy said, "that it has made a positive difference."

"Mandy," Cassie called out as she came into her older sister's bedroom, "supper's almost ready."

"Stay out. I'm on the phone," Mandy answered, laying on her bed surrounded by books and bed pillows.

"Are you talking to Mark?" Cassie smiled as she wiggled back and forth.

"None of your business!" Mandy shouted. "And next time knock."

"None of your beeswax," Cassie giggled. "I know anyway."

"Get out!" Mandy yelled throwing a pillow at Cassie. "You don't know anything!"

Cassie slowly walked out of Mandy's room still listening to her sister's conversation.

"Close the door Cassie," Mandy said. "Close it!"

Cassie closed the door behind her and walked down the hall toward her bedroom. The door was open, and she thought she heard Patrik barking. "Patrik!" she called out, "Are you here?"

Her room looked empty, and she raced to her closet. "Patrik? Are you back here?"

The quilt that Nanny Phe had made for her lay on the closet floor, covered with reading books. The little door that opened to the eaves was ajar. Cassie knelt before the door and put her head into the opening. "Patrik? Patrik, are you here?"

Cassie could hear Patrik's muffled barking in the distance. "Why don't you come to me?" she asked. "I miss you."

Patrik's barking got louder, but not closer, and Cassie remembered when she first met him at Mr. Mike's hardware store. She learned to hear him speak through her mind's energy.

Are you trapped again, Patrik? Cassie asked through her mind's eye.

In the tree, Patrik replied. *The tree is locked. You have to open it the way I have shown you. You must use a crystal and surround the tree three times saying the magic words.*

Cassie ran to her bedside table and took out a folded tissue from the drawer. She carefully unwrapped it to reveal the crystal rock she had been given from Queen Epona. Holding it in her hands, she felt the tingling warmth of its energy rise up through her fingers.

I'm coming, Patrik. I'm coming to get you.

Cassie ran down the stairs and out into the kitchen.

"Daddy, we have to go get Patrik. You have to come quick!"

"What? What are you talking about?"

"Patrik! He's in the tree. He can't get out!" Cassie said. "It's locked!"

"Hold on, slow down," Daddy said. "Why do you think that?"

"Patrik was barking in my closet. He told me."

Mommy walked over from the stove and stood in front of Cassie. "Supper is almost ready. No Patrik games tonight."

"Please, Daddy," Cassie pleaded as she began to cry. "We just have to go. We can be quick."

Daddy looked back at Mommy, and then at Cassie's pleading face. "Put on your coat. I'll get the search light."

Mommy pursed her lips and shook her head. "Jack, you promote this. You make it worse."

"I promote peace and quiet for the rest of the night," Daddy said. "For you too."

Daddy flipped the backyard spotlights on and followed Cassie out the back door. He could see her running ahead of him, silhouetted by the lights from the house. "Cassie, wait for me!" he called shining the searchlight ahead of them.

Cassie ignored her father's request and reached the gate. She lifted the trowel from the rake, quickly pulled the gate to the side, and ran up to the doors of the potting shed.

"I said wait," Daddy said. "Stop."

"I have to hurry," Cassie said as she quickly patted each statue on its head, then touched the orb one held and the flower the other held. She placed the crystal from her pocket between the petals of the flower and lifted it safely to the ground.

"Is that necessary"? Daddy asked.

"Yes, Daddy."

Daddy opened the right front door and placed the other gnome statue in front of it to keep it open.

"Be careful," he said, shining the flashlight inside the shed. "It's dark."

Cassie walked to the back door and began to lift the rod. "We have to go to the tree," she said solemnly. "He's there."

Daddy groaned as he opened the little door in the back of the shed and swung it over. "Rod," he said holding out his hand to Cassie. "Wait for me, and no fooling around," he added sternly.

Cassie handed the rod to Daddy, who secured it to the keep the little door open.

"Thank you for waiting. You can go through now."

Cassie walked through the opening while Daddy bent down and angled under the door frame.

He stood up and pointed the search light ahead of them, "Hold my hand and watch the steps."

Cassie took Daddy's hand, and they proceeded slowly, carefully walking down the steps.

"We're here now Cassie. There's no Patrik."

"I have to go around the tree. You wouldn't let me do that before. Three times around while I say the magic words."

"Go very, very slowly. I'll walk with you and shine the light for you."

Cassie walked to the tree and placed her palms on the bark. She could sense the energy rising up from the earth and connecting with the crystal energy in the gnome's hand. She took a deep breath and began to walk around the base of the tree. "Tree of Light, World's Unite!" she yelled. "Tree of Light, Worlds Unite! Tree of Light, Worlds Unite!"

"I think we're done now," Daddy said softly.

"I have to go all the way around the tree three times." Cassie slowly encircled the tree saying the magic words until she had completed three rotations. "Patrik's not here yet," she sighed.

But we are done, Cassie. You've done what you know how to do. Mommy has dinner ready. It's time to go back."

Cassie lowered her head and walked to the steps.

"I'm sure Patrik will be okay," Daddy said reassuringly.

"He said he needed my help," Cassie said as she slowly trudged up the stone steps, pausing several times to turn back and look at the tree. *Please come to me, Patrik.*

At the top of the stairs, they both stopped. "Go ahead through," Daddy said motioning to the small door, "I'll be right behind you."

When Cassie was all the way through the opening, Daddy grabbed the door frame to propel himself through. His knees hit the floor, and he slid in the rest of the way. "Ugh!" he yelled feeling the wind begin to churn up his back, "Cassie! Get down," he yelled, pulling his daughter down beside him.

WHOOSH! WHOOSH! WHOOSH!

The wind blew through the shed, scattering the chairs. "Patrik, you're back!" Cassie squealed. "I knew you would come back!"

Daddy stood up and ran his fingers through his hair.

"Daddy, Patrik's free! He's back!" she said joyfully.

"I know that's what you believe honey. I do. Let's lock the doors and close up the shed again. We need to get back to the house."

"Wonderful!" Mommy greeted them as they came through the kitchen door. "Can we finally sit down and eat supper now?"

"Go wash your hands, Cassie, and come right back," Daddy said as he went to the kitchen sink, and she headed for the bathroom in the back hallway.

"I assume everything was taken care of out there, right Jack?" Mommy asked. "No more trouble tonight, right?"

"Cassie says Patrik is back if that's what you mean. And we have once again unleashed the whooshing winds from the magic tree. They blew through the potting shed and knocked everything over."

Cassie came back into the kitchen and saw her Mommy staring at her father.,

"Patrik's back!" Cassie said excitedly. "I knew we could help him."

"I want you to eat your supper Cassie. No more talk about Patrik," Mother said sternly. "Patrik's not allowed at the table."

"It's okay, Mommy, Patrik's had a big day. He's gone upstairs to take a nap on my bed."

After dinner, Cassie asked if she could go up to her room to spend time with Patrik.

"I guess so," Mommy said. "We'll come say goodnight later, when it's bedtime."

"Okay, Mommy," Cassie said from the stairway as she shouted, "Patrik, I'm coming!"

"Jack, I don't want all this Patrik foolishness at Christmas," complained Mommy. "Cassie will disrupt everything."

"Well let's see how it goes. He's just arrived, and there's still plenty of time for him to adopt good behavior. But yes, I'll keep an eye out for any unwanted activity."

Patrik, Patrik. Where are you? Cassie called out.

Cassie, come over to the closet.

Why are you in here? Cassie asked as Patrik lay on her quilt.

She sat down beside Patrik in the closet and began to pat his fur.

I'm so glad you're back. Are you all done with your work?

No. Not all done, but Archangel Uriel and Queen Epona have given me new information that will help us connect with Akaleia in Lemuria. I

15

brought back crystals for you from the Elemental Kingdom, he conveyed as he placed a group of crystals on her quilt.

How long have you known the Elemental Kingdom?

Patrik sighed and moved closer to Cassie so that his head lay in her lap. *This is our home now, Cassie, in Pine Cove. My home again with you. Even though we can travel between dimensions to different worlds and travel through time. My home is with you for all of our lifetimes.*

I love you Patrik, Cassie whispered.

We were both originally part of the Lemuria colony, Cassie. We came from star planets to bring a fuller life to Earth, the life that we were accustomed to experiencing. A life of love. I then came from Lemuria to the Elemental Kingdom.

Did we come from Cassiopeia? My star planet? Cassie asked. *Why don't I remember Lemuria? When you are in physical form it is hard to remember your past,* Patrik answered. *Your heightened intuitional and telepathic abilities, however, are your connections to that life.*

Sometimes I have dreams, Cassie replied, a*nd I think I remember things.*

You and I are meant to come together again and work for the highest good of all.

Cassie was quiet and began to think about a life beyond the life she knew. *Like my dreams,* she said.

Not a dream, Cassie. You are able to see reality in a different form.

Like the Elemental Kingdom? Cassie asked.

Yes. The Elemental Kingdom of Earth is ruled by Archangel Uriel. He is the guardian of the earth, and he has helpers. The gnomes are his primary helpers.

Cassie nodded. *Nanny Phe said the gnome statues are made of basanite.*

Yes, they are. The gnomes worked with Dr. Blake to mine basanite for his experiments.

Is that what Dr. Blake used to create his experiments?

Yes, basanite contains the crystals of transformation. The beings of the Elemental Kingdom work primarily with mindful energy. Thoughts are transformed into physical existence through the crystals. Dr Blake kept records of his work for others to follow.

The satchel, Cassie said, *and the Light Language. They are his directions.*

Yes. They are very important papers. They must be kept safe and protected.

Daddy says so, too. And Mommy isn't happy when Nanny Phe talks about a paper that was written at the university about Dr. Blake and our property. She sounds afraid.

We never have to fear the truth, Cassie.

I think she thinks someone would want to steal the papers. That's why they hid them in daddy's office.

"Cassie?" Daddy asked opening her closet door. "Are you doing your writing?"

"Patrik and I are talking. He is telling me about the Elemental Kingdom."

"Okay, honey. It's time for pajamas and bed. Can you wash your face and hands and brush your teeth?"

"Yes. Patrik will get into my bed."

"Sure, that's fine. I'll be back in a few minutes."

CHAPTER 2

Lights, Ribbons, Magic!

Patrik awoke from the same dream that had haunted his subconscious mind for hundreds of years. He was lying on the ground in the potting shed garden next to his master, Dr Edmond Blake. Smoke permeated the air as flames rose across the yard, engulfing the barn and the outbuildings. The air was hot and hard to breathe, and red sparks floated down upon both of them. Patrik repeatedly licked Dr. Blake's arms, trying to soothe his burns and stir him into awakening.

Dr. Blake please wake up. Please talk to me.

When Dr. Blake and Patrik had seen flames rising up the barn door from the kitchen window, Dr. Blake cried out, "Patrik, come quickly! Come quickly!"

They rushed outside to open the stalls and save their animals. Patrik barked out a warning as he herded them all out as best he could, knowing they would be safer in the woods. When Patrik ran back, Dr. Blake lay in the dirt outside the barn door where he had collapsed.

"Patrik," Dr. Blake whispered, "you are a good dog."

Patrik bit onto the collar of Dr. Blake's shirt and dragged him away from the fire and over to safety of the potting shed garden.

We are safe here, Dr. Blake, Patrik said as he licked the doctor's wounds and blisters.

Patrik suspected the fire had been intentionally set by a group of men from town who feared Dr. Blake's work and knowledge. Dr. Blake had published articles in medical journals about herbal therapies and using energy as a healing medium. His paper, "The Vibrational Forces of Nature," received criticism as well as interest from those who were open to new ways of thinking. His patients knew his therapies unexplainably helped to relieve many conditions and diseases, and they were grateful for his help.

There had been recent gossip escalating in Pine Cove from people who didn't understand Dr. Blake's work and didn't want to. They referred to his therapies as "sorcery".

When people came out to his farm, Dr. Blake purposefully talked about the work he was doing in the barn, as if it was no more unusual than tending a farm. He never discussed the potting shed, or the magic tree in the woods where the gnomes travelled back and forth mining basanite. Dr. Blake worked with the basanite, a form of jasper rock, to conduct his experiments and to extract energy crystals. Energy crystals were powerful in their abilities to create healing and transformation.

As the fire raged, Patrik knew most of the barn buildings were lost. Periodically, he heard the animals running through the woods and crying out in fear. His fur was singed, and his nose burned when he breathed. Loud voices shouted in the distance, and instinctively, Patrik inched closer to Dr. Blake's body.

"Patrik," Dr Blake whispered, "everything will happen as it should in time. You must wait for the child here, by the magic tree. You will be taken care of by the gnomes and light beings in the elemental kingdom. Thank you, my friend."

Patrik lay motionless, pretending to be severely injured as the men who started the fire stood over them.

"Are they dead?" one man asked as another rolled Dr Blake over on his back and kicked his side.

"He's not moving. Not breathing as far as I can tell."

"The dog is dead," the taller man said. "He'll never bite us again, that stupid mutt."

"Let's go back. No one will be out here till tomorrow."

"No one will care, either. No more witchcraft out here."

The men turned and began to walk away, their voices fading into the distance. Patrik lay still.

Dr Blake, Dr Blake ... Patrik called out in his mind. *Don't leave me.*

Patrik stirred and turned in his sleep, curling up closer to Cassie. She reached out and instinctively patted him, letting him know he was safe. As Cassie slept, she wondered how she and Patrik would be able to travel together again as Patrik had suggested, this time far away. Their travels had been limited to the borders of the Elemental Kingdom, where they met Archangel Uriel and Queen Epona, Queen of the Fairies. All their adventures increased Cassie's telepathic abilities and her work with energy crystals. Cassie knew their bigger mission beyond the Elemental Kingdom was to send energy to Akaleia, the High Priestess of Lemuria. Their crystal energy would reestablish vibrational connections to other worlds, specifically to rebuild transformational energy bridges to Lemuria. Cassie knew energy allowed connections of thoughts and actions, even though she didn't know how. She knew her mind wishes created things. When she purposefully sent out a mind wish, she knew that it started to create positive change. She never sent out a negative mind wish. She didn't know how.

Patrik smiled as he lay beside Cassie and heard her mind wanderings. He had waited hundreds of years as a spiritual being on Earth for Cassie to meet him here. Here in Pine Cove, Maine. Momentary sadness overtook him as he remembered the tragic fire and the death of his beloved master who had lived in this same house. And the barn, he whimpered, where now Millie's house and her new barn stood. Dr. Blake had foreshadowed the violence coming to him. When his intuition and visions became more vivid, he began to prepare Patrik for the future, the long future without Dr. Blake beside him to continue their work.

"Patrik, listen carefully," he would say, and then instruct him in what to do and how to do it. "Do not be afraid. You have magical gifts of knowing how to use crystal energy and manifestation, and you must carry those forward. You must wait. Wait here as a being of light for the child to come. She has the light inside her, like you. You will find her, and she will find you. Your powers together will bring much goodness into the world and beyond."

"Cassie," Mommy called to her the next morning from her bedroom doorway. "It's time to get up. You need to have breakfast and get ready for dance class."

Cassie rolled over in her bed and blinked at Mommy. It was early morning, and the darkness of winter shadowed her room.

"Are you awake?" Mommy asked as she came closer.

Cassie held her stuffed animals closer, her rabbit Elroy and her bear Merton. "Yes."

"Yes, you're awake? It's time to get up."

"Okay," Cassie answered. "Yes."

"Don't dawdle, now," Mommy added. "Put those old toys away and get dressed. Breakfast will be ready in a couple of minutes."

"Yes," Cassie replied again.

Cassie hugged Merton and Elroy closer, smelling their sweet familiar fur, then sat up to pat Patrik who was still sleeping beside her. Patrik wagged his tail and licked her hand.

I know Patrik, Cassie said sympathetically through her mind energy. *I know you have to go away again.*

Patrik placed his paw on her arm and whined softly. *I came to tell you and prepare you, Cassie. Akaleia is calling. We are getting closer to her now. I have continued to build energy connection with the crystals we gather. It is now time to extend our help to Lemuria to fully unlock all the dimensional forces so we can live in peace.*

Cassie was silent for a minute and then lowered her head. *I know we have work to do*, she admitted, *but how will we get back? You were locked inside the tree. It will snow and block the opening to shed!*

I was locked in, Patrik explained, *because of the absence of your life energy around the tree. You started to open the tree by saying the words and circling the trunk, but then you weren't allowed to continue.*

Daddy wouldn't let me, Cassie said. *He isn't happy down there.*

He is afraid for you, Patrik answered. *Then I called out to you in your closet portal, and you went back. The magic tree is open now for me and for us to travel both back and forth through the passageway.*

Will you be back soon? Cassie said hopefully. *Will you be back for Christmas?*

I will continue to use the crystal energy to prepare for our connection to Lemuria. I will be back with you at Christmastime. And I will have gifts for you and others.

Cassie looked down on her bed and the small pile of fresh crystals laying there.

These are for you to use in your practices at night gathering moonlight and for you to give to others as you wish. Always make sure you keep at least one and allow it to absorb the Light energy to magnify its powers.

They have magic, Cassie said. *Will they give others magic?*

The magic is for all of us who believe, Patrik answered. *And they may be useful for those who need to believe.*

If I give one to Poppy, will she see you?

The crystal energy helps everyone to see more, Cassie. Even you.

If I call to you, will you hear me?

I am always able to hear you, but I am not always able to answer you. I also need to

protect you. You have not come into your full powers yet.

You will be gone a long time, Cassie said as she nodded her head.

Remember, Cassie, time is only real in the human world. Our time is always present, past, and future in the same moment. Time can be whatever you draw to you. Whatever you desire to experience will be your present time.

Okay. Cassie sighed. *I will miss you, and I will look for you.*

I will be in the familiar form that you know, Patrik answered. *I will talk to you, and you may call to me whenever you want. I will hear you and answer you when I can. Remember, all things happen in Divine Order and in Divine Time.*

What are you going to do there? Cassie asked as Patrik prepared to leave. *Is it the same work we do in the Elemental Kingdom?*

When we are in the Elemental Kingdom, we gather more crystals. Crystal energy propels all thoughts, actions, and words into form, a manifested physical form. I believe I can now direct that energy in ways to help Akaleia and propel us on our journey.

The potting shed, Cassie nodded, *and the gnomes. That was where Dr. Blake did his crystal work.*

Yes, agreed Patrik. *The gnomes were his underground workers. They mined basanite and brought it to Earth through the magic tree. Dr. Blake planned to use the crystals of energy from the basanite stone to help humanity.*

Can I go with you? To Lemuria?

Not yet. This time I have to go by myself. I need to test how far I can travel as a half physical, half spiritual being. I need to make sure it will be safe for you to travel when we go together. Your being is much denser than mine.

Do you know how to get there?

Archangel Uriel and Queen Epona have created a map for me beyond the Elemental Kingdom. I have practiced travelling on the paths that are closest to the borders of the Elemental Kingdom. This time I am going to go as far as I can with their guidance and communications from Akaleia.

I will miss you, Patrik.

I will miss you, too. Remember that time is an illusion, and I am never gone far. Continue to place your crystals in the moonlight to energize them. They will send energy to me to reach Lemuria and come back to you.

I will, Patrik. I promise.

"Cassie!" Mommy called out from the bottom of the stairs, "Come down now. Breakfast is ready!"

Cassie kissed Patrik on his head once more and patted his fur. Patrik jumped off Cassie's bed and crept into the portal through the little door in the closet. From there, he would enter the tunnels to the magic tree to begin his journey. Patrik had told Cassie he would be going a long way and be gone for a long time. Cassie knew Lemuria was an ancient civilization, an original civilization on Earth. Beings of Light came to Lemuria from celestial realms to establish a new colony and bring Light and Love into the world. As it existed in ancient times, it now existed in another dimension. Like the Elemental Kingdom, Patrik had told her, but deeper and farther beyond.

Patrik travelled quickly to the Elemental Kingdom and was still filled with crystal energy when he arrived. He met Archangel Uriel and Queen Epona in the field of flowers where the stream flows between the trees, a place also known to Cassie from her previous travels. Together, the three reviewed the map they had created and the path to Lemuria.

Akaleia has communicated to us that access is now open to Lemuria, Archangel Uriel told Patrik. *You may encounter some obstacles, but you will be able to pass through them. Once you have started your journey, you cannot stop. Keep focused on your destination.*

I'm ready, Patrik answered. *I look forward to meeting Akaleia again after so many lifetimes and working to reconnect our bridge.*

Patrik and Queen Epona walked to the edge of the fields of flowers, until the air turned into a fine mist that lifted Patrik into a cloud. He remained weightless as he looked ahead and flowed into the unknown. When he was deeper into the dimensions of the inner earth, Patrik felt a loss of balance and began to tremble. The air had shifted, and he thought he was in a maze, or a storm, perhaps, or some type of power field that was causing him to stutter in his progress. The vapor about him was increasingly hotter, and at times he thought there were flames of orange tongues surrounding him.

Are these guiding me? he wondered, *Or are they trying to prevent me from moving ahead?* Patrik closed his eyes and allowed the crystal energy to pull him into the unknown.

Akaleia, he called out, *please send me guiding messages.*

When the movement stopped, Patrik realized there was a solid surface underneath him. The air smelled sweet and was calm again.

Patrik, Akaleia said as she glided towards him, *you have come to Lemuria.* Akaleia stood in a waving gown, tall and regal. Her elongated head and arms surrounded Patrik in a gesture of love and welcome. *I am so thankful you are here.*

Patrik embraced Akaleia in his mind's eye, sending feelings of gratitude and love. *I am overwhelmed to see you. I didn't know if we would ever be together again.*

We have always been as one in many lifetimes, Akaleia acknowledged. *Now, light years ahead, we have the chance to renew energy work on Earth together.*

Cassie sat at the wooden table in the kitchen eating cereal with banana when her daddy came through the back door with Ned.

"How far did you get?" Mommy asked, handing him a fresh cup of coffee.

Daddy took the leash off Ned and gave him a pat, "Good dog Neddie," he said. "We, you know, went up the driveway."

"He's limping again, Jack," Mommy answered. "You should bring him in to see Millie at her vet office soon and have her take a look at him."

"Yeah, we'll get to that," Daddy said lifting his head and patting Ned again. "Cassie, are you ready to go get Christmas decorations today?"

"Uh huh," Cassie replied, taking another spoonful. "Can Poppy come too, Daddy?"

"Yes, I guess so. Mommy can ask Twirla at dance class if it's okay."

"You're a brave man, Jack Murphy. Two on the loose."

Daddy laughed. "They stay pretty close together."

"Cassie, do you have your bag and shoes for class?" Mommy asked. "Go upstairs and get your bag and shoes, please."

Cassie sat in the front seat of her Mommy's white Toyota Camry as they drove to Twirla's dance studio, *The Kick'n Leg*, in Pine Cove. "Pretty cold this morning, huh Cassie?" Mommy said, glancing at her.

Cassie looked up at her Mommy and then outside the window again. "It's going to snow."

"How do you know that? The weatherman on the news this morning didn't say that, and the sun is out."

"I can feel it." Cassie nodded.

"The window is closed, Cassie. How can you feel it?"

"It comes through me."

"Let's change the subject," Mommy said. "You and Daddy will have fun this afternoon together. I'm looking forward to getting all our Christmas decorations up, too."

"Patrik said he'll be back for Christmas."

"Of course, of course. Always have to include Patrik. You know I read in an article that as children get older, they become more aware of the differences between fantasy and reality. I am really looking forward to that!"

"Patrik's looking forward to completing our work."

Mommy shook her head and drove on in silence.

"Hey! Gratefully, we are here Cassie," Mommy said, pulling into a parking space in front of the dance studio. "Let's get your things."

"Cassie, hi!" Cassie's best friend Poppy shouted, skipping across the dance floor. "Did you practice your dance steps this week? I had a cold, so I didn't practice as much."

"We tried a couple times," Mommy interrupted. "Cassie has a short attention span. We'll see how she does."

Poppy walked with Cassie over to the chairs so she could change into her ballet shoes. "I know you'll do fine," Poppy encouraged her. "If you want to look at me, you can follow my feet."

"Okay." Cassie smiled.

"Did Patrik come today?" "No, he had to go away again, but he'll be back for Christmas."

"Can I see him then?" Poppy asked. "I promise to look really carefully."

"I don't know, Poppy. I'm going to try and help you. I think you will be able to hear his barking, though."

"Come on over this way, girls," Twirla called out. "Let's line up in our rows of four so we can start with ballet positions."

Cassie followed Poppy over to the middle of the room and stood beside her. "Listen to the music, Cassie," Poppy smiled, "and follow my feet."

When dance class was over, Cassie returned to the chairs to take off her shoes. She saw her Mommy walk across the room and stand next to Twirla. "Mommy's going to ask your mother if you can come with me and my dad to get Christmas decorations this afternoon," she said to Poppy.

"Can we play at your house after? Can we play school in the potting shed?"

"My daddy made us close up the shed for winter. He said we can't play out there because it's going to snow."

"Oh," Poppy said sadly. "Where will we meet Patrik?"

"He told me the tree will stay open for him to travel and he can come through my closet. My daddy said we can play school in my room."

"And my house too!" added Poppy. "And dance class with my dolls, that's always fun."

"Are you ready, girls?" Mommy asked coming towards the chairs. "Poppy, your mother said it's okay for you to come home with us. You and Cassie can go get Christmas decorations with Jack."

"Poppy, I'll meet you later this afternoon, okay honey?" Twirla said coming forward and extending her arms to Poppy. "Give me hugs, sugar."

"Okay Mommy," Poppy answered with a squeeze. "Is it a long day today?'

"No, sweetie, there's no more cheering dance practice till after the holidays."

"Ah, yes," Mommy sighed. "We're hoping Mandy gets her grades up in order to participate."

"I understand," Twirla nodded. "but those are the school's rules for all the athletes. If she wants to cheer badly enough, she'll do it."

"A life lesson." Mommy smiled. "Those can be hard."

"We all know that" Twirla agreed, "because we have all had our own experiences. But until you learn from them …"

"You think it won't happen!" exclaimed Mommy.

Twirla gave Poppy one last hug, "Time will tell."

"Time will tell all!" added Cassie. "That's what Patrik says."

"Let's go, now," Mommy directed as she ushered the girls to the door. "At least Patrik wasn't here today."

"Hello ladies!" Daddy called out as Cassie, Poppy, and Mommy came through the kitchen door. "How was dance class?"

"Good." Poppy giggled as she nudged Cassie.

"It was good!" Mommy answered. "And no Patrik incidents made it even better!"

"Patrik is travelling, Mommy," Cassie spoke up as Mommy looked over at Daddy.

"Twirla said there is no cheerleading practice today," Mommy added, ignoring Cassie's remark. "They are taking a Christmas break. Is Mandy up?"

"I've been upstairs once. Called out twice. She said she was stirring."

"I'll go up in a minute and get her," Mommy said. "It's a great day for her to study."

"That's exactly what I told her! She didn't seem excited. And I reminded her that we want to see her grades this weekend, to which she replied, *WHAT???*"

Mommy shook her head. "We definitely need to see them."

"WHAT??? WHAT???" echoed Cassie, grabbing hold of Poppy's arm and swinging it back and forth.

"That's very funny!" Daddy laughed.

"Are you going to Mike's?" Mommy asked as they headed out the door.

"Yes, he has that whole area beside his hardware store with trees and wreaths. We'll have lunch when we get back. I think there might be snacks at Mr. Mike's store, too," Daddy said smiling at the girls. "Let's go get in the Ford Explorer and collect some Christmas decorations!"

"And bonus, you get to catch up with Mike!" said Mommy.

The ride to Darby's store in Pine Cove was fairly quiet as Cassie and Poppy whispered back and forth in the back seat. Periodically, Daddy looked in the rearview mirror to see them smile and , which made him smile.

"I see you, Daddy!" Cassie shouted looking at his face in the mirror.

"Okay, girls," Daddy said, parking in front of the hardware store. "Go ahead and get out of the car and come around to the front. Be careful, there are lots of cars here today."

"Well look who's here!" Mike Cavanaugh shouted from the gate, "My favorite customers!"

"Cassie, Poppy, and I are here to get a tree and some decorations," Daddy said, walking across the row of cars and shaking Mike's hand. "How are you, buddy?"

"Really good, busy, you know, this time of year. Hello Cassie and Poppy, are you excited about Christmas?"

"I asked Santa for a bicycle and new dolls," Poppy said, "to be in my dance recitals."

"That sounds wonderful!" Mike said. "And what about you, Cassie?"

"I asked Patrik to come back for Christmas." She looked up at Mike. " He said he would be back by then."

"He's not here now?" asked Mike. "He used to spend a lot of time in my lumber yard."

"He's travelling," Cassie said seriously. "He has work to do."

"You know how it is with Patrik," Daddy said. "Always something new."

"Well Cassie, I hope he comes back for Christmas," Mike said. "I am still wanting to meet him."

"I'm going to get to hear him bark," exclaimed Poppy. "Just like Cassie!"

"That will be wonderful, I'd like that, too. Come on over this way." Mike gestured. "Let's see what special decorations we can get for you today."

"I'm thinking a tree about eight feet. Balsam fir, if you have it," Daddy said to him. "Plus some pine bough garland and three wreaths."

"Daddy, can we get some ribbons too?" asked Cassie.

"Yes, we need that. Do you and Poppy want to go over pick out a color? Stay where I can see you."

As Cassie and Poppy walked over to the racks with ribbons on them, Mike turned to Jack. "How's the potting shed doll house coming?"

"Good. I just have some finishing work to do."

"Let me help you. I'm over at Millie's tonight, and we've nearly finished the barn for winter. I'll come over."

"Thanks, that would be great. I need your advice on installing the closures on the little door in the back of the shed and the windows. I want to make it as real as possible, but those stupid windows in the shed don't open. I want to make them open with that pulley system you told me about."

"Maybe we can figure out how to really open them by doing the doll house." Mike chuckled. "I know you are trying to make it very authentic."

"I got a branch off a tree that's thick and tall to put outside the doll shed, like the magic tree. I'm trying to figure out how to make a little door in it. You know, Patrik's secret passage. Connie found these little toy figures of a girl and a dog. It looks like Cassie, although I'm not sure what Patrik looks like."

"You should ask Cassie," Mike said. "I'm sure she knows."

"Yeah, of course she does." Jack laughed. "Hey girls, what do you have there?"

"We got ribbons! We got a purple one with sparkles, and a red one with sparkles, and a green one with sparkles," said Cassie. "They match!"

"Does Connie go for eclectic?' Mike asked as Daddy nodded at Cassie.

"This is very artistic!" complimented Daddy. "Great job, girls. Nanny Phe will be thrilled with your ribbon talent."

"Poppy got three ribbons too, Daddy, so we would match across the street."

"That is so sweet," Mike said, bending down to them, "You know what, girls? Such a nice idea to match. You are good friends. I want to give you the ribbons as a little gift from Millie and me."

"That's nice Mike, thanks," Daddy said.

"I'll bring your tree around Jack. The wreaths and laurel you wanted are over on the right. Help yourselves to hot chocolate and cookies on the table."

"Sounds good, Mike. And I should be available after eight o'clock, if you ah, want to call me."

Mike laughed, "I do love Christmas Jack. It is the season of surprises."

The Ford Explorer was loaded with greenery, ribbons and a Christmas tree tied to the roof when Daddy backed out of the parking lot. "Let's sing a Christmas song on the way home, girls. What songs do you know?"

"The one about the sleigh," Poppy spoke up, "and the horses."

"Jingle Bells!" Daddy shouted. "Cassie, you know this one too. Can you sing it with us?"

"*Dashing through the snow, in a one-horse open sleigh ...*" Daddy sang out as Cassie and Poppy stared at him. "Okay, here it comes, you guys do the laugh part. *Laughing all the way! HaHaHa!*"

Cassie and Poppy laughed and swayed side to side as he sang.

"Here's a version I bet you don't know," Daddy said as he began to hum *Jingle Bells* again. "And Rudolph smells ... hum, hum, hum, and daddy laid an egg."

Peals of laughter rose from the back seat to accompany him as he turned the corner onto Bristol Road. "I knew that would get you to chime in!"

"Hum, hum, hum," Cassie mimicked, "hum, hum, laid an egg!"

Squeals of laughter continued as they drove down the road and into their driveway.

"You guys are better hummers than me," Daddy praised them. "Thank you for the entertainment. Go ahead inside. Mommy is going to have some lunch for you. I'll come in shortly."

"Can we take our ribbons in? Cassie asked.

"Absolutely! Go show Mommy what a great job you both did."

"Hey Jack," Mommy greeted him as he came in the kitchen door. "Lunch is ready. The girls already started."

"Thanks, Connie, looks good. Did the girls show you the ribbons they picked out?"

"They sure did. Very sparkly. Very sparkly."

"And they match!" shouted Cassie.

"Yes, the sparkles indeed match," Mommy agreed.

"Across the street, too!"

"Yes, Cassie. We'll just have to ask Twirla if she's on board with it."

"My Mom loves sparkles," Poppy chimed in. "She loves to put them on our costumes for our recitals and parades."

"I really like all your costumes, Poppy. They are very attractive," Mommy said.

"Are you going to eat Connie?" Daddy asked.

"I already had an early lunch when Mandy finally came downstairs."

"Where is she now exactly?"

"In the shower. She'll be out soon. I told her about the afternoon study plan."

"Great. I'll let her get going on that and sit with her before dinner to look at her grades."

"Merry almost Christmas!" Twirla sang out as she knocked on the back door.

"Come on in!" Mommy greeted her. "How was the rest of your morning?"

"Thank you for taking Poppy. It really freed me up. This was our last class till mid-January and there was a lot of follow-up work to do."

"You're very welcome," answered Mommy.

"She was wonderful as always," added Daddy. "And she's a good hummer, too."

"A hummer?" asked Twirla.

"Like this, Momma. Hum, hum, hum; hum, hum, hum; ha ha ha ha ha!"

"Well, my goodness!" Twirla exclaimed. "That's quite the humming!"

"And Daddy laid an egg!" Cassie squealed in laughter.

"This is almost too much," Twirla answered, trying to catch her breath. "I am sorry I missed the trip."

"We got ribbons!" Poppy smiled.

"And they sparkle!" Cassie added.

"So, we can match," Poppy confirmed. "We want to match across the street."

"What a wonderful idea!" Twirla responded. "I think you two are the very best of friends."

"You may want to see them first, Twirla," Mommy said. "To make sure, ah, they go with your decorating ideas."

"Oh, honey, I am sure they are beautiful. We'll make sure we match."

Daddy was standing beside the packages of decorations on the counter watching the conversation. "Twirla, I have extra garland, and maybe we could string it on both porches and hang the bows from there."

"Thank you, Jack. Great idea. Let me know what I owe you."

"Nothing. It's Mike and Millie's contribution to our holiday neighborhood decorating scheme."

"That is so nice! I think we need to bake some cookies for them as a thank you, don't you think so, Poppy?" Twirla asked. "Such good neighbors."

"And you make very good cookies, Twirla, I remember," Daddy said. "You too, Connie!"

"Good save, Jack," said Mommy as Twirla and Daddy laughed.

"Twirla, what are you doing next weekend? Do you have any plans? Jack and I were going to have a get together with everyone Saturday."

"That would be great. Let me know what I can bring."

"I'm going to see if I can still barbeque," Daddy added. "Even in the snow."

"We'll have other things, too," Mommy said. "We should have a backup plan in case we're snowed in."

"I make a wonderful chili, Connie, great with rice and corn bread. Let me bring that."

"Can we come, too?" asked Cassie.

"Of course, you can come, too!" Daddy answered. "And we'll invite Papa Ed and Nanny Phe, Linde and her family, and the whole neighborhood!"

"And Patrik, too!" yelled Cassie. "Patrik too!"

"How did it go with Mandy and the online grade check?" Mommy asked Daddy as she and Cassie worked to make a salad for supper.

"Not good, as you might expect. There are courses lacking homework and two have failing grades overall."

"Did you make a plan with her?" Mommy asked.

"No phone until the homework is caught up. That's just lazy," Daddy replied, waving the phone in his hand. "After that, I said we'll talk. She needs to show us she has caught up. She is going to ask her teachers on Monday if there is any extra credit she can do over vacation to make up the test grades. Especially math."

Mommy nodded, "Do you think we should get a tutor for her?"

"I think she needs to get her act in gear before she is in deep trouble."

"She thinks she doesn't want to be too smart," Cassie interrupted. "She said it's snobby. That's what she said on her phone."

"When did you hear that?" Mommy asked.

"Last night. She talks on her phone when she goes to bed."

"And you hear her?"

"I can hear everything, Mommy."

"What does that mean?" You can hear everything?" Mommy asked, raising her voice.

"It's like the snow I told you about in the car. It comes, and I feel it into words."

"Let's not talk anymore about these ridiculous things, Cassie. I'm tired of them."

Cassie lowered her head and did not reply. *Patrik,* she called out in her mind wishes, *please help my Mommy believe me.*

"Cassie, can you please go get your school bag so I can check for any schoolwork you need to do today?" Mommy asked the next morning after breakfast. "You have school tomorrow, and you want to help Daddy with the outside decorating today."

Cassie nodded and looked across the table at her father. "When are we going to decorate our Christmas tree?"

"Great question, Cassie Lynn! I think while you and Mommy go through your school bag, I'll bring the tree inside and set it up. You can help me put the lights on."

"How big a tree did you get, Jack? Are you going to be able to bring it in yourself?"

"It's about seven feet. They cut a couple inches off the bottom yesterday. I'll hammer the stand on in the yard and then bring it in. Of course, I welcome your opinion as to where it goes."

"Of course!" laughed Mommy. "I know it will be in the living room, but let me think a minute about which corner, or maybe in front of the picture window."

"It would be nice to see it from the road," Daddy replied. "Even for people driving by."

"Cassie, go get your bag and bring it down," Mommy said again. "Go now."

"Okay Mommy," Cassie replied as she headed for the stairs.

"You know I usually do this with her," Jack said to Connie. "This doesn't have to be done right now. We'll have time later today."

"I'll be fine, Jack, and I'm interested in seeing what she's doing."

"Okay, but you usually get frustrated with her."

"Do you think one day she'll be able to handle these things without being asked several times?" Connie asked.

"I think she has made great progress this year with Katie her magician teacher. Yes, I have faith that she will."

"That reminds me, will you call your parents and Peter about the party next weekend? Ask him to invite Katie?"

"He'll invite Katie. I believe they are together most all the time."

"Really?" Connie said raising her eyebrows. "All the time?"

"Don't pry.. I'm sure it will all evolve in good time."

"Yes, me too, but they need to be quick about it!"

"Your quick and their quick could be different, you know. They want to be sure this time around after their college breakup."

"That won't happen again," Connie said. "I'll call my sister Chloe for the party, too. Although I know she is coming for Christmas, so she may not be able to do both."

"Why doesn't she just stay a couple weeks till Christmas? Ask her if she can change her hospital schedule."

"I will, but I'm not hopeful. I'm just glad she's coming for Christmas!"

"I have my bag," Cassie said from the doorway. "Is Auntie Chloe coming for the party?"

"We hope so, Sunshine," Daddy answered standing up. "But right now, I'll let you two ladies go through your bag, and I'll get busy with the tree."

"YEAKS!" Cassie squealed several times while jumping up and down. "Patrik loves Christmas trees, too! He told me he wants to give everyone presents this year."

"There is no..." Mommy started to say as Daddy interjected, "What kind of presents Cassie?'

"I can't tell you because it's a surprise!"

"Okay, let me be surprised," Mommy said, shrugging her shoulders. "Let's go through your bag, please."

"These are my done papers," Cassie said opening folder, "and Miss Douglass said we could do this paper at home if we wanted to."

"Oh, I think we should do it Cassie. This looks like fun. Can you read the instructions at the top?"

Cassie took in a deep breath, looked squarely at the paper, and said very seriously, "Shade in the correct amounts of ingredients to make the cookies."

"That's right! Go ahead and take your pencil and do that."

As Cassie started to work, her Mommy looked through her completed papers and noted the corrections that were marked. "Cassie, what are you doing? That's not what the directions said to do."

"I'm connecting them to the cookies."

"But you're not supposed to do it that way. Look at the quantities and shade in the correct amounts. How many cups of sugar are needed?" Mommy asked, pointing to the pictured measuring cups.

"One and a half."

"So, can you shade in one and a half cups?"

Cassie began to use her pencil to shade in the bowl. "I put the sugar in the bowl the way Nanny Phe showed me," she said.

"Cassie, you've made squiggles all over the paper. Miss Douglass is going to tell you to do it over again."

"What's going on?" Daddy asked coming into the kitchen with the tree.

"Cassie's not doing her homework paper correctly, and I am showing her the mistakes."

Cassie looked up with tears welling in her eyes.

"You know," Daddy offered, "let's take a break from schoolwork and do some Christmas tree work for a while."

"That doesn't solve the problem, Jack," Mommy snapped.

"It solves it for a few hours, and I think you two need a break. Come on Cassie, let's do the tree lights."

Mommy shook her head and took in a deep breath.

"Mandy, lunch is ready," Mommy called out from the bottom of the stairs trying to keep her voice even. "Come on down."

"I can't come, ever!" yelled Mandy. "I'm doing the homework Dad said I have to do."

"What did she say?" Daddy spoke up from the living room where he and Cassie were taking the tree lights out of the boxes.

"She's working on her homework," Mommy answered.

Daddy stood up and walked to the hallway, "I'll go get her."

"Mandy, your Dad's coming up to check on your progress!" Mommy shouted as Cassie followed her dad to the staircase.

"You didn't need to warn her, Connie." Daddy smiled starting up the stairs. "I'm sure we can come to an agreement."

"Dad!" Mandy said in surprise as she came out of her room.

"I didn't like your tone. I thought I'd come check in with you."

"I don't like spending my weekend doing all this homework."

"You should have thought of that weeks ago, Mandy. This is your unfortunate pay back."

"It's just not ..."

"Stop," Daddy said sternly. "Before you go further, Amanda, think carefully about what you are going to say."

"Lunch is ready," Mommy called up the stairs. "Let's eat, and we can talk about something else, like Christmas!"

Daddy and Cassie took one of the lengths of laurel from the porch and some green twine and walked across the street to Twirla's house.

"Neighborhood decorating company at your service!" Daddy greeted them.

Twirla laughed. "I really like this. You're hired!"

"Poppy and Cassie, can you hold the laurel up for me?" Daddy asked as he started at one end of Twirla's porch and looped it up and down as he went along.

"I have the ribbons!" Poppy said excitedly.

"Why don't you and Cassie decide what colors you want to put where," Twirla said as the girls took them out of the bag.

"Does Patrik have a favorite color, Cassie?"

"He likes all colors," Cassie said, "but when we travel to the Elemental Kingdom, we are guided by red light. That's Archangel Uriel's light."

"I would like to see that, too!" Poppy exclaimed. "Can I see that when I get to see Patrik?"

"I'll have to ask Patrik."

"Okay, girls, let's bring those ribbons over here. Have you decided what colors go where?"

"We like this one first," Poppy said, holding up a red ribbon.

"That's perfect!" Twirla exclaimed. "Good choice."

Poppy held out the green ribbon, "And this one is second."

"And where is the last one?" Daddy asked.

"Right here, Daddy."

"Thank you," Daddy said as he reached out for the purple ribbon and tied it closest to the stairs.

"This looks really nice. Thank you," Twirla said. "Now we need to get your porch done!"

"This way, decorating crew," Daddy signaled to them. "Let's go across the street and finish up our house too."

CHAPTER 3

Creating Time

Patrik continued to move with Akaleia toward the Lemurian village. With every breath, he remembered the serenity of Lemuria, warm and tropical, and its oneness with all of nature. Tall palm trees shaded their route, and the fragrance of blooming flowers flowed from every direction. He felt calm and welcomed.

You have become acclimated to this new environment very quickly, Akaleia spoke to Patrik. *You have traveled through multiple layers of atmospheres.*

I remember feeling as if I were tumbling through a maze, and at one time, I thought there were orange flames all around me. Archangel Uriel told me to stay focused and not get distracted.

Akaleia nodded. *The dragons of the island continent came to escort you into the last dimension of your travel. They provide guidance and protection for those that are known to us. They also protect our colony from unwarranted intruders. As we evolved, so did other beings from other star systems and colonies. Some did not come in peace and harmony.*

Patrik watched the many animals that roamed freely about them. Antelope, goats, and chicken-like birds. *Are these animals part of someone's farm?*

The animals, birds, fish and all wildlife are not owned. We share them all in unity. I know you are familiar with the workings of a farm on modern Earth.

Yes, Patrik answered. *In my last lifetime on Dr. Blake's farm, he had domesticated animals, horses, cows, sheep, pigs, and chickens. They were all part of his ability to sustain his life, as well as produce from his vegetables, flower, and herbal gardens.*

In Lemuria, Akaleia continued, *our lives are sustained in a different way. Everything we need is provided for us. We also ask for our needs. Are you hungry, Patrik, or do you feel thirst?*

I don't know, Patrik answered. *When I think of it I feel a surge of energy that comes through my body and the thought goes away.*

You are being fed energetically Patrik. You are remembering.

As they walked forward, Patrik noticed that everything in Lemuria appeared circular. Other subtle bodies beside them were globes of light, energy beings that worked in circles within the circles.

Is this how energy is generated Akaleia?

These are beings still in transformation. They have only partially evolved from their celestial life.

Cassie sees colored orbs, and calls them her fairies, Patrick replied. *She plays with them in the yard with Linde and Poppy.*

Akaleia heard Patrik's words and unsaid thoughts. *Fairies are elemental beings, but they also evolved from celestial realms.*

How did we become separated? Patrik asked. *Crystal energy still exists here.*

As our colony evolved, other colonies rose up. Some were quite different from us and wanted different things. When we were no longer in unity, our energy became compromised and depleted. Some of us moved to different lands, while others chose to stay in this dimension. The Universe is asking us to come forward again and co-create the energy bridges between worlds. We need your energy to accomplish that.

I have remained a dog for hundreds of years in this lifetime, Patrik responded.

I do not see you as a dog, Patrik. You are a being of Light. Your golden energy surrounds you.

Patrik thought for a moment, then asked, *Will I be a dog again on Earth? Will I be Cassie's dog?*

Yes, Akaleia responded. *I know Cassie is very special to you. When you return to Earth, you will be in familiar form to her, but also retain what you have learned here. The ability to change form, to shape shift.*

Do you need that ability here?

Yes, she replied, *at times we change form as a means of protection, but also to experience it as a gift. By shape shifting we are able to function in all aspects of our environment. Earth, air, water, and even fire.*

Fire? How do you function in fire?

Akaleia turned to face Patrik. *We become dragons. We are the flames.*

On Earth we don't have dragons anymore, Patrik said, *not for millions of years.*

Lemuria is another Earth Patrik, the earth under the earth. Dragons on the above earth plane where you are from shape shifted too, to adapt. They are similar. They are salamanders.

Patrik nodded. *Cassie said the salamanders were tricked. They supported the flames in Dr. Blake's barn.*

There are salamanders as well as dragons that are not in alignment with the highest good, Akaleia explained. *They seek their own power and purposes.*

Do they try and prevent crystal energy connections? Patrik asked.

I do not know their exact purpose or intent with crystal energy. It does appear that overall, their intentions are to gain and manipulate power.

Control it and us, Patrik said.

There is much power to be gained from harnessing crystal energy, Akaleia agreed. *For now, our work needs to be kept secret.*

I understand, Patrik said.

"How are we doing for the neighborhood party tomorrow?" Daddy asked Mommy as she sat at the table writing more items on her to-do list.

"We have food shopping to do, some prep, and to clarify what things people are planning to bring," she answered without looking up. "I'm running out of time."

"You can make time," Cassie offered from her seat. "Patrik showed me how."

"I don't need to make time," Mommy said sharply, "I need to make better use of the time that I have."

"So, the party is tomorrow afternoon," Daddy said quickly. "Cassie, I know you will be a big help with that, and I have some things you can help me with too."

"Jack, did you get a hold of your brother? Are he and Katie coming?"

"He and his special person, that being Katie, Cassie's teacher," Daddy said winking at Cassie, "are both coming. And before you ask, he is bringing drinks for all of us and says that Katie will bring a dessert."

"Oh, she doesn't have to do that. She's our guest."

"She's our family, Connie. Maybe not officially yet, but family always brings things."

"Are they getting married?" Cassie beamed. "Can I go to their wedding?"

"Slow down, Cassie, you are going too fast," Daddy said. "Right now, we are only looking at what we need for the party tomorrow, okay?"

"Cassie, if you can modify time, try working on Uncle Peter." Mommy laughed.

"Okay, Mommy." Cassie nodded.

"It could work!" Daddy said. "And for that matter, Cassie, work on Mike and Millie too!"

Daddy walked over to the table, still chuckling, and picked up Connie's shopping list. "Cassie, you and I are going to complete the shopping while Mommy does the finishing touches on the house to get ready for the party. Tomorrow is supposed to be milder, Connie, and I am planning on barbequing and lighting the fire pit. I think we'll all be outside for a while."

"That sounds good, thank you. By the way, your mom is going to take Cassie over to her art studio this afternoon so they can do a project together."

"Nanny Phe?" Cassie beamed.

"Yes. She has something special for you to do together," Mommy said.

"What about Mandy? She should be helping us get ready for the party too," Daddy said.

"I'll get her up soon. Yes, she should help." Mommy smiled. "Things are better now that she's caught up on her homework and has her phone back."

"Okay, but she still needs to participate in chores, and I want to know what she's doing for extra credit over vacation to get those test grades up."

"She has two projects to do," Mommy said matter-of-factly. "I know she'll get them done."

"She asked Mark to help her," Cassie added. "He said yes!"

"How do you know that?" asked Daddy.

"I hear her."

"She talks that loud on her phone?" Mommy asked. "Cassie, I think you make things up sometimes."

Cassie lowered her head and remained silent.

Daddy moved over and put his arm around Cassie. "Honey, why do you think you know that?"

Cassie looked up and blinked back her tears. "She said you are mad at her. She said Mark is good at math."

"Okay, yes, that makes sense," Daddy answered nodding to Mommy. "We're not mad at her Cassie, we just know she hasn't been doing as well as she is capable of," Daddy added. "I'm not sure about Mark being involved though. She is supposed to do the work by herself."

"She has two weeks and two holidays to celebrate, too. Time is running out. Let's just get it done and over with and move on!" Mommy said sharply.

Daddy walked over to the back door and took a very deep breath. "Cassie and I are going to the store with your list. Text me if you think of anything else, okay?"

"I will. Cassie don't forget to keep your hands in your jacket pockets!"

"We are off on an adventure," Daddy said as they exited the house and walked onto the deck. "I am glad you're with me."

Jack and Cassie got into the Ford Explorer and drove out of the driveway to do their errands. "It's a long list, Cassie. We have three stops. We'll do the grocery shopping last so things stay cold, okay?"

"Okay, Daddy."

"So, tell me more about how you can create time. What you offered to help Mommy with."

Cassie lowered her head and remained quiet for a while. "Mommy didn't like what I said."

Daddy nodded as he spoke. "I think she doesn't understand how something like time can be changed. It makes her feel uneasy. But I would like to hear how it happens."

"Patrik told me."

"Is Patrik able to modify time?"

"Yes."

"Are you able to modify time?"

"Sometimes, and we can do it together too."

"And how do you do that?"

"I ask for it."

"Who do you ask? Is there a person in charge of time?"

"No," Cassie giggled.

"Cassie?"

"In my mind wishes. I ask for more time."

"Why do you need more time?"

"Patrik needs more time to do his work. And when I go with Patrik, we may need more time before we come back."

"Before you come back? Where do you go?"

"To the Elemental Kingdom."

"Oh, sure. Do you get an answer to the request to add time?"

"I feel the vibrations."

"The vibrations, is that the same thing as your Light language?"

"No, Daddy. Vibrations are energy. My mind wishes create the spaces in time."

"So, you ask for more time and then the clock doesn't move?"

Cassie giggled again. "It looks like it moves, but there are more spaces. Patrik says time can be anything we want it to be, past, present, or future."

Daddy looked over at his daughter and smiled. "You know Cassie, I need to spend some time thinking about the things you've just told me. It's a lot to take in."

"Patrik says you already know how to make more time because you are taking time to ask about it and think about it too."

"That Patrik, he is a clever one for sure. Tell him to keep talking to me through you, okay?"

"Patrik says, YES!"

Nanny Phe's car was parked in the driveway at their house when Jack and Cassie came back from shopping. Cassie ran out of the car to find her. "Nanny Phe!" Cassie shouted coming through the kitchen door.

"Hello, sweet love," Nanny Phe said, wrapping her arms around her. "How is Cassie Lynn today?"

"Good, Nanny Phe. Daddy and I went shopping, and we got things for the party!"

"I see there are lots of things going on for the party. I love the outside decorations too. Did you help with that?"

"Yes! And Mr. Mike gave us ribbons, so Poppy and I could match across the street!"

"I saw the matching ribbons. They look wonderful!"

"Hi Mom," Daddy greeted her as he came in the kitchen. "How are you?"

"Very well. Busy this time of year, but I do love the holidays."

"I hear you and Cassie have special plans."

"Yes we do, don't we Cassie?" Nanny Phe hugged her again. "Fun Christmas things!'

"Were you able to get everything we needed Jack?" Connie asked.

"Yup. Everything on the list. Just need to bring it in."

"I'll help," Connie offered. "Phe, you and Cassie can get going if you want."

"Okay, Cassie, let's get our creative juices flowing!"

"Do I have that?" asked Cassie.

Phe smiled "Of course you do, sweetheart. You create things every day."

"I can create time," Cassie answered softly as Mommy groaned behind her.

"And I want to hear all about it, Cassie! Let's get going!"

Cassie and Nanny Phe sat at the long wooden table in her art studio on high top stools. Nanny Phe was an artist, specializing in pottery. She had taught art to high school students for many years before she retired. Paintings and drawings hung on the room's rustic walls. Fired pottery pieces and art supplies were stored on numerous shelves.

"I thought you might like to make some Christmas gifts for your family today. Did you already have gifts?"

"I have some crystals that Patrik gave me. He said I could give some to people if I wanted."

"The special crystals, like the ones you put into the flower in the gnome statue?"

"Yes. But I always have to keep at least one for me."

"I think they are very special, Cassie. Do you know how many you might give to people?"

"Maybe four."

"So, I am thinking we might want to make gifts together that you could give to all the family, and maybe some special friends like Poppy and Millie. How does that sound?"

"Okay."

"We can take this dried lavender that was from my flower garden last summer. Doesn't it smell wonderful?"

"Like in the potting shed garden!"

"Yes, it brings back good memories doesn't it? And we can make little bouquets with Christmas ribbons to give to people. They say that if you put lavender under your pillow, you will have sweet dreams with the angels. What do you think of that?"

Cassie nodded and smiled as Nanny Phe started weaving strands of lavender together. "Here honey, let me show you how to do it."

"Can I pick out the ribbons, too?"

"Absolutely! Here you go. It's like braiding hair. Three strands. Over right, over left, to the middle, and repeat."

"I like this!"

"You are doing a wonderful job. I am so proud of you!"

Later that night, Cassie snuggled in her bed with Merton and Elroy and dreamed of Patrik travelling. She knew he was going far away this time, farther than he had been before and into another dimension. He was trying to reach Akaleia, the High Priestess who lived in Lemuria, whom Patrik knew from a very long time ago.

If I can manipulate time Patrik, can I make your trip go faster? Cassie had asked him before he left.

No, Patrik had answered. *Each step must be taken very carefully and slowly. I need to make sure my energy aligns with the vibrations in another dimension.*

I can send you energy through the crystals, Cassie had responded. *To give you powers.*

Yes Cassie, that is helpful. Trust that I am where I need to be as you are where you need to be, and all is well.

While Cassie slept, Jack and Mike stood together in Jack's garage workshop contemplating the finishing touches on the potting shed doll house. Jack had built everything to an appropriate miniaturized scale; the doors, the fireplace, the fence, the gate encircling the garden, and even the magic tree.

"This is so cool," Mike said, "I know Cassie will love it."

"I hope so. It's going to be a long winter with the potting shed locked up."

"Look how you made this little door open in the magic tree," Mike observed. "Is the hole inside it big enough for the dolls?"

"Yup, both little Cassie and Patrik can fit in there. Just the way Cassie tells us."

"I'm glad you made it the way Cassie believes it works. Nice, Jack."

"My mother even made these little clay replicas of the gnomes sitting outside the front doors of the potting shed. Incredible detail."

"Do you want to look at these windows one more time and see if we can get them to open the right way?"

"I'll follow your lead. I don't know the right way," Jack acknowledged.

"So according to the *This Old Barn* shows on PBS, in the old buildings, the windows were controlled by a pulley system. They didn't lift up from the bottom in the traditional way we think now."

"Why would they do it that way? It seems easier just to go over and lift up the sash and pane of glass," Jack said, thinking about how traditional windows work.

"Well, the idea was to promote cross ventilation as well as ventilation from the ceiling. The pulley allows the window to open from the top or the bottom by pivoting at the horizontal middle. That way they could optimize the flow of wind. If the doctor had the fireplace going to do his work, whatever that was, it would have added air coming in and exhausted any fumes from the fire that were in the room."

"I still don't understand why the windows were locked solid in the shed. Somewhere in the history of this house, someone was trying to keep something out."

"Or trying to keep something in," Mike grinned.

"There's something more to this," Jack admitted, "and maybe not a good thing."

"Well, we don't know, do we?" Mike answered truthfully. "They didn't give any clues as to the functionality of locking it up on the show. But I can rig this up like the shed was originally built so the windows open with the pulley."

"Let's do it!" Jack said enthusiastically. "Patrik, get ready!"

The next day was a mild December morning beginning with temperatures starting near 40 degrees. "It can only go up from here," Jack said as he sipped coffee with Connie and waited for the girls to get up.

"Anything you can think of that we need or haven't done?"

"I think we are all set, and people should arrive around four. That'll give the kids some time to play outside while there's still a little daylight left. We can put the spotlights on too."

"Chloe isn't able to come. She's going to take a couple days at Christmas, though. So, she'll be here Wednesday that week for Christmas eve, and be able to stay through the weekend."

"That's great!" replied Jack. "That'll give your sister plenty of time to relax as well as spend time with you and both girls."

"I want to talk with her about both the girls and get her advice."

"You think they aren't doing well? I mean overall, aside from Mandy's recent issues, I think they are doing fine."

"I think I would like a psychologist perspective on teenage rebellion and elementary age uncontrolled imagination."

"It's not uncontrolled," Jack answered softly, reaching out to hold Connie's hand. "but I admit it is very continuous. I think that may just be her normal."

"No, it's not normal, and I really value Chloe's opinion and perspective."

"I know. She has been very helpful to us several times. But let's get ready for today and a party with all our family and friends and get these kids up!"

"Ned's trying to get up, Jack. I can see him struggling in the hallway by your office."

"I'll get him. No problem."

"Jack," Connie started to stay.

"He's good, Connie. And I'm not ready. I'll take care of him."

The day became busy with party prep. As Jack had predicted, the weather was very mild, near 50 degrees, and the idea that they could enjoy some time outside became more feasible. Cassie spent most of her time out of her mother's way, helping her dad with various chores and standing on the fence to pat the horses as they came by. Millie was out in her yard as well and came over closer to Cassie and the horses.

"Hey, Jack," Millie called out to him. "Can Cassie come across the fence? I'd love to help her get on a saddle with Luna and walk them around the paddock if it's okay."

Daddy was moving deck furniture and wiping tables and chairs. He waved back in a form of acknowledgement. "Thank you, that would be great."

"Up and over the fence, Cassie," Millie told her, "or climb under and start from the ground, and we'll work your way up from there."

Cassie nodded, and then climbed down. She lifted her leg between the rungs of the fence at the lowest level, moved through to the other side, and stood up straight. "I know I can get across this way," she said confidently.

Millie laughed. "Yes, I remember, you have done that before. Come on over by me, and I will help you put on this helmet and get up in the saddle."

Cassie stood still and looked up at Luna, her tan face with a white star on her forehead, and her beautiful white mane that she tossed from side to side.

"Luna likes you, Cassie. See how she bends her head down to you. She wants you to come closer."

Cassie took Millie's hand and moved forward to stand beside Luna.

"Grab these reins, and put your foot in my hand, and I will lift you up to get on the saddle," Millie directed. Cassie held onto Millie and the reins with her left hand and put her left foot in the palm of Millie's hand. "Up you go," Millie said as she boosted her up. "Leg over the saddle."

"I did it!" Cassie said excitedly.

"Give Luna some neck pats now, she was a good girl for you."

Cassie leaned to the side and patted Luna's neck. "So soft."

"She is a softie for sure," Millie answered. "I want you to keep holding the reins and grab hold of this, this is called the pummel, with both hands."

Cassie put the reins in both her hands, took ahold of the pommel, and looked over at Millie.

"That's perfect. I have a hold of Luna's reins down here, too. And now I am going to lead Luna very slowly around the paddock. You hang on now."

Cassie smiled as they proceeded around the paddock, walking parallel to the fence. As Luna took steps forward, her motions created a side-to-side movement, and Cassie bobbed up and down with the pace. "I think you are doing great, Cassie; you are really getting the hang of this. You let the horse be the lead."

Cassie smiled again and began to feel the energy emanating from Luna's body touching her hands and legs above the stirrups.

Thank you, Luna, Cassie spoke through her mind.

"Neigh, neigh," Luna spoke up, shaking her mane.

"Luna's happy. Horses do that when they're happy. I think you make her happy."

"She says I'm her friend. And Patrik is her friend."

"Where is that Patrik these days?" Millie asked as she walked. "He hasn't been around as much."

"Patrik's travelling. He has work to do. He said he will come back for Christmas."

"I hope so. He always makes for an interesting day. Luna and Kai seem to know when he's here too."

"They do! They see him."

Millie smiled. "You know Cassie all animals have a very heightened sense of perception. They know things before we know them. They have intuition. Do you know what that is?"

"No," Cassie said.

"Well, hearing is a physical sense, through your ears. Intuition is hearing through a spiritual sense, but we understand it through our minds. What they call a sixth sense. It means an ability to know before things happen or to be guided by inner messages. I think you have intuition."

"You do?"

"Yes, a very heightened intuitive sense. You can tell me what you know, or the horses know, any time you want."

Cassie smiled. "Are you and Mr. Mike going to get married?"

56

Millie laughed, stopped walking, and looked up at Cassie. "Why would you ask that?"

"It feels like it," Cassie answered.

Millie smiled and nodded. "Well Cassie, like I said, I think you are very intuitive. Time will tell, I guess."

Cassie came into the kitchen after riding Luna to find several people busily working with food preparation.

"Hello, Miss Cassie!" Nanny Phe greeted her. "I heard you were riding a horse over at Millie's house. How special!"

"Luna likes me," Cassie answered.

"Oh, I am very sure of that!" Nanny Phe said. "Horses have that sixth sense."

Cassie's eyes twinkled as she smiled again. "Intuition. Millie said that animals and I have intuition."

"Cassie, go wash your hands, please, and then come back. We have some helpful things you can do," Mommy directed.

"Okay, Mommy," Cassie replied, walking toward the bathroom in the hallway.

"Surprise!" Chloe shouted as she came through the back door. "I couldn't stay away."

"Auntie Chloe!" Cassie exclaimed running back to hug her.

"Hello, my friend Cassie, loving on you!"

"Chloe, wow," Connie said reaching out to hug her sister. "I am so thrilled you're here!"

"Me too, Connie. Family. Important times."

"Chloe, so glad to see you!" Nanny Phe spoke up as Papa Ed and Jack nodded from the counters where they were cutting up vegetables.

"Couldn't resist, huh?" Daddy joked.

"Where's Mandy?" Chloe asked.

"Holler upstairs, she'll come down if you're here," Daddy said. "And maybe she'll actually start helping with something."

"Jack, enough. She's done a lot of schoolwork today," Mommy said.

"We'll see," Daddy replied. "Time will tell."

"Time can tell all!" Cassie said.

"Oh, stop you two!" Mommy pleaded. "This gets old really fast."

"Hello, everyone," Peter announced as he and Katie came into the kitchen.

"Peter! Katie!" Mommy greeted them. "Welcome. Come on in."

"We decided to come over and help if we can, because, you know, we have skills!" Peter proclaimed. "More than just building outdoor decks."

"You so do!" Daddy laughed giving his brother a hug. "Glad you came over."

"I brought some dessert things," Katie said, holding a tray in front of her as Nanny Phe and Mommy reached out to help her.

"So good to see you again, Katie," Nanny Phe said. "I hope you are having a good school year. Cassie is very happy in your class."

"And we're so happy with Cassie's progress in school," Mommy added. "You have done a tremendous amount of work."

"Well, actually, Cassie has done all the work. She's very invested in learning," Katie replied.

"And as I was asked, here's some assorted beverages too," Peter said holding out a cooler.

"Over here, Peter." Papa Ed motioned, standing beside what he called his drink station.

"Hi Pop," Peter greeted him with a hug.

"You doing okay? Papa Ed asked. "Are you off on semester break now at the university?"

"Yeah, it feels really good. I have planning work to do for classes next month, but Katie and I can spend much more time together."

"Excellent!" Papa Ed said. "We're all getting together for Christmas too, right?"

"Yes, and then we are taking a trip to Virginia to see Katie's parents for New Year's."

"I'm sure they'll love having you," Mommy said. "It's good to spend time with family."

"We'll see." Katie smiled.

"I'm going outside to make sure the grill will start," Daddy said, "and others will be here soon. I plan to start cooking in about an hour if that works for the rest of the food, Connie."

"Yes, I think that will work out fine."

"Excellent, we are on a schedule!"

CHAPTER 4

The Vibrations

More guests arrived in the later afternoon before the sun set. Jack's friend and co-worker, Dan Compton and his family, Paula, Mark, and Linde drove onto the driveway, waving to neighbors who were walking over from their houses. Ivy and Jim Morgan brought more gifts from their bountiful gardens, this time preserved vegetables and fruits.

"Cassie," Daddy called into the kitchen. "Poppy and Linde are here. Come on out and say hi!" Cassie started for the back door.

"Grab your coat!" Mommy yelled as she turned on the back spotlights. "So grateful that you did these back lights for us Ed."

Cassie, Poppy and Linde met in the backyard and stood together. "Let's play tag," Poppy said. "You run, and I'll be it!"

Mike and Dan stood with Jack at the grill. "It's warm here," Mike said, holding his hands out as Millie moved inside carrying the food they had brought.

"I heard that Mandy asked Mark if he would help her with math assignments over the holiday vacation," Dan said to Jack. "Is that good with you?"

"I'm okay with it. We'll need to talk about some guidelines, especially with Mandy. I heard about it in a very roundabout way."

"Mark came and told me upfront. He wants to make sure everything goes well, and you give permission. You know, he cares about her."

"Yes, I do know that, and I appreciate that. Mandy has not been so forthcoming, however."

"You do what you think is best, Jack," Dan said. "Whatever you feel work's best."

"I wish I knew what that was," Jack answered. "I don't know how she got into this mess with her grades. Even being warned that she might lose her spot on the cheering squad didn't seem to ignite a fire. I'm not sure what she needs to make changes, so it won't happen again."

"Mark is very good at math. I am sure he can be of help. I am sure he will stay very serious about it."

Jack laughed. "And that is the maturity I want Mandy to adopt!"

Dan smiled. "Well, he is a couple years older. Experience is a great teacher."

"Daddy, Look!" Cassie cried out. "Look at the moon!"

Daddy looked across the yard towards the potting shed and saw the full moon rising over the roof.

"Wow, Cassie, that is beautiful."

"Nanny Phe said next week is the winter "sol-tis" too, the shortest day of the year," Cassie added. "Some people have ceremonies. Can we have a party then too?"

"We can light a candle in the house, if you want. That would be okay."

"Okay," Cassie said. "I'll tell Nanny Phe. Maybe she'll light a candle, too."

"The moon is beautiful," Mike called out. "Look how it frames the potting shed and the garden."

"It's like summer daylight," Cassie said. "Daddy, can we open the gate and go into the fairy garden?"

"We're good here at the grill," Dan offered, "Go ahead if you want."

"Okay, Cassie, for a little while you can play in the garden. I am not opening the potting shed."

Daddy walked over to the gate and lifted the trowel from behind the spade so the girls could enter.

"We need to go down to the tree, Daddy. The moon is lighting up the tree."

"I don't want to do that," Daddy said.

"Please, please," the girls begged.

"Patrik might be there, too," Poppy said. "Right, Cassie?"

"I'll come with you, Jack. Safety in numbers." Mike smiled, holding a big flashlight in front of him. "Dan is managing the grill, and Peter started the fire pit on the deck for you."

"You sure about this Mike? You know some of the strange happenings."

"You know, I have always been intrigued by this magic tree idea since we rescued you and Connie from the locked shed that night. I'm in! This is great!"

"You are not helping, Mike," Daddy said. "There's nothing down there."

"Of course, there is! Are you kidding? Don't you feel it? As soon as you open that gate you can feel it. Let's go, the girls are ahead of us."

Jack, Mike, Cassie, Poppy, and Linde slowly made their way through the inside of the dark potting shed following the flashlight's beam. Mike guided them all to the back door and lifted the handle and rod so Jack could secure it. Mike knelt down and inched his way out first, then held the light in place for the others to follow. As soon as they emerged, they saw the bright moonlight illuminating the stairs and the forest floor.

"Wow!" Daddy exclaimed. "I had no idea. I've never been out here in a full moon."

Every step, bush, branch and lasting oak leaf was highlighted by the moon's glow.

"Let's go this way girls," Daddy said as Mike took Linde's hand to help her down the stairs.

"This is where Patrik opened the door to the magic tree!" Cassie exclaimed as she held her hand out to touch the bark. "You can feel the vibrations."

Poppy and Linde moved forward to the tree and began to touch the bark.

"I want to do that, too," Mike said. "Jack have you ever tried this?"

"No, I haven't."

"Give it a try."

Daddy slowly moved closer to the magic tree as the girls began to dance around it. "Cassie, don't say the words."

"What words?" Mike asked. "There are words?"

"No. Yes. Not really," Daddy answered, holding his hands out to touch the bark.

"I feel a tree," Mike said. "A solid tree."

Daddy took a very deep breath. "Okay tree," he said, "show me your hidden door."

Mike stepped back as Daddy moved his hands down to touch the place where Cassie had said the tree had opened up into a cave. Immediately, his hands began to tingle and feel warm. He paused a moment, not sure of what he was feeling, as the sensations continued to travel up through his arms and to the center of his chest.

"Okay! Nothing here. We're done."

"Are you all right? Mike asked him. "Did you really feel something?"

"Come on, girls, quickly. Everyone back up," Daddy called out to them. "Time for the party!"

The dining room was set up as a buffet with plates and utensils at one end, followed by all the bowls of food. Grilled steak and chicken, Twirla's chili and cornbread, a lasagna from Millie, and salads of all types. Nanny Phe and Paula, Linde's mom, helped the three younger girls get their plates and get settled at the small table in the kitchen.

"We have little Santa's elves at our table!" Poppy said excitedly, looking at the toys in front of their seats. "They're so cute!"

"I made them for you girls," Katie said. "An elf for each of you!"

"Thank you, Miss Douglass," Poppy and Cassie said together.

Katie smiled. "Let's keep this our little secret at school, okay?"

Others walked out to the deck to eat at the outdoor table or sit by the firepit, while some chose the living room. "Come keep me company, Peter," Katie said following Chloe, Mark, Mandy, Mike and Millie, as they headed outside.

"Absolutely!" Peter said, grabbing a bowl filled with tortilla chips for them all to share.

"Your tree is beautiful, Connie," Nanny Phe said as they sat in the living room, "and you have such pretty ornaments."

"Thank you, Phe. Actually, Jack and Cassie decorated the whole tree," Connie said. "I just told them where I wanted it to be placed."

"Ah, a supervisor. Good for you," Papa Ed chimed in. "Every good job needs a supervisor!"

"The tree is from Mike's store," Jack added. "He has great trees."

"We went over there, too," Dan said. "Paula and Linde and I. Mark wasn't interested in shopping with us this year. He did help me bring it in the house, though."

"Always good to have some extra muscles around!" Jack added.

"Poppy had a wonderful time with you and Cassie," Twirla said, "and our outdoor decorations look wonderful!"

"That was all the girls' idea," Jack said, "and Mike donated the ribbons and the laurel."

"Did you see our house?" Ivy Morgan asked. "Mike's been over there too. Our ribbons match all along the street! Millie's house, too!"

"Just say Mike and Millie's house, Ivy." Her husband Jim smiled, as people in the room chuckled. "Soon enough for those two."

"What's soon enough?" Mike asked from the doorway. "I came in to get a little refill on my plate, and I couldn't help but overhear."

"You are a lovely couple," Phe replied, "and you know it, too."

Mike smiled, "Millie is a very wonderful woman."

"Are you blushing, Mike?" Dan laughed. "Jeez, get on with it! Don't spend too much time thinking on this."

"I can help you, Mr. Mike," Cassie offered, standing next to him. "I can create time for you."

Mike knelt down to be eye level with Cassie as others whispered, and Connie tried to shush her.

"I appreciate all your help," Mike said honestly. "You can give me all the time you want."

Cassie smiled. "Okay," she said as she headed back to the kitchen table, "But Patrik says you're busy at work so it might not feel like extra."

"We have had way too much of this today," Connie complained. "She's offering to make time for everyone. Ridiculous!"

Jack got up and motioned to the group. "Can I get anyone anything? I'm going to check on the deck people. And if anyone would like to come sit by the fire out there, it's really a mild night."

"With a full moon!" Mike echoed.

"How are you girls doing out here?" Daddy asked the kitchen table group. "May I get anything for you?"

"Cookies!" Linde shouted.

"That's a good answer. We'll have cookies and other desserts in just a little bit. If you want to grab your coats, you can come outside again. We'll make room for you on the deck."

The girls ran to get their coats and then followed Daddy across the kitchen.

"Hello, everyone, how is everything out here?" Daddy asked, opening the back door for the girls to come out.

"Come sit for a while, bro." Peter invited him.

"Come on, girls." Chloe motioned to them. "Come sit by the fire with us."

"Everything was wonderful Jack," Millie said. "You and Connie throw great parties."

"Thank you. I'll be sure to tell Connie, too," Daddy said, as he made his way to the couch at the corner of the deck where Mark and Mandy were finishing their plates.

"Mark, can I get you a refill?" Daddy asked him as he sat on the couch with Mandy.

"No, thank you, Mr. Murphy. It was great. I'm good."

"Mandy, why don't you go grab a couple more sodas for you and Mark, please," Daddy said nodding to her.

"Ah, okay," Mandy responded. "I'll be right back, Mark," she said, moving past him.

Jack took a seat in a chair across from the couch. "So, Mark, how is school going for you?"

"Really good, Mr. Murphy. I am on the basketball team, too, so you know, it's busy."

"I do know how that is. Your dad and I used to play as many sports as we could."

Mark took a deep breath and looked up at Jack. "Mandy asked me to help her with her math project over the school vacation. I want to make sure that's okay with you."

Jack nodded. "Thank you, Mark. I appreciate that. I have heard about that potential plan from Connie. Well, actually, from Cassie. Do you think you can help her?"

"I know that when she has questions and we, you know, talk on facetime, I can answer her questions or help her find the answers."

"So, you think this is a serious thing, like being a tutor."

"I do."

Jack laughed as he thought to himself… *Well, I'll probably hear that answer again later in life.*

"Okay. I'm good with it. You can come over whenever it is best for both of you. The dining room table is always cleared off, and that will give you plenty of space to do your work. Do you know that she has things she has to finish over vacation?"

Mark nodded. "She already talked to me about them."

"Well, that's encouraging. Glad to hear it. Thanks, Mark."

"Bringing desserts out for everyone," Nanny Phe announced, carrying a plate of cookies, as Twirla followed behind her with dessert bars, napkins, and small plates.

"Come get comfortable, everyone, there's plenty of room," Daddy called out.

"Jack, this deck was a great idea. I am enjoying it now, but building it last summer was a pain," Peter complained. "It took a lot of hours to get this done."

"And I do thank you very much Peter. I couldn't have done it without you."

Katie squeezed Peter's hand, "I think you can probably do anything you set your mind to."

"Time will tell," Peter said, kissing Katie's hand.

"Time will tell all!" Cassie shouted, as people laughed in the background.

"A lot of focus on time this weekend," Daddy said. "I will just say that it does go by quickly. It's almost Christmas. Where did the fall go?"

"Twirla," Chloe asked, "How was your trip to New Orleans in October? And how goes settling your property? I hope it all went well."

"It was complicated, as I expected it would be. The property is now officially settled and taken over by the city. Glad to be done with it. When I was in New Orleans, though, I was given an artifact that was found in the basement of the property, a petrified doll."

"In your building?" Mommy said in disbelief. "That's scary."

"Like a voodoo doll?" Peter asked. "Something living was petrified?"

"I don't believe in voodoo, casting spells and hexes," Twirla answered. "I believe, however, that at one time, the doll was used as a form of protection, to ward off evil. In New Orleans, we take those things very seriously."

"I would certainly be cautious," Chloe said. "These things give me the willies!"

"Willies? I haven't heard that saying in a long while." Ed smiled.

"I think it aptly describes it!" Millie added. "I have the willies too!"

Twirla smiled at the group, "Apparently, they found a very old burial ground under the building."

"Fascinating!" Peter shouted. "What did they do then?"

"There really wasn't much to do. A burial ground is a sacred and historical site. They restored it as much as possible and put a small park there."

Daddy leaned closer to the fire. "What happened to the doll?"

Twirla laughed. "Actually, I brought it back with me. I want to bury it in my flower garden to be restored by the earth angels."

"That is a wonderful idea!" said Phe. "Adding positive energy to its new habitat."

"Guess you'll know in spring if your garden feels the same way about it," Mike said. "Maybe it will keep all the bugs away!"

"Hopefully we all won't have to find out if it doesn't go well," Mommy added.

"Connie, you can't believe in all this witch stuff, do you?" Daddy asked her.

"Given the number of strange things already happening here in that potting shed and tree, I think a certain amount of caution is very wise."

Cassie stood up from the couch. "Patrik says everything is meant to be, and we are all where we belong. He says time will tell!"

Mommy groaned as Twirla reached out to Cassie. "Thank you, honey. That is always good advice. Please tell Patrik to keep an eye out though, okay?"

"Patrik is working. He's travelling to Lemuria."

"What's Lemuria?" Daddy asked. "Is this something new?"

"No, Daddy. Remember, I told you. He's going to meet Akaleia, the High Priestess. We need more information before we go there."

"This is just craziness," Mommy said sharply. "You're not going anywhere!"

"I know Lemuria," Peter chimed in. "It's an ancient civilization. It was a continent in the Pacific, maybe 500,000 years ago, before Atlantis. It is believed that the inhabitants came from constellations, star planets."

"Like Cassiopeia, Uncle Peter!" Cassie exclaimed. "My star planet."

"Yes, just like that, sweetie!"

In Lemuria, days and nights flowed into an expansion of light and dark with no concept of time. Akaleia and Patrik spent their waking hours relearning about each other and the evolution of life in Lemuria and life on Earth. What was apparent in both worlds is that some beings choose to become their higher selves and promote good in the world, while others choose an unfulfilled life where they are never happy. Those beings live and breathe negativity, judgement, and evil.

Happiness comes from within us, Akaleia said, as they stood among the beauty of the gardens. *We have to find our own happiness.*

When Dr. Blake died, I lost my happiness, Patrik admitted. *I was lost in an unfamiliar world.*

Akaleia nodded. *It is hard to wait for the Universe to align us again. We often think we are ready to move forward before our path and purpose are clear. Do you know your life purpose, Patrik?*

I know that Dr. Blake told me to continue his work with the crystals. I know that as I searched and found the Elemental Kingdom again, I started to find my previous lives. I know I am meant to work with you and Cassie to build energy connections between dimensions.

But on Earth, Patrik? Do you know your purpose on Earth?

I am meant to collect as much crystal energy as possible and help Cassie enlighten others to its powers. It can be used to promote good in the world.

As you and Cassie bring information forward, be aware that others may want to use it for their own purpose and powers. In the wrong hands, crystal energy could be very dangerous.

I will remember that, Patrik said.

This is a school, Akaleia said, showing Patrik a ring of large stones laid out in a circle. *All ages are educated here at the same time. The elders are our teachers, and all information is conveyed to promote growth, healing, and the ability to create a higher good for all. Since there are no constraints of time, learning is a lifetime accomplishment.*

Christina, Akaleia called out as a floating smaller being with golden hair moved forward.

Patrik, this is my daughter, Christina. She most often resides in the home of Telos, in the modern-day Mount Shasta. I have asked her to come spend time here again in Lemuria.

Patrik spoke greetings to Christina and felt vibrational goodness emanating through her. *You look familiar to me,* he said.

Christina is Cassie's older sister, Akaleia clarified. *It has been many lifetimes since they have been together.*

Patrik smiled as he said, *then Cassie is also your daughter, Akaleia.*

The Sunday neighborhood Christmas party was a huge success. The group conversations around the firepit gradually drifted off as it became later, and people began leaving with gifted plates of extra food, warm memories, and a feeling of Christmas cheer and merriment. "Merry Christmas!" they called to out to each other. "Hope to see you again soon."

"That was wonderful!" Chloe said as she helped Connie clean up the last of the kitchen dishes.

"If you don't know where something goes, just put it on the dining room table, and we'll put them away tomorrow," Connie suggested. "I think we've all had a big day, and you know what? I'm tired!"

"Great neighbors and friends, Connie. This is such a good neighborhood."

"It really is, you know?" I admit I was hesitant when we moved from Ohio last June, but everyone has been so welcoming."

"Here comes the last of the party goers," Chloe joked as Mandy, Jack, and Cassie came through the back door.

"I believe everyone has gone home, now," Daddy said. "We were out there for quite a while talking with Dan's family, and of course the walkers."

"You mean the next-door neighbors?" Mommy quipped.

"Yes, they like the idea of walking each other home now, and Jim made it clear that he was in charge of the flashlight. Tonight, they sang Christmas carols all the way!"

"I taught Poppy and Linde a new trick!" Cassie spoke up. "How to talk to the fairies in the wintertime."

"I don't know, Cassie, do you think they got it?"

"Yes," answered Cassie. "They will remember."

In order for Cassie to travel safely with you, Patrik, we need a much stronger crystal band of energy, Akaleia said. *In many ways crystal energy protects us.*

Patrik blended his being with Akaleia in a gesture of love and farewell. *Thank you, Akaleia.*

We will continue our mission and Dr. Blake's work and send to you what you need to expand the pathway.

Cassie, I have started my journey back to Earth, Patrik messaged her. *Please continue to send crystal energy and positive thoughts.*

Cassie climbed into bed with Merton and Elroy and thought about Patrik. He hadn't arrived yet, and she wondered where he might be in his travels back to Pine Cove for Christmas. She could hear Mandy and Chloe talking in Mandy's room. Mandy continued to be very upset about the restrictions her parents had put her on and the school projects she had to do over Christmas vacation.

Cassie reflected and paused, then sent out a mind wish, *Please help Mandy finish her projects. Please give her more time to do them.*

Cassie turned over on her side and opened her bedside table drawer. She took out a shiny crystal wrapped in tissue. She had two tissues now, one for the crystal that Queen Epona had given her, and one for the crystals that Patrik had given her earlier in December.

She carefully unwrapped a crystal and placed it in the moonlight on her windowsill until it began to glitter. She reached out and brought it to her chest, closed her eyes and created her mind wish.

Patrik, I am sending you energy again, Cassie said. *I want you to use this energy to travel back to me. I want you to be here for Christmas.*

"You seemed to have had a good time tonight, Mandy," Chloe said across Mandy's bedroom as they were getting ready for bed, "and some time together with Mark."

"It was like I was finally able to do something again! My Dad has been awful about my grades. He even took my phone away for almost a week!"

"I'm sure that was very difficult for you. Did it motivate you to get caught up?"

"No, I was angry!"

"But then you got caught up."

"And now I have these stupid projects to do over vacation," Mandy continued. "He says I can't do things with my friends unless I work on the projects every day, like every day! And it's supposed to be my vacation!"

"I'm sure your dad is thinking about what's best for you so you can have a fresh start next semester."

"And the school! You know what they did? They put me on probation and said I might not be able to be a cheerleader anymore. That's just wrong!"

Chloe nodded. "There's a lot going on isn't there? It must be stressful."

"How can I keep up with cheering, anyway?" Mandy answered exasperated. "My dad won't even let me go to the gym with the other girls."

"It sounds like you have a list of things you have to do, which are the two school projects; and a list of things you want to do, which is to be with friends. Is that right?"

"Yes."

"And what do you think is your priority?"

"The things I want to do."

Chloe laughed. "Of course, you do! But you can't do them unless you do the things you have to do first! I gathered from the conversation tonight that Mark is going to be helping you, at least with your math project."

"At least I get to see him."

"Mandy, how did this all happen anyway? When I was here at Halloween, you seemed to be doing okay in school. Did something change?"

"Mandy?"

"People said I was snobby because I was seeing Mark."

"How does that make you snobby?"

"Because he's a junior and on the football and basketball teams, and I'm just a freshman."

"What did you think?"

"I just wanted, you know, to fit in."

Chloe smiled. "I do understand, Mandy, but you have to pick your real priority. Do you want to be on the cheering squad or "fit in," as you call it?"

"Cheering."

"So, then you know what you have to do."

"I don't like it."

Chloe laughed again. "Of course, you don't! You don't have to like it; you have to do it!"

CHAPTER 5

Open the Door

Cassie's mind wandered as she slept in varying dream states. She visualized Patrik travelling away from Lemuria, very far away, and the energy her crystals gave off propelling him forward. She saw Patrik in a mist, speaking through his mind's eye. He looked calm but asked her something. *What? What, Patrik?*

Cassie turned in her bed saying, *Show me ...* but she couldn't understand what he was trying to show her. *I'm here, Patrik. I'm listening.*

Then it was dark in her dream. Dark like the depths of the winter, dark like the depths of the ocean. She saw Patrik waiting for her just like the first day they met in Mr. Mike's lumber yard. Cassie cried out, *Patrik! Come closer ...* "Patrik! Patrik! Come closer!!

"Cassie, Cassie," Daddy said softly, gently shaking her shoulder, "Cassie, you had a dream. Wake up honey. It's Daddy."

Cassie rolled on her back and looked up. "Daddy? What are you doing here?"

Daddy smiled. "You had a dream. You were calling out for Patrik."

"Is Patrik here? I couldn't reach him."

"No, honey, it's still nighttime. Everyone is sleeping."

"He said he would be back for Christmas."

"I'm sure he's trying. Patrik's pretty good at getting where he needs to go."

"He needs me to help him, Daddy. He needs me to travel, too."

"Cassie, listen to me. Patrik is fine. He's fine. He needs you to get some sleep, so you'll be ready for Christmas."

Cassie sat up straight and reached under her pillow to retrieve her crystal rock. She held it in both hands, brought it to her chest, and laid down in her bed again.

"Is that your special rock?" Daddy asked softly. "The one from your bedside table?"

"Yes."

Daddy pulled the blanket up around her shoulders and kissed her forehead. "Let's all try and get some sleep now. This morning will be here soon. Let's try and get some sleep."

School vacation started the next day, and the usual Monday morning routine was substantially slowed. Both Mandy and Cassie were allowed to sleep in. Chloe had gone back to Boston after the neighborhood party and was planning on returning for Christmas week.

Jack was only working half a day on Monday, and then he was going to be on vacation through New Year's Day.

"I just want to check on the internet system security from the weekend," he told Connie at breakfast. "Dan and I are seeing new attempts at breaches. It won't take me long." Jack got ready for work, walked Ned, and headed for the back door. "I'd let Cassie sleep in as long as she wants. She was having wild dreams last night."

"I sort of heard some of that, and then you got up. Thank you, Jack."

"She's all worked up about Patrik being away and not coming home for Christmas yet," Jack said.

Connie shook her head. "Please stop talking like you actually believe that story."

"I think the important thing is that Cassie believes the story. I am trying to support her until she matures into the next developmental phase of her life. When she doesn't need to make fantasy her reality."

"Did you come up with that by yourself, Jack?"

"Chloe may have made that statement at one time," Jack confessed. "I found it reassuring."

"I think when Chloe's here over Christmas, we should talk with her again about Cassie's current behavior. Her input would be reassuring to me."

"Okay, everybody," Mommy announced after they had all come down for breakfast. "It's the day before Christmas Eve. While we are mostly ready, any unfinished preparations should be completed today, so we can enjoy tomorrow and the town square festivities."

"Does she talk like this frequently?" Chloe asked Mandy. "I mean, I know she can be a little controlling at times, but this is revealing."

"She gets stressed out around holidays and parties," Mandy answered. "So, we usually just do what she says."

"So, what kind of things would we need to get done today, Connie? What do you need help with?" Chloe asked.

"I'm good with my list," Mommy replied. "I do plan to make a dessert for Christmas dinner at Phe's house. Maybe a pie, no, probably a cheesecake."

"Okay, Mom, that sounds good." Mandy nodded.

"I like cake," Cassie said. "I can lick the spoon."

"I like to do that too, Cassie!" Chloe exclaimed. "Connie, what do you feel we all need to do today to be free for tomorrow, and at what time tomorrow?"

"Yes. I forgot to tell you about tomorrow."

"How about if we start with today," Chloe said. "Today first."

"Is Daddy coming home early?" Cassie asked. "Daddy can help."

"Yes, he'll be home early, and he can help. You all need to finish any shopping and wrapping today."

"Oh, shopping." Mandy smiled. "I'm in."

"Do you need to shop, Amanda?" Mommy asked. "Don't you already have your presents? Are they wrapped?"

"Cassie, what about you?" Chloe asked turning towards her niece. "Do you have presents?'

"Yes."

"Phe had her over to her studio the other day, and they made gifts," Mommy said.

"That is so sweet," Chloe said. "So, are you all set Cassie?"

"Yes, and Patrik gave me gifts."

"Patrik doesn't make gifts, Cassie!" Mandy snapped at her sister. "He has paws."

Mommy and Chloe burst into laughter as Cassie sat up straighter in her chair, "Patrik can make anything he wants to. He just asks for it!"

"Okay, enough now," Mommy intervened. "Let's get back to today's plans."

"I will volunteer to take anyone shopping who would like to go. We'll have fun and get out of your hair for a while," offered Chloe.

"Me, me!" Mandy waved across the table.

Chloe turned and looked at Cassie. "Cassie, would you like to come shopping with us?"

Cassie shook her head. "I have work to do with Patrik."

"She can help me with the Christmas dessert until Jack gets home," Mommy said. "I'll keep her busy."

"Let's get going then. Connie, when we get back, you can fill us in on tomorrow," Chloe said standing up from the table. "I do love Christmas!"

Cassie spent most of the morning happily writing in her closet with Merton and Elroy. Instead of creating a story, she quieted her mind and listened for messages from Patrik through her mind's eye. She remembered her dream from last night. She remembered Patrik standing in the mist trying to tell her something. *I am here, Patrik. Waiting. Tell me what I need to know.*

"Cassie? It's Daddy. Are you in there?" he asked opening her closet door. "What are you doing, honey?"

"I am listening to Patrik."

"Is he talking with you today?"

"I'm writing what he says."

"Is it the Light Language again?"

"He needs me to do something for him," Cassie answered. "Something important."

"Okay, well maybe you could do that later. How about if you come down for lunch, and then help me and Mom with some things."

"I miss Patrik."

"I do have to say that it is more fun when Patrik is here. So, in that way, I miss him too."

"He says there is something I need, to help me help him."

"Do you know what that is?" Daddy asked patiently.

"No. He's trying to show me."

"Okay honey. Let's go downstairs now."

Cassie stood up somewhat reluctantly and placed her writing book on her quilt. "Stay here and listen," she said to Merton and Elroy. "I'll be back soon."

Mommy planned to fill the afternoon with last-minute decorating and had written out a list of items to pick up at the grocery store.

"Come on, Cassie," Daddy said after lunch. "The grocery store awaits!"

The grocery store was filled with last minute shoppers, and the checkout line was long. "You did a good job being patient, Cassie, thank you," Daddy praised her.

Next, they proceeded to the flower shop where they bought a flower centerpiece for both their dining table for Christmas eve and Nanny Phe's table for Christmas day.

"I like the shiny balls," Cassie said, "they match the sparkles on our ribbons outside!"

"Yes, they do! Let's put these in the car and go say hi to Mike," Daddy said. "We can walk over to his store. It's right up the street."

"Jack, hi! And Cassie too, so good to see you. What are you doing out and about?" Mike asked, shaking Daddy's hand.

"We are doing a few last errands and thought we'd walk up to say hello."

"Cassie, are you all ready for Christmas?" Mike asked, bending down to her. "Do you think Santa will be good to you?"

"I need him to help Patrik come back for Christmas. That's all I asked for."

"Do you know where Patrik is Cassie? Maybe I could ask Santa too."

"He's in Lemuria. He went to see Akaleia. He's trying to come back but he needs something."

"Do you know what he needs?" Mike asked glancing up at Jack.

"No, but he's trying to show me. I know when I see it, I will know what it is."

"That sounds like a big gift, Cassie. I will also ask Santa for you."

"Thank you, Mr. Mike," Cassie said, reaching out to touch his cheek.

"You are a special little girl. Always remember that."

"Mike, what are you and Millie doing tomorrow, Christmas Eve? Do you want to come over for a while?"

"Let me ask Millie, but I think that would be great! We're both working most of the day. Are you sure Connie wants more company after you just had the party?"

"It's more like an open house than anything formal. We'll do a buffet thing with some appetizers and food."

"I love it. Can we bring anything?"

"Not that I can think of," Daddy answered. "But at some point I will need some lifting help, if you know what I mean."

"Roger that," Mike answered. "I got you covered."

That night everyone sat at the dinner table talking about what they had done during the day.

"Supper is great, Connie, thank you." Chloe spoke up. "Really good."

"We saw Twirla at the mall, and Peter and Katie too," Mandy said between chewing. "They had a great time at the party."

"What did you all do at the mall?" asked Daddy.

"Shopped," Mandy said matter-of-factly. "Shopped."

Daddy straightened in his chair and turned towards Mandy, "And did your day include any time working on your school projects?"

"Mark's not available till Thursday. We are going to meet then."

"I didn't ask you what Mark did on your projects today."

"Here's a plan," Chloe spoke up quickly. "Mandy and I are going to go through her assignments tomorrow morning, early, before the Christmas Eve festivities start. We are going to work on a plan and outline the work she needs to do with a schedule."

"That sounds great!" Mommy said. "Mandy always does better with a plan."

"Don't we all?" Chloe said. "I think a plan is absolutely needed."

Cassie looked up from her plate. "Patrik needs a plan too."

"Oh, Cassie," Mommy said with a sigh.

"What kind of plan does Patrik need?" Chloe asked. "Do you know?"

"He needs a plan to get back to me for Christmas."

"Well, why don't we talk about that tomorrow morning too? We'll take all that you know and put it into a map, so to speak, for Patrik to follow. How does that sound?"

"Good."

"You're going to be busy tomorrow, Chloe," Daddy said.

"I like busy, and it's too cold to go to the beach."

"Connie, what time do the things in town start?" Chloe asked.

"About one. It's just for a couple of hours. They have Christmas caroling and strolls, last minute time with Santa, and shops where the kids are given little presents."

Chloe nodded. "Cool. It gets everyone in the mood."

"Then we'll come back and have a simple dinner and maybe some people dropping in," Mommy added.

"I'll help with food prep, and when the girls aren't doing their plans with you," Daddy said, "they can help too!"

"Looking forward to it!" Chloe exclaimed. "I get to have a real Christmas this year!"

On the way to her bed, Cassie opened her closet door and picked up Merton and Elroy from their place on her quilt. "Come talk to me," she said. "Are there any messages from Patrik?"

Her green composition book was opened to the page she had been writing on, but there were no new writings.

"He didn't tell you anything more," she said sadly. "It's okay. Thank you for trying."

Cassie brought her stuffed toys over to her bed and tucked them in under the blankets by the window. "You'll be warm here," she said patting them.

"Cassie, are you ready for bed?" Daddy asked coming into her room. "Teeth brushed; face washed?"

"Yes, Daddy."

"Any new news from Patrik?"

"No Daddy. Merton and Elroy didn't have any other messages either."

"Do you have your crystal?"

Cassie reached over and opened her bedside drawer and took out a tissue that held the crystal from Queen Epona.

"Why don't you take out the tissue with the ones that Patrik gave you? Maybe that will make a better connection for communication."

Cassie reached over and put back the first tissue and took out the second one.

"Six."

"Wouldn't six transmit more energy than one?"

"I think so."

"Well try it tonight. Put them under your pillow. I'll come in again if you have bad dreams, but I think you are going to have a good night's sleep."

"Okay, Daddy," Cassie replied, holding the group of crystals in the tissue in her hand.

"Do you think Patrik will come back?"

"I think Patrik will always be close in your heart. And your heart is right here," Daddy said pointing to Cassie's chest. "We hold everyone we love in our hearts."

Cassie nodded as Daddy kissed her forehead, "Good night, sweetheart, and sweet dreams."

Cassie drifted off into a deep sleep, holding the tissue packet of crystals tightly in her hand. She repeated in her mind wishes, *Patrik, come talk to me. Come home.*

Her dreams once again focused on Patrik, but this time she saw him walking out of the mist. *Patrik…*

Patrik's voice was clearer: *Cassie, open the door. Put me in the tree. Put me with a crystal in the tree. Close the door.*

Cassie sat up, startled. She looked around her room as the waning moonlight shone through her window. She reached out and touched Merton and Elroy and breathed a sigh of relief, then searched her sheets for the crystal tissue packet.

Under your pillow Cassie.

"Patrik?" she said out loud.

Cassie reached under her pillow and grabbed the tissue packet of crystals and brought them to her chest.

Cassie, open the door. Put me in the tree. Put me with a crystal in the tree. Close the door.

The crystals were warm against her skin and began to glow in the faint moonlight.

I hear you, Patrik. Help me find the door.

"Oh, good morning, everyone," Chloe sang out coming into the kitchen about 6:30 Christmas Eve morning. "Am I early? The girls aren't up yet?"

"You are early by Mandy's clock for sure. Cassie seems to be sleeping in too," Jack said.

"Did she have dreams again last night?" Chloe asked.

"Not that we know of. I think she had a restful night."

"That would be good," Chloe replied. "If she's sleeping well, then she's more relaxed."

"While you're here, Chloe," Connie started, then paused. "We, ah, we would like to talk with you about the girls and how you see them behaviorally. You know, how do you think they're doing?"

"Okay," Chloe said. "But the short answer is they are doing well and are going to be fine. They are doing fine."

"They have issues," Connie said.

"We all have issues Connie."

"But these issues are interfering with their lives, their growth!"

Chloe took a deep breath. "Connie, I know you only want the best for your family and trust me, please, when I tell you they are developing normally, normally at their own pace. Like all of us, they learn from their experiences."

"Well, that's not helpful," Connie said. "What do we do to create positive experiences for them?"

Chloe furrowed her brow and paused before she spoke again, "You are helping to create positive experiences every day in both their lives, and very much so! But you can't control the outcomes of their experiences. You can guide them, and you are doing a fabulous job with that. But you can't control how they go through life."

"I can't believe you are telling me that all of this is normal," Connie said. "Mandy is on probation, in danger of failing this semester, and being kicked off the cheering squad. Cassie, well she lives in her own fantasy world, and we know what trouble that is."

"We do?" Jack asked.

"Yes, Connie. The basis of all of that is true."

"Chloe," Jack offered, "Do you think this will all pass by in time?"

"When we talk about time, well yes. Except that our personal timeline and the reality of time as a measure of when things will occur may be two different things."

"Oh God," Connie groaned. "The time thing again."

"Look guys. As humans we develop in processes. We learn by doing. Each of us does that in our own way and in our own time."

"How can we speed that up?" Connie asked very seriously.

"Each of us has our own clock," Chloe said.

"You need to ask Cassie about her time thing, Connie," Jack added. "It's very interesting."

"That's so ridiculous!" Connie shouted.

"I would ask that you trust in each girl's own experiences," Chloe said. "Continue to support them in the ways that you are doing. Have patience, and trust in their abilities and judgement."

"And try and get through the day-to-day trials and tribulations," Connie added.

"Probably some," Chloe replied. "And rejoice in the good times too! Each day brings positive moments and love of family!"

"Hello, Sunshine!" Daddy called out to Cassie as she made her way to the kitchen table in her pajamas and bathrobe. "How did you sleep?"

"Good."

"Here's some juice to help you get started," Mommy said, placing a glass on the table.

"Thank you," Cassie said.

"Did you have any dreams?" Daddy asked.

"Patrik told me what to do, but I don't know what it means."

"What did Patrik tell you to do?"

"Open the door. Put me in the tree. Put me with a crystal in the tree. Close the door."

"Is it the magic tree? We've looked down there before Cassie, but we've never found a door in the tree."

"I couldn't see it. I asked him to show me the door."

"And he needs this to come back for Christmas?"

"Yes."

Chloe stood by the sink and cleared her throat. "Sorry, little tickle," she said looking back at Daddy and raising her eyebrows. "You know Cassie, Christmas is a magical time. You never know what might appear to help you out."

Cassie looked up at Auntie Chloe, "Christmas is tomorrow."

"Yes it is, but you know there is as much time as you want, right Cassie?" You have to ask for it, remember?"

"My goodness," Daddy said leaning back in his chair. "I never would have thought of that."

"It's a magical time," Chloe said. "For all those who believe."

Chloe began working with Cassie after breakfast to create a plan for Patrik to come back from Lemuria.

"I'll get Mandy up soon," Mommy said. "She does need to get that plan done for her schoolwork."

"Yes indeed," Daddy said. "She needs to get it done this morning."

"Cassie, remember when we were out in the potting shed last summer and we drew maps of our homes?" Chloe asked.

"Yes."

"Let's start with where that map ended and work backwards to home."

"For Patrik to follow," Cassie said as she and Chloe started to draw the places Cassie could remember on the drawing paper at the dining room table.

"What were the words Patrik told you? What do you need to do?"

Cassie nodded, "Open the door. Put me in the tree. Put me with a crystal in the tree. Close the door."

"So, we need to include the potting shed and the magic tree too, right? Where are we going to put that?"

"I'm going to put it here," Cassie indicated pointing to the bottom right corner. But I'm going to put our house over here, not together."

"Okay. Why do you want to put them apart?"

"Because sometimes Patrik and I can travel through my closet."

"Oh, so there are other ways to access the magic tree."

"We go to the tunnels in the tree through my closet."

Chloe nodded, "A portal. Where do the tunnels take you?"

"I think Patrik needs more energy to come back," Cassie said ignoring Chloe's question and drawing a new square to represent their house. That's why he wants me to use a crystal."

"Where do you want to put the crystal?"

Cassie carefully looked at her new map. "In the house. Daddy said we can't go down to the magic tree in winter anymore."

"How far do you think Patrik has been able to come back? Can you tell when he talks with you?"

"He came out of the mist, but it's still cloudy."

"Is that what the Elemental Kingdom looks like?" Chloe asked.

"No, he's not there yet."

Chloe looked at the map. "Draw your crystal where you think it should be honey."

"What are you drawing here, Cassie?" Chloe asked as she turned back to the map they had created.

"I'm filling in the Christmas decorations and the presents!"

"Where did you decide to put the crystal?"

"It belongs under the Christmas tree. I put it here."

"You know best, Cassie. Follow your intuition."

"I'm ready to start our plan, Auntie Chloe," Mandy said from the doorway.

"Great! You'll need your laptop so we can look at the assignments. After that, we are all going into town, remember?"

"Oh, okay, I guess," Mandy said turning away from the dining room. "I'll be back."

The celebration in Pine Cove was very festive. People were caroling on the town square, and shops were providing cocoa or hot cider with baked goods.

"Okay, everybody in the house," Daddy directed when they came back from the town activities. "What a great time that was!"

"There were so many people there too!" Mommy said. "I didn't know I knew so many people!"

"I'm upstairs," Mandy said dashing by them.

"Mark," Cassie giggled. "Mark is going to call her."

"Cassie, you don't know that for sure," Mommy said. "She has lots of friends."

"I know what I heard her say," Cassie replied. "She told him."

"This is such a pretty coastal town," Chloe spoke up. "I find things I like here every time I come,"

"You should come more often!" Mommy said sincerely. "That would be fine with us."

"Thank you. I always appreciate your hospitality and the hugs from this little one," Chloe said wrapping her arms around Cassie. "What prep work do you need to do for the buffet?"

"I have some things in the freezer to heat up. And Jack picked up a couple platters from the deli today too. Very casual."

"Are your parents coming over Jack?" Chloe asked.

"Probably for a little while. They'll have something to eat and say hello. They are doing Christmas dinner tomorrow so they will be busy early in the day."

"Jack, will you go down to the freezer and bring up the frozen food labeled EVE?" Mommy asked.

"Sure, how many packages do you think I am looking for?"

"Cassie, will you help Daddy bring things up from the freezer, please? He's going to need another hand."

"Okay Mommy," Cassie said as she started to follow her father to the door by his office.

"Careful on the stairs," Daddy reminded her. "Hold onto the railing."

The cellar was a dark place even when the lights were turned on. Daddy made sure Cassie got safely down the stairs, then walked over and lifted the cover on the freezer. "Let's see what surprises we have in here for tonight!"

Cassie walked farther into the cellar and over to one of the outside walls. She put her hands on the field stone foundation and felt their ridges.

"What are you doing,?" Daddy asked.

"There is something behind this," Cassie said seriously. "It moves."

Daddy walked over to the wall where Cassie was standing and put the palms of his hands on the large field stones. "I don't feel anything."

"Don't open it, Daddy. Keep it closed."

"Okay, I won't. Let's get the food upstairs for your Mom now. She's waiting."

Daddy gave Cassie two bags of cookies and pulled out a lasagna, and 2 loaves of Italian bread. "This is it I think," he said. "Let's go up."

Cassie walked to the stairs while still looking at the wall. "Keep it closed," she repeated.

"No problem, Cassie. It's closed. Let's go celebrate Christmas!"

Connie had started the stove oven and the wall oven. The frozen items were immediately put in to begin to cook.

"It only takes about an hour, an hour and a half at the most," she explained.

"How did Mandy's planning session go this morning," Daddy asked Chloe as they all stood in the kitchen.

"It was a teachable moment for me," Chloe said. "I learned a lot."

"What did Mandy get out of it?"

"Yes, well, clearly it helped organize and prioritize her projects. She has to dig in to find some answers, but truly, I don't think they are that hard."

"So, you think she can work off this plan?"

"Absolutely. Her biggest obstacle will be allocating time to focus on the work and not get distracted."

"Can you send me a hard copy of your plan? I think we are going to need to keep on top of this to be successful."

"Sure Jack. But why don't you ask Mandy to send it to you. She is the one responsible for the work, after all."

"Yes, that's true. I will do that."

"Cassie," Mommy called up from the bottom of the stairs, "come on down. Poppy and Twirla are here and Nanny Phe and Papa Ed."

"Can I go up?" Poppy asked.

"Oh, sure honey. Just get Cassie and come back down for the party."

"Are you all ready?" Twirla asked Connie. "Everything done?"

"Gosh, I hope so! I can tell you I'm done! What about you? Did you finish the doll costumes you were making?"

"I did! They're wonderful! And I can't wait till the girls see what Santa brings. They'll be so surprised," Twirla said. "I can hardly wait!"

CHAPTER 6

Christmas Wishes

The dining room table was set up for the Christmas Eve buffet with meat and cheese platters, rolls, and salads. "About a half hour more for the hot items," Mommy told everyone. "Cassie and Chloe, why don't you bring down any wrapped presents you have for all of us, and put them under the tree?"

"Great idea," Chloe echoed. "I'll ask Mandy while I'm up there."

Cassie walked up the stairs to her bedroom to find the gifts she had made with Nanny Phe, and to decide who she was giving the four crystals to. She had given it careful thought, and although she could think of many people who would think a crystal was a nice gift, she wanted to give them to people she felt would believe in them and use them. She asked Patrik for guidance, but he told her to follow her heart. In the end she decided on Poppy, her Daddy, one for Peter and Katie, and one for Mr. Mike and Millie to share.

Nanny Phe had helped Cassie wrap the lavender bouquets in tissue paper and tie them with green ribbons. Cassie smiled knowing she had a gift for everyone.

"Hi Cassie," Poppy called out as she entered her bedroom. "Are you ready for Christmas?"

"Patrik isn't here yet. I'm waiting for him."

"When is he coming?"

"I don't know. But he told me to do something for him, and I have to wait to find a door." "What kind of door?"

"A door in a tree, but it's not the magic tree behind the potting shed."

Poppy thought for a moment. "Patrik will show you, Cassie. And I can help you too. He'll be back."

"Cassie, Poppy," Mommy called up the stairs. "Come on down. There is food ready, and guests have arrived."

Cassie and Poppy walked down the stairs and into the kitchen where Nanny Phe and Papa Ed greeted them. "Have you had a wonderful day?" Nanny Phe asked. "I saw you at the Christmas Eve festival."

Cassie hugged her grandmother tightly, "Patrik isn't here yet."

"But I think he will be soon," Nanny Phe replied. "This is a magical night."

"Ho, Ho, Ho, Merry Christmas!" Daddy called out as Peter and Katie came in the kitchen door.

"Hello girls," Katie smiled at them. "So good to see you! Are you enjoying your Christmas vacation?"

"We have lots to do," Poppy replied. "And when Patrik comes we'll have even more to do!"

"I bet that's so!" Katie said. "He hasn't been to school lately, so you'll have lots of things to catch up on with him."

"Patrik's been working," Cassie said. "He's been away."

"Well, that explains it. Tell Patrik if he wants to come back to class, he's welcome as long as he's quiet."

"I help Patrik be quiet too," Poppy declared. "We both help him behave."

"Come on, girls," Twirla called from the dining room entry. "Let me help you get some plates for dinner and get settled."

"Everything looks so wonderful, Connie," Twirla said. "Thank you for doing this."

"It wouldn't be Christmas if we weren't all together," Connie replied, smiling at her friend. "And all together, we do have a big family!"

"Hello Mike and Millie!!" Cassie heard her father call out from the kitchen. "You're just in time!"

People stayed for several hours enjoying the food, company, and stories about their favorite Christmas memories. Stacks of brightly wrapped presents for members of the family were already under the tree, "But Santa doesn't come until tomorrow!" Mommy chimed in.

"Oh, I think we'll all be very excited when we see what Santa brings," Twirla said with a wink.

Cassie inched over to Poppy and whispered, "I'll be happy when Patrik comes back."

People began to leave soon after the desserts were shared, saying their goodbyes and wishes for a Merry Christmas the next day.

Mike and Millie stayed later than the other guests, standing in the kitchen and talking with Jack and Connie. Cassie and Mandy had gone upstairs much earlier, and Chloe said her good nights, adding that she would check in on Cassie and make sure she was settled into bed.

"Are you all ready for bed, Cassie? Face washed; teeth brushed?" Chloe asked.

"What if Patrik doesn't come home, Auntie Chloe? What if he is lost forever?"

Chloe sat down on the edge of Cassie's bed and brought Merton and Elroy up closer to Cassie's chest. "Cassie, I know it's hard to wait for things that are so important to you. Christmas is like that, don't you think? It's only one day, and then we have to wait a whole year again for it to come. But it always comes back again, doesn't it?"

"Yes."

"Christmastime is filled with magic. Everything is possible," Chloe spoke softly, waving her hands in the air. "The magic is here. In this room and under the Christmas tree. Believe. And believe in Patrik too, because you know he is trying really hard to get here."

"Okay."

"I love you sweet Cassie, and I will see you in the morning for cocoa and presents!"

96

"Okay, Mike," Jack said, grabbing his jacket from the peg in the hallway. "The time has come to retrieve the potting shed doll house."

"I can hardly wait to see this," Mille said to Connie. "Mike has been talking about it since Thanksgiving. Secretly, I think they like playing with it too!"

"They have clearly had a good time. Jack insists they know how to open the windows in the real potting shed now. Come spring, they're on it."

Connie walked over and opened the kitchen door as Jack and Mike came across the deck from the workshop carrying the house. "Jack, this is really big!"

"And heavier than I expected it to be too," Jack said. "You all set Mike? Easy around the door."

"Got it, buddy. Keep going."

"Wow!" Millie exclaimed. "I had no idea. Will you make me one?"

Mike chuckled, "You want a potting shed?"

"No, a barn with some horses. I think you guys could go into business together. We could have a whole Pine Cove Village; Darby's store, Twirla's dance studio. I bet you'd make a lot of money doing that."

"This way, Mike. Let's set it down over here by the big window. Cassie will have room to play with it in the morning."

"Here's the little figures and shed furniture," Connie said coming across the living room. "This is going to be so special."

"Oh, look at the little Cassie and Patrik!" Mille exclaimed picking up the two figures. "And this must be Poppy!"

"Shhhh.." Chloe cautioned coming down the stairs, "I can hear you upstairs. Oh, my goodness! Look how cute this is!"

"Chloe, we are not staying up all night playing with this," Connie said.

"But we could." Chloe smiled.

"Can I play too?" Millie asked.

"Ladies," Jack addressed them, "We need to get some sleep. Morning will be here soon. Children will be out of bed."

"Yup," Mike agreed. "Time to go check on the horses one more time, Millie, and button up the barn for the night."

"Are you going to come to my mother's for Christmas dinner tomorrow?" Jack asked. "I heard her ask you tonight."

"We'll see," Mike said. "Millie has to go into the clinic tomorrow and check on the animals. Hopefully there will not be any emergency calls."

"If my day goes well," Millie replied, "we'd love to come by."

"Then it's all set. We'll see you tomorrow!"

"Thank you for all your help with everything, Mike. I couldn't have done this without you," Jack said, hugging his friend.

"My pleasure, really. I can't wait to see Cassie's face!

Mike and Millie said their goodbyes and proceeded up the driveway and around to Millie's house, then down her driveway towards the barn. Snow had begun to fall softly, and a thin layer of white covered the backyard. Millie looked up and felt the crystals falling on her face, "I love this beautiful night."

Mike reached out and gently brushed away the snowflakes from her cheeks. "You are beautiful," he said, leaning forward to kiss her.

Luna and Kai neighed softly as they heard the barn door open and footsteps coming closer.

"Hey guys," Millie greeted them. "Got everything you need? We came to say good night."

Both Mike and Millie opened the gates to the stalls and started to pat down each horse. "Time for bed," Mike said as his arm slid down the side of Luna. "Almost Christmas."

Millie placed her hands on Kai's neck and let them slide down his back. "You're a good boy Kai. We love you."

"Millie," Mike said as she came out of the stall, "Millie, I want to ask you something."

Millie smiled and walked forward, standing in front of Mike. "Okay," she said softly. "Okay."

Mike smiled. "You are the love of my life. I want to ask you to marry me."

"Well Michael Cavanaugh, you big warm bear. You will have to ask me."

Mike drew in a deep breath. "I don't have a ring."

"I don't need a ring," Millie said. "Try again."

Mike reached out and grasped both Millie's hands and knelt before her. "Millie, I love you with my whole heart. I want to spend my life with you, forever. Will you please marry me?"

"Yes," Millie said muffled by Mike's kisses. "Yes."

Cassie awoke with a start, "Patrik? Patrik?"

Cassie, open the door. Put me in the tree. Put me with a crystal in the tree. Close the door.

Cassie sat up and scanned her room. It was still night. The room was dark and when she looked out the window, the backyard was dark also.

Patrik? Are you here?

Cassie, open the door. Put me in the tree. Put me with a crystal in the tree. Close the door.

Where is the door? Patrik, where is the door?

Follow the magic, Cassie.

Cassie blinked as she tried to become more awake and absorb her surroundings. She listened again and tried to understand what she had just heard. Reaching under her pillow, she grabbed the crystal rock that lay safely underneath it. It was warm, and Cassie brought it up to her chest. *Where is the door?* she mind wished quietly. *Show me the door.*

The crystal began to glow brightly in her hands and cast a beam into the bedroom. Cassie got out of bed, and as she did, the light expanded into the hallway. Cassie followed the light. As she walked, each step seemed to increase the length of the light ahead of her and extinguish the light behind her. She followed the trail to the front stairs where the beam shifted downward. Cassie took a deep breath and grabbed the railing with one hand. She kept the crystal tight in the other, and slowly proceeded down the stairs. The light turned to the right and into the living room. Cassie walked forward, mesmerized by the Christmas tree and decorations shimmering in the crystal light. *Show me the door,* she mind wished again.

The light guided her toward the big window. "Ah!" Cassie cried out kneeling on the rug and reaching out to touch the roof of the potting shed dollhouse. The crystal dropped to the floor and continued to illuminate all of it. "Patrik? Are you here?"

The dollhouse was mounted on a large board that had been painted to contain a garden area. Two miniature gnome statues stood outside the front doors of the potting shed on stone steps. Cassie lifted the front of the roof and pulled on a knob that moved the whole front over to one side. Inside, two small figures sat on chairs at a table. She picked them up and realized they looked like her and Poppy. A fireplace was built in the corner and a small door was in the back of the room that opened when she lifted the metal rod. She then saw that a large tree branch was mounted on the board behind the house. Cassie placed her 'Cassie doll' back inside the shed and moved it through the small door to the stairs. She then crawled around the board, so she was at the back of the shed, and walked her Cassie doll down the mounted stone steps. "Patrik!" she shrieked embracing the dog figurine in front to the tree.

Cassie, open the door. Put me in the tree. Put me with a crystal in the tree. Close the door.

Cassie opened the little door in the front of the tree branch and placed her Patrik doll inside, then reached around the shed to pick up the crystal from the living room floor. The crystal glowed brighter in Cassie's hands and sent a beam to the magic tree. Cassie brought the crystal to her chest, *Please bring Patrik home,* she mind wished again. The crystal fit snugly in the tree with Patrik. She closed the door and closed her eyes. "Tree of Life, Worlds Unite; Tree of Life, Worlds Unite, Tree of Life, Worlds Unite," she said aloud. When Cassie opened her eyes the crystal light was no longer shining from inside the tree and the living room was dark.

"Cassie?" Daddy said, coming across the room. "It's not Christmas morning yet, honey."

"I did what Patrik asked me to do, but he hasn't come back yet."

"What did you do?"

"I opened the door. I put him in the tree. I put a crystal in the tree. I shut the door."

"Patrik asked you to do all those things?"

"Yes. And now I'm waiting."

"Can you wait in your bed?"

"I guess so."

"Cassie, you told me Patrik has been travelling. Someplace far away."

"Lemuria," Cassie said softly.

"It's going to take him a long while to get back, don't you think?"

"He's been coming for a while. He just needed more crystal energy to get back."

"Well, I think we should give him some more time. Remember what you said about time? We can create the time we want. Why don't you go back to bed and create some time for Patrik if you think he needs more time."

"Patrik and I can shorten time too, Daddy."

"So, it could go faster?"

"Yes."

"This night is getting shorter even as we speak. Let's go back to bed and wait for morning, please."

"Okay. Patrik can come through my closet too."

"Amen to that! You'll be in bed and know right off. Up we go."

Daddy followed Cassie up the stairs to her room and tucked her into bed again.

"Okay, you have Merton and Elroy right here," Daddy said bringing the pair back up under Cassie's arm. Are you all set now?"

"Can you open the closet door?"

"Yup, last thing, Cassie," Daddy said as he walked over and opened the door. "Sleep well now."

"Daddy, will you tell Patrik to come home please?"

Daddy took a deep breath and walked over to sit on Cassie's bed again. "Patrik," he said calmly. "We miss you. Cassie misses you very much. Please come home."

"Thank you, Daddy."

"Goodnight, Sunshine. See you in the morning."

Connie had coffee ready for Jack the next morning when he came in the door from taking Ned outside.

"It's cold out there, today," he said. "Coffee is just what I need."

"Should we get everyone up for Christmas presents?" Connie asked. "I'm surprised Cassie isn't up yet."

"She was up in the middle of the night," Jack replied. "She found the potting shed doll house. It was a big hit. We were up for a while."

"I slept right through it!" Connie said with a smile. "Glad she liked the doll house."

"Maybe you were dozing sweetheart; I don't really think you missed it."

"Morning, guys," Chloe said coming into the kitchen. "Coffee ready?"

"Right here," Connie said, handing her a steaming cup.

"Merry Christmas and thank you," Chloe replied wrapping her hands around the mug.

"Merry Christmas," Jack and Connie both said as footsteps sounded down the stairs.

"Cassie." Jack nodded. "I am very sure it's not Mandy."

Connie, Jack, and Chloe took their coffees into the living room where Cassie was busily exploring all the features of the potting shed doll house.

"The windows open!" she exclaimed. "They know how to open!"

"Any news from Patrik?" Daddy asked while Mommy shook her head at him.

"No, but I'm opening all the windows," replied Cassie.

"Cassie, this is so much fun," Chloe said coming to kneel beside her. "I would love to play with you."

"Cassie, have you seen your new bicycle that Santa brought you? It's red. You like red," Mommy interrupted. "You should come look at your bicycle."

"We could play school, Auntie Chloe," Cassie said happily. "We could sit at the table."

"Can I be Poppy for now?" Chloe asked. "I'll sit here. Are you the teacher?"

"Yes. Let's learn more about the magic tree today."

"Okay. Is that what you wrote on the chalk board?"

"I didn't write on it," Cassie said.

"Jack, did you write on it?" Chloe asked.

"No, what does it say?"

Cassie looked closer. "It's Light language. It says, I'm home!"

Chloe looked at Jack and Connie. "I didn't write on it," Daddy repeated.

"Patrik, where are you?" Cassie pleaded. "Show me."

The crystal light began to shine from inside the tree, casting a dim light into the back of the potting shed dollhouse.

"He's barking!" Cassie shouted. "Are you here?" she asked as she opened the door to the magic tree.

"Right here!"

Cassie laughed as she fell back on the floor. "Patrik, you're back!"

"Maybe this wasn't a great idea, Jack," Mommy said sarcastically. "I think you built another open door to fantasy land."

"Come on, Mandy! Everybody's waiting for you to come downstairs to start opening presents," Chloe called out as she entered her bedroom.

"I'm coming," Mandy groaned turning her head back into her pillow.

"No, you don't!" Chloe said pulling the bed covers off her, "Up, up, up!"

"Arrghhhh …"

"I know that's a yes. It's Christmas! Joy, Joy, Joy!"

"I'm getting up, Auntie Chloe."

"Show me. I'm not leaving until you do. Here's a sweatshirt," Chloe said holding out Mandy's sweatshirt in front of her.

Mandy slowly stood up and grabbed her sweatshirt. "I hope this is worth it."

"Why are you so grumpy? It's Christmas!"

"I'm not going to get what I wanted."

"Mandy. Getting what you want is not really what Christmas is about."

"Well, I deserve to get what I want."

"Really?" Chloe asked. "That's quite the statement. Let's talk about that later, but for now, let's go downstairs and open presents!"

Nanny Phe was at her back door to welcome them for Christmas dinner as they got out of the Ford Explorer.

"Hello, Cassie and Mandy! Come right this way," she greeted them.

"Merry Christmas!" Daddy called out to her as he and Mommy grabbed some presents from the back of the car to bring in.

"That one's mine, Jack," Chloe said, "I can take that. And this bag has all the presents Cassie made for everyone."

"That's very thoughtful of her," said Daddy as he walked over to the house. "Looks like Peter and Katie are already here."

"Hello, everyone," Mommy called out coming into the kitchen.

"Twirla just drove in," Daddy said. I'll stay here by the door and wait for them."

"Let's put the presents over here by the tree," Phe said as she motioned to Chloe and Connie. "My goodness there's a lot!"

"Hi Cassie," Poppy called from the doorway. "Is Patrik here?"

"No Patrik," Mommy spoke up. "No Patrik allowed."

"Oh, Connie, that's okay," Phe said. "I love dogs."

"Patrik came home, Poppy," Cassie said excitedly. "He's resting at our house."

"That's wonderful news Cassie!" Nanny Phe smiled at her while Poppy clapped her hands. "He's been gone a long time. Everyone should be home for Christmas."

"Twirla, let me take your coat," Papa Ed offered. "Can I get you something to drink?"

"I got it covered, Dad," Daddy said, coming out of the dining room.

"Why don't we open presents before we eat," Nanny Phe said. "There's plenty of time."

"Peter's Santa!" Daddy cried out. "I called it first. Where's the hat?"

"Jack, you're such a big twerp," Peter replied, taking the hat.

"Let me see, Peter," Katie asked. "I do love a Santa!"

"And I know you do!" Peter said with a wink. "Let's have some elf helpers. Cassie and Poppy, would you like to be my elf helpers?"

Poppy and Cassie stood up readily as Peter called out names and handed the presents to the girls to deliver. Soon everyone had packages open, and the room was filled with wrapping paper and ribbons.

"Really!" Mandy screamed. "Nanny Phe and Papa Ed, really?"

"It comes with a strict contract," Daddy said sternly as Mandy took her new phone out of the box and jumped up to hug her grandparents. "And it can be taken back if you do not live up to the expectations of the contract."

"This is great!" Mandy shouted. "It's just what I wanted!"

"You need to listen to your father, Mandy," Papa Ed added. "We won't have a problem taking it back if necessary."

"Cassie," Twirla said across the room, "Poppy got a bicycle from Santa for Christmas."

"It's blue," Poppy said, "and I have to learn how to ride it."

"I got a red one," Cassie said.

Poppy smiled at her friend. "We can learn to ride together!"

"Well, we need to wait for the snow to melt, to make sure it's safe," Mommy said.

"The driveway will melt between storms, Connie," Daddy said. "They can learn to ride in the driveway."

"And once they are comfortable," Twirla began to say when Mommy interrupted her, "And careful. Helmets are required at all times."

"Yes, of course," added Twirla, "then we could all go to the park and ride on the trails."

"Katie and I could come, too," Peter said. "We could ride over and meet you."

"Great idea Peter!" Daddy exclaimed.

"And then you can ride over here for a picnic," Nanny Phe told them all. "That will be a wonderful day!"

"Knock, knock," Mike said from the kitchen doorway. "I hope we're not too late."

"Come on in, Mike and Millie," Papa Ed welcomed them. "Here, let me take your coats. You're right on time. We're just finishing presents."

Mike and Millie came into the living room with "flowers for the hostess," Mike said as he handed Phe an evergreen arrangement in a glass bowl with a candle.

"This smells wonderful!" Phe said, "Thank you so much."

"That's my bag, Uncle Peter," Cassie said reaching out her hand. "I have gifts for everyone."

"Beautiful, Cassie. Beautiful," Nanny Phe encouraged her.

"First, I have gifts that Nanny Phe and I made. They smell good. If you put them under your pillow the fairies from the potting shed garden will bring you sweet dreams," Cassie announced as she handed out the lavender bouquets to everyone.

"These are so pretty, thank you!" Katie said as she shared it with Peter to smell.

"A breath of spring." Chloe smiled.

"Does this really work?" Mandy asked.

"You have to put it under your pillow," Cassie said, "and believe."

Mandy shrugged, "I don't believe."

"And these are gifts from me and Patrik," Cassie said putting her hand in the bag and pulling out four crystal stones. "Patrik gave me these from the Elemental Kingdom. You can make wishes with them. They are very powerful."

"Oh boy," Mommy said shaking her head, "here we go."

106

"I have a special present for you, Poppy," Cassie said, holding out one of her crystals in the palm of her hand. Poppy's eyes lit up as she reached out and took the crystal. She drew the crystal to her chest and closed her eyes, "I wish that I can see Patrik. Or at least hear his barking."

"That's very special, Poppy," Twirla said.

"Thank you, Cassie," Poppy added with a hug.

"And this one is for Uncle Peter and Miss Douglass," Cassie said holding it out to them. "You can make any wish you want."

"Cassie, you and Poppy can call me Katie when we're not in school. We're friends and family."

"I sure hope so!" Daddy shouted. "We've been waiting on you two!"

"Jack, stop, that's not polite," Mommy scolded him. "Let them enjoy their time together."

"Thank you, sweetheart," Peter said giving Cassie a hug. "We love it."

"We'll have to think of a special wish," Katie added, "together."

"And thank you also, Connie," Peter said as Katie's cheeks blushed. "We are absolutely enjoying our time together at our own pace."

"And this one is for you, Mr. Mike and Millie. To share. Patrik says you can have one wish."

Mike took the crystal from Cassie's hand and placed it in Millie's hand as he held it close with his. "Mike and I are getting married!" Millie blurted out. "We are!"

"What? Congratulations! This is wonderful!" people called out as Daddy shook Mike's hand and Chloe embraced Millie.

"We just thought it was the right time," Millie spoke up as she looked at Cassie, "everything fit together."

"Absolutely!" Papa Ed called out. "You have been right for each other from the beginning!"

"Do you have a wedding date?" Mommy asked.

"Oh, no, we haven't really had time to talk about that yet," Millie said.

"Soon though, we're bursting ready!" Mike said as everyone in the room laughed, and Mike held Millie close to him.

Cassie smiled at Mike and Millie. "That was my wish," she said, "for you to be together. You still have one wish you can make."

"We will consider that carefully, Cassie," Mike said. "Thank you."

"Daddy, this crystal is for you," Cassie said as she placed the last one in his hand. "Patrik says to hold it close, and when the time is right, you will know the wish you need to make."

"Thank you," Daddy replied. "I will treasure this."

"That's all the crystals I have to give away," Cassie announced. "I had to save one for me."

"Beautifully done, Cassie," Nanny Phe spoke up. "You have shared things that are precious to you with everyone. That is the true spirit of Christmas!"

Cassie climbed into her bed Christmas night with Patrik lying beside her and Merton and Elroy under her arm. "Thank you for coming home, Patrik," she said as she patted his fur. "I missed you."

"You found the door Cassie, you did exactly what I asked and needed."

"Did you find Akaleia?"

"Yes. We have a lot to talk about. There are connections to Lemuria which you must help us strengthen, and connections to Telos which you will need to create."

"What's Telos?" Cassie asked.

"It is another colony that was started when Lemuria began to fail. It began to sink into the ocean. Some Lemurians migrated there."

"Is it going to sink into the ocean too?"

"No, it is located inside a mountain, Mount Shasta."

"Why do you need me?"

"Telos needs a human presence to be able to move from the colony into the earthly mountain. Telos needs an ability to communicate directly between the Lemurians and human beings."

"But you can communicate with human beings."

"Cassie, I need you to know how special you are, to be able to navigate both worlds as one being. You do not have to transform to do it."

"But how will I know what to do?"

"You will always be guided," Patrik said. "Time. We must be present to time."

"Will you need to travel again?" Cassie asked.

"We will need to travel together. We need your help; first in Lemuria. Our travel will require a much longer period of time."

"I have two crystals left. One from you and one from Queen Epona," Cassie said. "I gave four crystals out, and I told them they can each make a wish."

"Yes. Wisely done. You have chosen well."

The potting shed doll house stayed in the living room after Christmas, "for now," Mommy had determined, "until we find room upstairs."

"There's room inside my closet," Cassie said. "Patrik would like that."

"No, I want you out of that closet, Cassie. It's not healthy."

"What's not healthy?" Daddy asked coming into the living room.

"Being in her closet for so much time."

"Well, it's like a secret fort, Connie. I had one in my Mom's backyard and spent days there. She used to let me sleep there too."

"Not helpful, Jack."

"I can be helpful," Daddy said with a smile. "How about if Cassie and I go upstairs and measure her room to determine where it will fit best."

"Okay. Try that," Mommy said.

"C'mon, Cassie. Let's get the tape measure in my office and we'll start by measuring the potting shed house to see how big it is."

"Okay, Daddy."

As Daddy and Cassie measured the board the house was mounted on in the living room, Mandy and Mark worked on her school projects at the dining room table. "How's it going in here?" Daddy asked them.

"Good," Mandy answered turning in her chair. "We've done four of the steps."

"How many steps are there?" Daddy asked.

"Well, ten. We're stuck on number five."

"What's the question?" Daddy asked coming over to them.

Mandy moved her paper over to Mark. "Mark can tell you."

"I think the question is asking us to use two formulas," Mark explained. "But when we try to combine them, we get a very abstract number. It doesn't make sense."

"I'll tell you what," Daddy replied, "Help me move the potting shed doll house upstairs, and if you want, I will help you take a look at the problem."

"Done," Mark said, quickly getting up from his chair and walking into the living room.

"Did you really push your job off on Mandy and Mark?" Mommy asked when they all came back downstairs.

"It's a diversion. I was listening to them, and they were stuck on a formula. This may be a way to help them," Daddy said, putting some popcorn in the microwave. "Consider it a study break."

"We'll see," Mommy said. "Don't let them divert for too long."

"I like popcorn, Daddy," Cassie said, standing beside him in the kitchen.

"Me too, Sunshine! Almost done."

Daddy got out bowls for everyone as the microwave beeped. "It already has butter on it, Cassie."

"That was nice of you to let them know where they could find the formula they needed," Mommy said to Daddy at dinner. "And thank you for working with Cassie to determine the closet was too small for the dollhouse."

"It was a bit of a tricky math problem. I'm glad I could help," Daddy said. "Tomorrow's supposed to be a nice day outside. I'm hoping to start helping Cassie learn to ride her bike."

"Don't you think it's too soon? It's going to be cold."

"It's winter. We'll dress warmly. Besides, in the beginning I'm going to have to hold onto her bike all the time. I won't let go."

CHAPTER 7

The Potting Shed Dollhouse

Cassie cuddled in her bed with Patrik, glad he had returned home for Christmas.

Patrik, tell me all about Akaleia and Lemuria. Is it nice there?

Patrik placed his head in Cassie's lap. *Lemurians came to earth a very long time ago, more than you can count. They came from star planets to create a loving world. A world like the one they lived in.*

Did they do that? Did they create that? asked Cassie.

Initially they created a continent of settlements in what is now Australia. It mirrored their star planet. It was filled with love and acceptance. Lemurians are tall, graceful beings of Light and Love with long flowing hair. They move in a way similar to Queen Epona and Archangel Uriel.

Cassie nodded. *Like they are flowing through a cloud.*

Yes, you remember.

Where are they now? messaged Cassie.

Over many hundreds of thousands of years, Lemuria sank beneath the ocean. But Lemuria still exists Cassie, which is where I go. It is in another dimension of existence, of being, like the elemental kingdom.

Did they all drown?

No, Patrik reassured her, *no. Prior to the sinking of their continent, the ancient Lemurians became aware of their destiny and used their mastery of energy, crystals, and vibrations, to hollow out a vast underground city in another area of earth. This land is called Telos.*

Does Akaleia talk to you?

She talks in the same way that we talk. Lemurians have all evolved their sixth sense, like you and I, which allows them to communicate through extra-sensory perception. They communicate and travel by mind energy. It is the same energy that we use. They are our family.

The week after Christmas was busy for everyone. Cassie and Poppy spent several days playing with the potting shed dollhouse and equal time at Poppy's house with her new dance dolls and costumes.

"Patrik hasn't let me hear him bark yet," Poppy complained. "When do you think I can hear him? Will you talk to him and ask him for me Cassie?"

"Patrik hasn't needed to bark. He only barks for special reasons."

"Oh, okay. Will you tell me when he does bark so I can listen too?"

"Yes. Patrik will know when the right time is."

Daddy took advantage of the sunny weather to help Cassie learn how to ride her bike.

"It's a process, Connie. One step at a time. Don't worry. Cassie will do fine."

"Okay, if it's in the driveway, as long as you are with her and hanging on to the bike."

"Got it," Daddy said. "For now, that works."

Cassie ran through the kitchen and out to the garage to get her bike.

"Okay, Cassie, let's start by getting your helmet on correctly," Daddy said at the start of their lesson. He then watched Cassie put on her helmet and connect the straps.

"The round part goes in the back, and if you leave the straps where they are, they shouldn't need to be adjusted each time."

"Okay." Cassie smiled.

"Next step, Cassie. Bring your bike around so that the bike leans up against your right leg."

"Like this?"

"Yes, great job! I'm going to hold on to your bike. Put your leg over and get on the seat. Okay?"

"It's like getting onto Luna, when Millie took me riding."

"Perfect. Now just sit on the seat a minute. Do you feel comfortable? Are your feet flat on the pedals?"

"Yes."

"Start pushing the pedals, Cassie, and I will hang on. Get the feel of it."

"I'm doing it!" Cassie cried out.

Mark was over almost every day to help Mandy finish her school projects and Chloe was back on the weekend to stay through New Year's Day.

"I love having everyone here and all the time off," Daddy said. "Maine, the way life should be."

Mommy smiled. "You said that before we moved here last year. I'm glad we are here too. I didn't realize how nice it would be to have family around, especially at all the holidays."

"It's supposed to snow tonight," Daddy said looking out the kitchen window to the back yard. "It'll be good to have some snow to play in."

"I hope you are as cheery about the snow when you are cleaning it all up," Mommy said.

"Patrik will help me," Daddy retorted, "I think he has a big bushy tail."

It did indeed snow that night and into Sunday morning. Cassie awoke with the sun just crossing her window ledge and looked out onto the back yard. Snow had blanketed everything in pure white crystal goodness. "Patrik," she said out loud. She could hear voices coming from the kitchen and wondered if Patrik would remember snow. But Patrik was no longer in her bed and did not respond. Cassie quickly got up and dressed in warm clothes and hurried down the stairs to the kitchen.

"Probably a foot or more," Daddy said to Mommy. "Lots to play in!"

"Is the snowblower all ready?" Mommy asked. "Ned won't be able to go out until you have cleared some snow."

"Yup. I'm going to start it and clear a path as soon as I finish my coffee." Daddy grinned, raising his cup. "When the girls come down, tell them to get dressed and come out to help shovel."

"Of course, Jack." Mommy laughed. "Sure. Maybe Cassie, but don't think she'll shovel. Play probably. Mandy doesn't move very early in the morning as you know. Chloe might be your best bet. They won't be up for a while though. Just saying."

"Got it," Daddy said. "I'm on it."

"It snowed!" Cassie said jubilantly. "Can I go outside? I think Patrik's outside."

"Come have a cup of hot chocolate and then you can go out. You can have breakfast when you come back in."

"Okay, Mommy," Cassie said grabbing the mug. "I think Patrik wants to play in the snow too!"

By mid-morning the driveway, walkways, and deck were all cleaned off. The sun began to shine brightly, and melted remnants of snow piles were left on the side of the driveway. Connie had fixed breakfast for everyone, and Jack took the opportunity before they ate to take Ned out for a quick walk.

"Hey neighbor," Millie called out from the fence as she watched Luna and Kai prance about the paddock.

"Millie!" Jack said. "Great snow!"

"Yes, it is!" Millie replied. "Fluffy too. Mike's going to clear some space for the horses to walk around out here."

"Hey, Jack," Mike greeted him coming across the paddock. "You need to get one of these buddy," Mike said pointing to the bobcat snowplow. This works great!"

"I see that. Certainly, food for thought," Jack said. "Or I could pay someone to plow the driveway."

"Not as much fun." Mike grinned.

"Jack," Millie said, "I see that Ned's having some problems walking. I'd be happy to take a look at him."

"Well, you know, he is getting older. We just go slower, a little at a time."

"Jack," Millie said again, walking closer to the fence, "there's lots of therapy we have available now. Call my office this week. Let me help you and Ned."

Jack stood for a moment and then nodded. "Thanks Millie, I'll do that."

Chloe and Cassie sat in Cassie's bedroom playing with the potting shed dollhouse.

"I wish I had more dolls, Auntie Chloe," Cassie said. "All my other toys are too big."

"What other kind of dolls?"

"I want a Nanny Phe doll, and a Chloe doll, and an Archangel Uriel and Queen Epona doll. And I need some fairies for the garden and some gnomes."

"Wow! You have given this a lot of thought," Chloe said. "That would help us have more adventures and stories to tell."

"Yes. More funner."

Chloe laughed. "We all need more funner in our lives Cassie! Let me see what I can come up with."

"Good morning, Mandy," Daddy greeted her as she came into the kitchen. "You pretty much missed breakfast and all the snow shoveling too!"

Mandy reached for the juice in the refrigerator. "Sorry about that, I guess."

"There'll be more opportunities, don't worry," Daddy quipped.

"Yeah, ugh."

"Are you all done with your math projects? Your make-up work?"

116

"Ah, mostly, yes."

"Mostly what do you have left to do?" Daddy asked. "Do I need to get involved?"

"Jack," Connie said turning from the sink, "Mandy has worked really hard on her projects. There is one whole week left to finish them too."

"Amanda? What's the status," Daddy asked again.

"Mark is coming over on Monday. He says we have three more steps to do on the math project. And I have to recheck my history paper and send it in."

"What's your history paper on?"

Mandy took a sip of juice. "It's my Ancient Civilizations class. Some far-off lost land stuff."

"Like Lemuria!" Cassie shouted from her seat at the table. "Like the Lemurians and other beings of Light."

"What? Where did you hear all that Cassie?" Mommy asked.

"Lemuria was actually a place," Chloe spoke up. "Thousands of thousands of years ago, before Atlantis."

"Is that what your paper is about Mandy?" Mommy asked.

"Gosh, no! It's like Egyptians or something."

"Glad you have another week left Mandy," Daddy offered. "I think you're going to need it!"

"Phe? This is Chloe. Hi! Are you shoveled out?" Chloe asked on her cell phone. "Glad to hear it. I was wondering if you would like to help me find a store in the area that would sell some more of the small dolls for Cassie's potting shed."

"Yes, that's right. Cassie has a list. Yes, we can both go with you tomorrow! Super, thanks. See you in the morning!

"Jack let's talk about New Year's Eve," Mommy said at lunchtime. "I know we invited most everyone over when we were all together on Christmas day at your Mom's house. Oh, I have to call Ivy and Jim. You should call Dan and Paula."

"Yes, I'll do that. What's on the menu?"

"Will you go shopping tomorrow? I started a list. I'm thinking a bunch of pick-up foods. People can pick and choose what they want. Chicken wings, a couple salads, some nachos and subs. I haven't finalized yet."

"Okay, yes, I'll go shopping. I'll call Peter to bring the beverages too. He's always good at that. You can work today on finalizing the list and what you want."

"Jack, Peter and Katie said they were going to Virginia for New Year's," Connie replied. "They won't be here."

"They went this weekend, instead. It was a short trip apparently, and not so pleasant. They're coming back tomorrow," Daddy said. "Cassie, do you want to come shopping with me tomorrow?"

"Actually, Cassie and I have plans tomorrow," Chloe said. "We're meeting Phe around ten."

"Oh?" Mommy said with surprise. "What's that all about?"

"You'll see. It's a surprise," Chloe said with a wink to Cassie. "How about if we all go sledding this afternoon? Where's the best place Jack?"

After lunch, everyone piled into the Explorer with several sleds and a toboggan in the back. "No excuses Mandy," Daddy said to her. "You are coming too."

Connie had called Twirla, and she and Poppy planned to meet them at the town park where there was a sledding hill.

"This will be great fun!" Daddy told everyone. "I haven't been here since I was a kid."

The area was fairly crowded when they got there, and Jack found a parking spot off to the side of the road. "We have to walk up from here," he said. "Everybody grab a sled. Hey Twirla and Poppy!" Daddy greeted them as they walked up the hill towards them.

"What a great day for sledding," Twirla exclaimed. "And the snow is perfect!"

"I'm not sure why I came, Dad," Mandy complained walking up the hill.

"To be part of the Murphy fun family Christmas!" Daddy shouted. "You remember the movie right? National Lampoon Family Christmas?"

"Daddy, those were all weirdos, not like us. Remember?"

Daddy laughed. "Oh Mandy, every family is a family."

"Mandy, hi!" a voice called out from across the hill. "Come on over, we're all here!"

"Bye," Mandy said quickly as she sprinted over to her group of friends taking a sled with her.

"Come find us when you're done!" Mommy shouted as Mandy left them.

"Over here," Twirla said. "There's some spots over here."

"Wonderful! Let's get a plan going," Mommy said.

"I think this is more about spontaneity," Chloe said as she grabbed the toboggan and asked Cassie, Poppy and Twirla to jump on.

"Away we go!"

Cassie and Chloe sat in Cassie's bedroom playing with the potting shed dollhouse and the new dolls and accessories they bought on Sunday.

"You guys have been up here a long time," Mommy said coming in the doorway. "Are you going to do this all day?"

"Ah, yeah, I think so," Chloe said. "Do you want to play with us?"

"Not really."

"We bought a doll for you too, Mommy. And one for Daddy."

"I saw all that yesterday. You have a doll for everybody."

"And the fairies and gnomes, too!" Cassie said excitedly. "Everyone plays together nicely."

"I'm glad to hear that!" Mommy said turning away in the doorway. "I'll let you know when lunch is ready."

"Okay, thanks," Chloe replied. "Cassie what do the gnomes do?"

"They work in the mines, under the earth."

"What do they mine?"

Cassie picked up one of the gnomes, "They bring up the rocks. The basanite rocks. What the gnome statues are made of."

"Are the rocks valuable?"

"They have special powers. They have crystals in them."

"Do you know what the special powers are?"

"Yes. Patrik tells me. You can make wishes with them. I gave them to people at Christmas so they can make wishes."

"What about you? What do you use the crystals for?" Chloe asked.

Cassie looked up at Chloe. "They have energy. I can send the energy to Patrik, and we can use it to help build the connection to Lemuria."

"Wow, that's very powerful indeed!"

"Patrik and I are going to need to go to Lemuria. It's a long way and we need a lot of crystal energy. He's been there before."

Chloe nodded. "Have you gone anywhere?"

"I've gone to the Elemental Kingdom. That's where Archangel Uriel and Queen Epona are. But I didn't need the crystals to come back."

"Did Patrik need them?"

"Yes, to come back from Lemuria."

"Cassie, when do you think you and Patrik are going to travel to Lemuria?"

"Patrik will tell me. He says we have to wait until there is a space in time."

"Time. There's the time again." Chloe smiled. "Cassie keep me informed, okay? I love to hear all about Patrik and your travels. Let me know if there are any plans for you to travel, will you please?"

"I can send you mind messages, Auntie Chloe. I know you can listen."

"Yes, I can listen, and I will hear you. I will make more of an effort to listen. Anytime."

"I'm going to start the fire pit later on," Jack said to Connie on New Year's Eve.

"Don't you think it's too cold tonight for people to be outside?" Connie said. "It's winter."

"I think there are some hearty people who would love to be outside. The stars will be out. Clear and crisp."

"I'll plan on entertaining those who wish to be inside. That's more my comfort level."

"Hi folks, can I help prepare anything for tonight?" Chloe asked coming into the kitchen.

"Are you and Cassie taking a break from your doll play?"

"Yes, actually. We have played out many scenarios and had a lot of fun over these few days. Cassie as you know, is very imaginative!"

"Oh yes, we do know that. It never ends," Connie said.

"She talked again about Lemuria. She said she and Patrik will have to travel there."

"What?" Jack asked turning back from the kitchen door.

"When she was lost in the woods last summer, she followed Patrik, right?" Chloe asked.

"Yes. She said she heard him barking and followed him into the woods."

"What do you make of this Chloe? Should we be worried?" Connie said.

"I don't think so, not right now. I would watch for any behaviors that indicate she is withdrawing, even in an imaginative way. She's telling me all about it, so she's not trying to keep it a secret. I'd be more concerned if she was trying to keep it a secret."

"This dollhouse is not a good idea," Connie said. "I don't like it."

"It's not the dollhouse," Jack replied.

"I think the dollhouse is actually helping her," Chloe said. "Through that play she is expressing more of what she believes and experiences. Real or unreal, keep her talking."

"When can you come up again?" asked Connie. "Soon, I hope."

"I have to go back later tomorrow, and then I'll look at my calendar. I can let you know."

"I think you should just move up here," Connie spoke up. "You can see patients here too."

"It's a possibility," Chloe said. "My contract is coming up for renewal this spring."

"That would be wonderful," Jack said. "Make it happen!"

People began arriving in the late afternoon, giving Poppy, Cassie and Linde time to play outside in the snow. Jack put the back spotlights on, and Peter, Katie, and Chloe started making snow forts with them.

"Come on Mandy, grab your coat. Let's go outside," Mark said to her. "It looks like fun."

Mark grabbed a shovel from the deck as he and Mandy proceeded down the stairs.

"Shovel, good idea Mark," Peter said. "Jack, do you have more shovels?"

"In the garage," Daddy said.

Peter proceeded to the garage as Mike came down the driveway driving his bobcat.

"Jack!" he called out, "How about if I make some big piles for everyone?"

"You do love your toys," Daddy laughed. "Sure, go for it. Everybody out of the way for a few minutes!"

Mike started scooping up snow, pushing it forward, and making several big piles. He then proceeded to make paths through the middle and around the yard for people to walk on. "That'll keep everyone busy for a while," he said backing the bobcat out and parking it over by the garage.

"Hey Mark!" Peter yelled as he threw a snowball at him and hitting his jacket.

"Let's have teams!" Mark said. "No throwing snowballs at the little kids though."

"Let's just make forts and play fox and hens," Katie said. "Peter? Can you restrain yourself?"

Peter laughed. "I will, yes."

"I'm not buying it," Daddy shouted as he hit Peter in the back with a snowball. "That was for Mark. He owed you one."

"Children!" Connie called from the back door, "I'm talking to all of you. Food's ready!"

"Connie, everything looks wonderful as always," Millie said walking around the dining room table.

"Twirla and I will get plates for the girls," Paula offered, "You do whatever you need to do. Do you want them at the kitchen table again?"

"Yes, that's fine."

"I'll sit with them," Chloe offered. "I love their conversations!"

"Do you want to sit outside, Mark?" Mandy asked, handing him a plate. "It's warm with the fire going."

"Sure. We can talk about making plans for tomorrow to finish your math project. Does that work for you?"

"Oh yeah, I guess so."

"Mandy, it's not going to take you that long to finish. You'll still have some free time this week."

Mandy shrugged, "I still have my history paper to write."

"That may take some time."

"Yes, but it doesn't have to be perfect."

"Mandy! This is your grade for the whole semester. And for cheering!"

"Yeah, I know. And I know that if I just sit down and write it, I'll get it done."

"So?"

"Tomorrow, after we finish the math project."

"I'll call you later to make sure," Mark nodded. "Sometimes you need extra motivation."

"Oh, it's warm out here!" Mommy said, coming out later onto the deck with others from the house.

"Plenty of room for everyone," Daddy said. "Seats in the back."

"Hey everyone, Mike and I have set a date for our wedding."

"Oh wonderful!" Nanny Phe said as Cassie clapped her hands.

"When is it?" Mommy asked. "I need to save the date!"

"You all need to save the date," Mike told them. "Valentine's Day!"

"Goodness, that doesn't leave much time for planning," Mommy spoke up.

"It will be small," Millie said.

"Do you have a venue in mind?" Papa Ed asked. "I know a lot of people in town, and I'd be happy to ask around for you. At least I could go scout them out."

"That would be really great," Mike said. "With Millie and I both working fulltime, we are somewhat limited."

"Valentine's Day is actually a Saturday this year," Millie said. "But we could be flexible too."

"Let me see what I can come up with first, then we can talk," Ed said.

"What about a dress, Millie?" Twirla asked. "Connie and I can go with you to look."

"Yikes!" Millie shrieked. "There are a few things to get done!"

"I would be happy to help you with flowers," Phe offered as she looked around at the big circle of friends, "Everything will be wonderful, Millie, no worries. Everything in good time."

"Mom, do remember the graduate student you met at the library?" Peter asked.

"Anna, yes. Do you know her?"

"I know her husband. He's a geology professor at the university. I meant to tell you all before Christmas, but he said Anna's thesis was accepted and published."

"What?" Daddy said loudly. "We were supposed to see the final version before she submitted it."

"She doesn't need your permission, Jack," Peter said. "It's based on her research."

"Well, there might be things in it we don't want to be made public," Mommy added. "About the doctor and his experiments."

"Connie, that was several hundred years ago. It doesn't reflect on you," Ed said.

"Have you seen it, Peter? What did it say?" Daddy asked.

"No, I haven't seen it. He said she just got the notification of acceptance."

"You know, Anna and I had a lovely relationship last summer at the library. I'll give her a call," Phe offered. "I'm sure she would be willing to share it."

"Thanks, Mom," Daddy said. "This was unexpected."

"Is she writing about Patrik?" Cassie asked. "He knows everything!"

"I am sure not!" Mommy said sharply. "Patrik is not in the research!"

"Well, let's talk about something different. What's everybody's New Year's resolution?" Daddy asked. "I'll start. I am going to buy a bobcat like Mike's when I grow up, and then we can build a ski ramp!"

"You are not. I know you; you are not going to grow up!" Mommy retorted as everyone else laughed.

"Okay, who's next?" Daddy called out.

"I'll be next," Twirla said. "My resolution is to create new dance routines that will win the state trophy for the cheering squad!"

"That would be great!" Mandy said excitedly. "I'll be there!"

"I'm counting on it, Mandy," Twirla replied. "We need you!"

"What about you, Connie?" Millie asked. "We've talked about your interest in teaching riding lessons to children several times."

"Oh, goodness," Mommy replied. "Yes, it's been on my mind. Spring. A goal for spring."

"I'm going to ask you again in March, then," Millie said. "I think you would be super with the horses and the kids!"

"Do you have a resolution, Cassie?" Daddy asked.

"Patrik and I are going to finish building the bridge to Lemuria."

"That sounds like a big project," Daddy said. "Let me know what your plans are, okay?"

"I think it's time for us early birds to start home," Ivy said. "Jim and I want to wish you all a Happy New Year!"

Dan stood up from the couch, "Us too. It's getting late for Linde. Mark, we'll see you at home."

"I have my car," Mark explained as Mandy reached out to hold his hand.

"Poppy, another half hour and then we'll head over to our house, okay?" Twirla said.

"That will be bedtime for Cassie, too," Mommy said.

"I think the real question is who will stay up till midnight?" Papa Ed asked as he and Phe stood up. "Don't think it will be me or Phe."

"Let's put another log on the fire," Daddy said, "and we'll see who stays up or not!"

As midnight came nearer it began to snow. "Here it comes," Mike joked, "a little frosting on a wonderful holiday."

Most everyone had left earlier, and the people who remained were huddled by the fire. Mark and Mandy sat together on the couch beside Mike and Millie. Cassie had been tucked into bed by Chloe, who had also sat with her for a while to get Patrik settled. "He likes you, Auntie Chloe," Cassie said. "He knows you believe us."

"Yes, Cassie, I do believe in both of you."

Outside, Mike held Millie's hand in his. "Keep me warm," she smiled up at him.

"I don't like January," Mommy announced as she came out of the house with some small fleece blankets for people to wrap up in. "It's too cold, too dark, and too snowy."

"Well, that about sums it up," Daddy replied. "It is all of those things. But, then we get February, which has more sun and more melting."

"That's very hopeful, Jack. We'll see how it all turns out, especially after you have cleared snow a couple more times." Mommy smiled. "What if we have a blizzard the weekend of the wedding?"

"Oh, Connie, think warm and sunny!" Millie exclaimed.

"Let's think positive," Daddy said. "We have what, six weeks until the wedding?"

Mommy nodded, "Yes, January is a long month."

"We have plenty of time." Mike chimed in. "It's going to be perfect!"

"Is Cassie all settled in?" Jack asked Chloe as she came out onto the deck. "You were up there a long time."

"We were talking for a while. She's sound asleep now, and I think I dozed off too!"

"You're just in time for the countdown," Mommy said. "Okay everyone, ten, nine, eight," they all called out, and then, "Happy New Year!"

Daddy stood and moved over to hug Mommy and give her a kiss. "Happy New Year," he said, "May this next year be as happy for us."

"Amen to that!" Chloe called out as Connie and Jack hugged her.

"And happy when you move up here!" Jack said.

Mark and Mandy stood up also. "I need to be heading home," Mark said. "Thank you very much, Mr. and Mrs. Murphy."

"You're very welcome, Mark, it's always good to see you," Daddy said. "We like having you here a lot!"

Mark smiled as Mandy laughed. "I'll be right back," Mandy said. "You know, walk Mark to his car."

"Drive carefully, Mark" Mommy said as she and Daddy turned back to sit by the fire.

"We probably should give them a minute or two before for we go," Mike said to Millie.

"Not too many minutes," Connie added as everyone chuckled.

"Remember being young?" Chloe asked. "Everything was magical."

"I'm feeling pretty magical right now, Chloe," Millie said squeezing Mike's hand.

"Okay, let's get going," Mike said. "Morning will come soon, and we have a wedding to plan!"

"I'm back," Mandy said coming up the stairs and passing Mike and Millie. "Goodnight, everyone," she said, heading to the door.

"Goodnight, Mandy," Daddy said, "and Happy New Year to all!"

CHAPTER 8

Wedding Bells

The next Saturday was spent taking down some of the Christmas decorations, the Christmas tree, and putting things away. Cassie sat at the kitchen table at lunch with her parents. "Why can't we leave the tree up longer?" she asked. "It's still pretty."

"It's starting to shed needles as it dries, Cassie," Mommy said. "It makes a big mess."

With Cassie's insistence, the bare Christmas tree was taken outside and leaned up against the potting shed iron fence. Cassie said she could decorate it with peanut butter pinecones and birdseed treats that Nanny Phe would help her with. "The birds will be happy there," Cassie said, "like the fairies in the fairy garden!"

"We'll leave the outside decorations up longer," Daddy said. "We can still turn the lights on at nighttime for a while."

Chloe had returned to Boston, but promised to keep them informed of any changes she was able to make in her schedule or her contract.

It snowed again, and again, and the days were frigid. Jack was back at work, the girls were back in school, and each of them had a good report card when the first semester grades ended in mid-January.

"Good grades, Mandy! Thank goodness that semester is over with!" Mommy said at the supper table one night.

"Now just keep your grades up," Daddy added. "The same rules still apply."

"You did a wonderful job too, Cassie," Daddy praised her. "We are all very proud of you,"

"And Patrik!" Cassie said. "He helped me, too."

"I think things are better now that the girls are back in school," Mommy said. "Mandy is caught up in her homework, and Cassie is back in the structure of Katie's classroom. I like structure."

Daddy laughed, "Yes, I know you do. But more importantly, Cassie loves going to school and being with her friends and Katie."

"Structure is good, Jack," Mommy continued. "Certainly, good for young girls who are learning and growing. It gives them a sense of security."

I think it gives you a sense of security also."

"Maybe. We all need that."

"I have appreciated all the help with the snow," Daddy said changing the subject. "The guy who is plowing the driveway is doing a good job. I really couldn't get it done and get to work on time."

"It's a lot of work, Jack. It's really been snowy," Mommy said.

"I need to get a bobcat like Mike's. I know it's expensive, but in the long run, I think it will save us time and money."

"I'd like to get through one winter before we decide, but if you want to look around for pricing go ahead."

"I'll do that," Daddy said.

"Let's see how this winter plays out, okay?" Mommy continued. "We can compare plowing cost to cost of the bobcat. And the cost of the time it would take you. Then we can talk."

"Okay, that's a good idea. I know the wedding is coming up. Do you have a date planned for looking at wedding dresses with Millie?"

"We are planning on going this coming weekend to a couple of bridal shops in the Portland area. I'm sure she'll find something. I am looking forward to it. Girls' day out."

"I will keep that in mind," Daddy said. "Take the whole day. I'll hold down the fort with the girls. Why don't you ask Twirla if she would like Poppy to come over too?"

"I will do that," Mommy said. "I know Cassie will love that, too."

"Have you heard from Chloe again?" Daddy asked. "Is she coming up?"

"She can't clear her appointments until February. She'll be up for the wedding and is thinking of taking vacation when the girls have school vacation in February."

"That would really be great! Maybe she can line up some interviews while she's here. She said her contract is up for renewal."

"Yes. She didn't say anything new about that though when I talked with her."

"I'll try and be patient," Daddy replied.

"Time will tell!" Cassie added. "If we think it, and say it, it will be!"

"Good morning, Cassie, are you ready for breakfast?" Daddy asked as Cassie came into the kitchen the next Saturday morning.

"Yes," Cassie said with Merton and Elroy in her arms.

"Did your friends want to come down to breakfast too?" Daddy asked turning in his chair to answer a knock on the back door. "Mike! Millie! Hi! Come on in."

"Hope we're not interrupting," Mike said. "We know it's kind of early. Have you been out yet? It's freezing!"

"No interruption at all," Mommy said. "Can I get you some coffee?"

"Sure," Millie replied. "We came over to ask you something."

Mommy poured coffee and got a glass of juice for Cassie as everyone sat at the kitchen table, "Here we go," she said, "cream and sugar right here."

"We are still planning parts of our wedding," Mike started, "and Jack, I wanted to ask you if you would be my best man."

"Of course, Mike, thank you!" Daddy replied, "I'm honored."

"And Connie, I wanted to ask you if you would stand up with me, too, and be my best woman."

"Yes! Thank you, Millie. I would love to!"

"And we want to ask Cassie and Poppy if they will be flower girls," Millie continued. "Would that be okay with you?"

Cassie raised her head and looked at Mike. "Yes!" she shouted, with a huge smile.

"Well, yes!" Mommy said. "How sweet of you to include them."

"They are very wonderful little girls, and very special to us," Mike said. We haven't asked Twirla yet, but I think she'll say yes, too."

"Have you talked with my dad lately?" Daddy asked. "About plans for a venue?"

"He is such a sweet man," Millie said. "We have a couple of appointments lined up this weekend. Ed says they all know we are looking at Valentine's Day. They will cater for us too, so we don't have to do anything except pick out a menu."

"Sounds like everything is well organized and under control," Mommy said. "And you already have your dress Millie, so that's perfect!"

"Jack, it's just a suit and tie for us," Mike said.

"Oh, okay, good. Easy."

"And Connie, you can wear whatever you want. You've seen my dress."

"Cassie," Mommy said, "let's talk with Twirla and we can all go shopping together for dresses for you and Poppy."

"Okay, Mommy. What about Patrik?"

"No Cassie," Mommy said firmly. "No Patrik at the wedding."

"Luna and Kai can't come to the wedding either, Cassie," Millie said sympathetically. "Maybe Patrik could keep them company?"

Cassie smiled again, "Yes. Patrik would like that."

"Looking forward to this wedding very much!" Daddy exclaimed. "This New Year is off to a great start!"

"How is work going this week, Jack?" Mommy asked while they all sat down to have dinner one night.

"Good, complicated, and lots for Dan and I to keep our eyes on. We're still having those random security breaches. The IT support person that Chloe's hospital uses returned my call. They're having the same security problems with their operating system. Unfortunately, they also can't retrieve any meaningful data to problem solve."

"Do you and Dan have to change your system out again? That was a lot of work last year. Months of work."

"And very expensive," Daddy replied. "No, we are planning to continue to frequently change the codes. Maybe we can stay ahead of the hackers, and they won't be able to find a way in."

"Is it like Light Language, Daddy?" Cassie asked.

"No, your father is talking about computer systems," Mommy replied, "not your squiggle letters."

Daddy put his fork down and looked across the table at Cassie. "Why do you think it might be like Light Language, Cassie?"

Cassie lifted her head, "You showed me on a printed sheet one time. You told me you used symbols."

"You remember that do you? Yes. I printed out a copy of the codes from the computer system for you."

"And you drew a picture with lines that connected everything. You said you had a firewall, but it wasn't a real fire."

"You have a very good memory, Sunshine. Is Light Language made up of symbols too?

Cassie nodded and then paused. "They mean things. They have to come through an opening."

"Like getting through a firewall?" Daddy asked.

"Oh Jack, really?" Mommy laughed shaking her head. "You can't be serious."

"Cassie," Daddy said looking intently at her, "what happens if you change the way a symbol looks? Does it mean something different?"

Cassie looked up, "It makes room."

"I'm done," Mandy said. "I don't know what you are talking about. Can I be excused?"

"Yes Mandy," Mommy replied. "I'm confused, too."

"I think it's very interesting," Daddy said. "Cassie, when it makes room, what happens?"

"It's like time. You can make time in between. Then you can make anything happen in the space."

"Wow, you have given me a lot of things to think about. Thank you. Let's talk some more again, okay?"

"Yes."

"I think dinner's over," Mommy said. "Jack, let's talk more again, okay?"

Cassie played with Patrik, Poppy, and the potting shed dollhouse every day after school. When Poppy came over, they raced up the stairs to begin playing school inside the little house. They created new stories and adventures with all the dolls and were always disappointed when Mommy called up the stairs to say that it was time for Poppy to go home.

"I still haven't heard Patrik bark yet" Poppy complained. "That was my wish."

"Wishes take time. Patrik knows you made your wish. Maybe he is saving it up till he thinks you need it."

"Oh, okay. That sounds good." Poppy nodded. "Patrik knows best."

Sometimes at night, Patrik told Cassie stories of his previous life with Dr. Blake, Archangel Uriel, Queen Epona and Akaleia. Cassie began to understand the large length of time Patrik had been in his "in between" life on earth, and even more years of his existence in other worlds prior to that.

You have other lifetimes, too, Patrik told her. *You will remember them in time.*

Cassie moved all the potting shed figures around; to the house, to the classroom, to the garden, to the magic tree. When she put figures into the magic tree, they would sometimes magically travel, ending up in her closet or coming out of the portal door. She moved the basanite statues from the stairs and moved the gnomes to look like they were working in the mines again, bringing up the rocks for Dr. Blake. In addition to all the figurines Chloe had bought for her, she had also bought two horse statues to represent Luna and Kai.

"We'll have to ask your daddy to make a barn next, Cassie," Chloe had said when she was up at New Year's as she put the Millie and Mike dolls over beside the horses and next to the fairy garden.

Patrik stayed close to Cassie in the day and sometimes travelled at night to the Elemental Kingdom.

Can I go with you, Patrik? Can I travel with you?

Not now. It uses more energy for you to come with me. We have to save energy for our trip to Lemuria.

Sometimes, Patrik brought back crystals from his travels to the Elemental Kingdom. Cassie would fold them in tissues and place them in her bedside table drawer with the others. *Queen Epona sends these to you*, Patrik would say, or *Archangel Uriel has given these to you.*

Patrik, how many crystals will we need to get to Lemuria?

I don't know. I didn't use any to get to Lemuria, but I needed more crystal energy for the last part of the trip back to you. That's why you had to help me come through the potting shed doll house.

Cassie thought for a few moments and nodded her head. *You needed more energy the closer you got to the physical world. You became heavier closer to earth.*

Yes, that's true, Patrik said. *You are more of a physical density than I am. You will need even more crystal energy to travel farther.*

Do I become lighter when I get closer to the other dimensions?

Yes. I know you become lighter when you grab hold of my neck mane that rises up. That is how we can travel together.

When I grab hold of your mane, I feel like I am floating in a mist, Cassie said.

You are beginning to know how to transform, dear Cassie. You are learning how to change from one state of being to another.

"Cassie, the sun is out, and the snow has melted from the driveway. It's January thaw!" Daddy said excitedly one weekend. "Let's get our coats on and practice riding your bike."

"Okay," Cassie said jumping up from the kitchen table and running to the hallway.

"Grab some mittens, too," Connie advised. "And a hat!

"Okay Cassie, I know it's been a while since we were able to be out here. Show me how you get ready to ride your bike."

"Okay," Cassie said, wheeling her bike around and putting her helmet on. "Like this?"

"Very good. Okay, climb up on the seat and put your feet to the pedals, and I will hold on. All set?"

Cassie grabbed hold of the handlebars and nodded.

"Start pedaling!" Daddy called out.

Cassie peddled as Daddy held on to the back of her bike and walked fast to keep up with her. "You're doing great! Keep going!"

Cassie pedaled all the way up the driveway with Daddy jogging beside her, "Stop peddling when you get to the end," he said. "Do you remember how to put the brakes on and stop the bike?"

"Yes, Daddy."

"Okay, show me. Let's go one more time. When you get to the end of the driveway, pretend I'm not here, and you are stopping yourself."

Daddy balanced the bike as Cassie mounted it and once again leaned forward, grabbing the handlebars. Cassie pedaled faster and more forcefully up to the end of the driveway, then moved the pedals backwards to stop.

"Terrific!! Are you ready? Do you want to try by yourself? I really wasn't hanging on much. You did all the work."

"You want to let go?" Cassie asked.

"Only if you're ready," Daddy said. "Do you feel ready?"

"Yes," Cassie answered. "Patrik and I are ready!"

"Let's go!" Daddy yelled as Cassie took off down the driveway towards the house with Daddy trailing behind. "You did it!" he shouted. "Go Cassie! I'm so proud of you!"

"Hey Connie," Daddy said one morning, "I meant to tell you that my mother called. She got hold of Anna, the one who wrote the thesis. She said she would give my mom a copy. They are going to meet for lunch."

"That's great news. But how do we know how much of it has been shared already?"

"I don't know. But I can ask my mom to get more specific information."

"That would be good, Jack. I'm concerned people will want to pry."

"Like how? What would they be interested in?"

"The same things the people who burned down Dr. Blake's barn were interested in. They think there is something to find, something that is valuable or gives them power."

"I really don't think there is anything to worry about. And besides, the satchel is in my office drawer, locked up. No one knows it's there."

"Let's just be mindful of things that may happen, okay? We need to pay attention."

"Okay. I'm with you. Everything is going to be fine Connie, you'll see."

Patrik lay on Cassie's bed the morning of Mike and Millie's wedding.

I'm sorry, but you can't come, Cassie messaged him. *You need to go and keep Luna and Kai company.*

"Cassie, are you finished getting dressed?" Mommy asked, knocking on her door.

Cassie looked up, "I was just helping Patrik."

"Here, let me help you," Mommy said, walking behind Cassie to zip up her dress. "Where are your shoes?"

"Right here, Mommy," Cassie said, picking her shoes up off her bed.

"I need to do your hair, too. Bring your shoes downstairs, and we'll finish up everything down there."

Cassie patted Patrik and walked to the doorway. *I'll be back later.*

"Cassie, come on," Mommy called out. "You too, Mandy, let's get going! We don't want to be late."

Cassie and Poppy stood together behind Connie in the hallway of the restaurant where the wedding was being held. They were dressed in identical dresses with different colored sashes. Poppy's sash was pink, and Cassie's was yellow. Between them, they held a large basket of flowers with ivy that trailed over the sides. People had already entered the function room and taken their seats. When the doors were opened, Cassie saw several rows of chairs placed in front of big glass windows.

Poppy reached out and held Cassie's hand. "We look like twins." She smiled. "We have the same dresses!"

"You both look so pretty," Millie told them. "And remember, I'll be right behind you."

"Wait for me to tell you when to go," Twirla added. "Then follow Connie down the carpet to the front by the windows."

When the music started, Connie began to walk forward toward Mike and Jack.

Jack smiled at her. "Beautiful," he whispered.

Cassie and Poppy came quickly forward with big smiles and giggles as Mike waved to them.

"Perfect!" he said to them as they stood to the side, and Millie began to walk to the windows.

Mike stepped forward and extended his hand as Millie reached out to grasp it.

"I love you," they said together.

February's brilliant sunshine continued to melt snow and ice on the driveway and in the yard. Cassie and Poppy were able to ride their bikes more often; sometimes with Jack and sometimes with Twirla helping them. They both needed to practice turning their bikes while they were riding them. At the end of the driveway, they needed to easily curve around and start back towards the house.

"Cassie, if you can't make the turn, put your brakes on and stop the bike," Daddy reminded her. "Then, wheel the bike around till you can get on again. It just takes practice, honey."

"Okay," Cassie said. "I'll go again."

"Poppy, look at you!" Daddy called out. "Good job. You'll both be riding by yourself very soon. Just in time for spring!"

CHAPTER 9

March Madness

"Mommy, Poppy is coming over with her bike so we can ride together in the driveway," Cassie announced one Saturday in March.

Mommy looked out the kitchen window and scanned the backyard. "I don't know Cassie. There's still a lot of snow and ice out there."

"But there's no ice on the driveway," Cassie said, "and the sun is shining!"

"What's up?" Daddy asked, coming in the back door. "He's okay," he said quickly, helping Ned across the threshold.

"Cassie wants to ride her bike."

"Poppy is coming over with her bike too, Daddy. Please?"

Daddy looked from Cassie to Mommy, then back to Cassie. "Let your mom and I discuss this for a moment, okay?"

"That's Poppy," Cassie said, hearing a knock on the back door. "She's here for me."

"Well, why don't you put your coat on and go outside with her. Your mom and I will be right with you."

Cassie ran to the closet in the hallway, grabbed her coat, and headed for the door.

"Cassie, wait," Mommy said. "You need a hat and mittens."

"Okay," Cassie sighed, as she headed back to the hallway and rummaged through her winter basket on the shelf.

"Good, thank you," Daddy said to her as she passed through the kitchen again. "We'll be right with you."

The storm door banged behind Cassie as she proceeded outside, then turned to look through the glass panel where she could still see and hear her parents talk in the kitchen.

"Connie, you are going to need to let her ride her bike by herself sometimes," Daddy said. "She has been doing that independently now for several weeks."

"I know Jack, I just think she isn't ready."

"Ready for what?" Daddy countered.

"How to handle it."

"The driveway?" Daddy said. "She needs to continue to practice. Poppy will be there too, and I'll be close by in the garage."

"What if she falls?"

"Didn't you fall once or twice when you learned how to ride a bike? And we never wore helmets! And you rode horses too!"

"Okay, okay. I get it," Mommy said, shaking her head. "But sometimes she just does things without thinking. And that dog of hers! He is always trouble."

"Patrik, I will remind you," Daddy said, "is an imaginary dog."

Mommy pursed her lips and folded her arms across her chest. "Cassie doesn't think so."

"No. Cassie doesn't think so," Daddy agreed. "But let's get back to bike riding. I'll talk with them both about helmets, safety, and staying in the driveway. I'll be serious, I promise."

Mommy laughed, "You are still a kid at heart Jack, and seldom serious. But okay, just keep an eye on them."

"Will do," Daddy agreed kissing Mommy on the cheek and heading for the door. "It'll be fine, you'll see."

"Girls let's get your bikes turned around, and we'll go over the bike rules," Daddy said to Cassie and Poppy. "Where's your helmets?"

"Right here," Poppy said pointing to her head.

"Right where it belongs! Cassie? What about you?"

"Coming!" Cassie yelled, running from the garage with her helmet in hand.

"How are you doing riding your bike, Poppy?"

"Good, and I can go fast!"

"I've seen you. Yes, you are fast."

"Right here, Daddy," Cassie spoke up handing her helmet to him.

"That's great. Go ahead and put it on please."

Cassie looked at her helmet and turned it around, so the rounded edge was facing her, then placed the helmet over her hat. "It doesn't fit good, Daddy."

"Let me adjust the straps for you," he said, as he loosened the straps to fit better over her bulky winter hat. "How's that?"

"Good," Cassie nodded as she started to get on her bike. "Can we ride now, Daddy?"

"Yes, you both have been very patient. I'll be in my workshop in the garage if you need anything. Have fun and stay in the driveway please," he said to them as he waved to Mommy in the dining room window.

"Let's go fast!" Poppy yelled, as she proceeded to ride up the long driveway with Cassie pedaling behind her.

Cassie stopped halfway up and turned to watch her dad walk down the driveway. Luna and Kai were out in Millie's paddock, and they trotted over to the fence shaking their manes. Daddy stopped and patted the horses, extending his hand to reach down their necks. He waved to the girls and continued walking to his workshop.

Cassie and Poppy rode together to the end of the driveway. Poppy was able to turn her bike before the road started and begin to pedal back. Cassie had to get off her bike and wheel it around. "I'll wait for you," Poppy offered. "We can still ride together."

Back and forth they rode several times, until Poppy said, "Let's take turns being leaders. I'll start, and you can follow me wherever I go."

Cassie nodded and started to get back on her bike. "I'm coming!"

"Follow my trail!" Poppy shouted, as she weaved to one side of the driveway and then the other. "I'm going up to the top now."

Cassie pedaled hard, trying to weave her bike after Poppy, bobbing her head up and down and concentrating on the pattern Poppy had made before her.

"I can't see you!" Cassie yelled as her helmet slipped down her face. "Wait, Poppy!" she yelled taking off her helmet. "I have to fix it!"

Cassie tugged at the helmet straps, trying to make them tighter. She suddenly saw Patrik running down the street.

"Patrik!" she shouted getting back on her bike and starting to pedal. "Patrik!"

"Cassie, stop!" Poppy yelled to her. "Put your helmet on!"

Cassie focused on Patrik and saw a car coming down the road behind him. "Stop, Patrik, STOP!" Cassie screamed as she crossed the driveway and entered the street. "STOP!"

Patrik ran towards Cassie as the car closed in on him, almost on top of him. "Patrik!" yelled Cassie, turning her bike towards the car and skidding on the winter sand.

The car brakes screeched as it swerved in the opposite direction. Cassie fell from her bike and was propelled into the granite post that held up their mailbox. Her head hit the stone, and her bike lay twisted on top of her.

"Cassie!" Poppy cried out, "Get up!"

Cassie lay motionless on the street, while Poppy stared at her face in disbelief. Her eyes were turned upward, and trickles of blood dripped from her nose. "Help! Help!" Poppy yelled, as she looked both left and right, wondering if she should run for help or stay with her friend.

"Poppy, go get help!" Ivy Morgan said, getting out of her car. "Quickly!"

Poppy ran down Cassie's driveway calling for help as Jack came quickly out of the garage.

"Cassie ... she fell!" Poppy managed to say as tears streamed down her face.

I know you're here, Patrik, Cassie conveyed to him through her mind messages. *You have to help Poppy; I can't get up.*

145

Patrik began to bark in acknowledgement of Cassie's request, as he crouched by her side and licked her hand. *You are alive and will be well, Cassie. All will be well. Help is coming.*

Cassie could hear Poppy crying out and footsteps running, but she couldn't speak or see. Instead, she sent more vibrational messages to Patrik, letting him know she could hear, and feel him, but could not move.

It's time to go Cassie, Patrik said, *it's the time to travel further.*

Cassie felt everything spinning around her, and her mind floating above her body.

"Cassie!" Connie cried out kneeling on the ground beside her daughter. "Are you all right?"

"I'm calling 911!" Jack shouted running up the driveway with Poppy beside him.

"Poppy, go get your mother. Hurry!" Connie told her.

Ivy Morgan stood by her car trembling. "She came out into the road so fast and swerved right in front of me. And then, dear God, she skidded into the mailbox."

"Jack's calling 911; we'll get some help. It'll be all right."

But they'll know, Cassie replied, *they'll know I've gone. And they'll think I am lost again like the last time and search for me in the woods.*

No Cassie, it will be different this time, Patrik said. *They will wait patiently by your side till you wake up. It will seem like a long time to you as we continue to travel far away, but in Earth's time, it will be short. Time expands and contracts as we desire it to be. We can use this dimension of your consciousness to find Akaleia again.*

Cassie mentally agreed with Patrik. Her intrinsic energy merged with her spirit as she once again floated above her body. Patrik's mane had risen up in a handle about his neck and she reached out to take hold of it.

There will be some obstacles on our trip, Cassie. Just keep your eyes closed and focus. Hold on to me. You are safe.

146

"Connie, Jack! Oh God," Twirla yelled as she ran up to them. "Poppy, honey, come over by me now, out of the way."

"Cassie couldn't see, Momma, and she took, she took her helmet off," Poppy sobbed. "And she went fast to save Patrik."

"I can hear the ambulance," Jack announced.

"It's okay honey. Cassie has to go to the hospital where they can take care of her," Twirla comforted.

"Patrik's with her too, Momma," Poppy whispered between breaths, "I heard him barking."

Twirla squeezed her daughter's hand. "Let's pray for her."

"Please let Cassie wake up," Poppy whimpered, "please wake up."

"Oh, Jim!" Ivy called out to her husband as he ran up the street from their house. "Cassie is hurt!"

Jim ran over to Ivy and put his arms out to comfort her. "It's going to be okay, Ivy, we have to trust in that."

"Here's the ambulance," Jack said. "Let's have all of you move out of the way so they can come closer."

Do you know where Akaleia is, Patrik?

Yes, , far away, in another layer of our world, under our world. Like the Elemental Kingdom we have traveled to before, we can exist in both worlds.

What if I miss my family?

We can be in contact with them whenever you want. I will hear their needs and tell you.

Can I come back if I want to?

Yes, you can be anywhere you want to be. Remember, time is a creation of the mind, as long or short as we desire; and as recent, past, or future as we manifest. Remember your purpose Cassie, our purpose, and trust in it.

Cassie grabbed tighter onto Patrik's handle as she continued to hear Poppy crying and speaking her name, and Twirla saying, "It's okay, honey. Cassie is going to be okay. She has to go to the hospital now."

Cassie heard people talking, and then her father said, "This is how she landed, no one has moved her. She skidded on her bike into the post."

We have to go now, Patrik messaged her as he rose up on his strong back legs and pulled Cassie on his back. *We have a long way to go.*

Do you know the way, Patrik?

I know the way; I have lived there, and at one time you have lived there. It is the home of our origin, Lemuria. Akaleia is in Lemuria.

Cassie and Patrik travelled together into the ethers of other worlds, in what looked like fog and felt like a weightless existence. Time became immeasurable, and Cassie thought she was in a long sleep. There were times when Cassie felt hot and thought she saw flames, but she was not burned as they sped through it.

You can open your eyes, now, Patrik messaged. *We are in Lemuria.*

Cassie opened her eyes and blinked. The area around her was lush and green and smelled sweet. She breathed in its fullness of life and released her hands from Patrik's mane to stand up.

Patrik, stay with me.

"Yes, I am here with you."

As Cassie continued to look around, her vision became clearer, and she realized that both she and Patrik were a flowing energy instead of a physical form. *We don't look the same, Patrik.*

We are in the same form as the beings of Lemuria. We are all one form now.

Beautiful flowers bloomed from grassy areas and birds flew above them singing melodic songs of happiness. Cassie breathed deeply and felt life's energy flowing through her.

Lemuria is a very large and beautiful continent, Cassie. All things grow here in all ways.

I think I like it here, Cassie communicated. *It feels friendly.*

Come this way, Patrik indicated as he moved forward. *We will be meeting other beings soon.*

The ambulance crew worked smoothly and swiftly around Cassie, assessing her vital signs and maintaining her body alignment to protect her neck and spine. "Cassie," they called out to her, "Can you hear us?"

"She lost consciousness," Jack said. "Is this temporary?"

"We'll take her to the emergency department," the paramedic said, "and ask you to follow us. The doctors will be able to run more tests and get further information."

"Okay, yes, thank you. We'll be right there." Jack nodded.

"We'll see you at the Emergency Room," the driver said to Jack and Connie as they were getting back into the truck.

Jack took out his phone and called his parents as Twirla reached over and hugged her friend. "Everything's going to be all right," she said, "She's in good hands."

"Mom?" Mandy cried out running down the driveway, "What happened?"

"Mandy, where have you been?" Connie said sharply. "You didn't hear all this?"

"I was in my room. I heard something; I just figured it was going on down the road."

"Cassie has had a bike accident and needs to go to the hospital. She's unconscious."

Mandy's eyes welled up with tears, and Twirla moved closer to offer support to her. "She's going to be okay, honey. Let's all stay together while your parents go to the hospital."

Jack put his phone in his pocket and turned to the group, "Thank you, Twirla. Phe is also coming over to be with you, Mandy, and Papa Ed is going to meet us at the hospital. We'll be in touch from there when we know more."

"Okay," Mandy whispered as she wiped tears away from her cheeks.

"We'll stay with her," Twirla replied. "You all go on to the hospital."

"Connie, we need to get going," Jack directed as he started up the driveway. "Go get your purse. I'll get my car. I have my phone."

"Thank you," Connie said hugging Twirla and then Mandy.

"It's going to be okay," Twirla said again. "The angels are here. They are all around her."

"Do you know when she will wake up?" Connie asked the Emergency Department physician who was updating them on Cassie's progress.

"No, I'm sorry I don't. She has had a very significant concussion, and the impact of that can vary, especially among children. The good news is that her vital signs remain stable. She's breathing on her own and oxygenating well. They are doing a Cat Scan of her head now in Radiology. I'll let you know the results when we have them."

"Did she say anything to you?" Connie asked with a trembling voice.

"No, Mrs. Murphy. She is still unconscious."

Nanny Phe parked her car in the driveway and walked into the kitchen where Twirla, Poppy and Mandy were sitting at the table.

"I'm here now, Mandy. We'll all stay together. It's going to be okay honey," Phe reassured her as she stood up and hugged her tightly. "We just have to wait now and trust."

"She was bleeding," Poppy spoke up, "there was blood on her face."

Twirla put her arms around Poppy's shoulders. "She'll be taken care of in the hospital, honey."

"These things take time to assess, Poppy," Phe said. "Time to get the tests she needs and the results. Your friend Cassie is a very strong little girl. She'll be playing with you again soon."

Patrik, are my parents worried about me? Cassie messaged as they continued to walk together in Lemuria.

It's been a very short time on Earth Cassie. They are with your physical body. You are being cared for in the emergency department of the hospital.

Am I all right?

You are in a deep sleep. You will awaken in time.

Can I hear them or see them?

Your physical abilities to see and hear on earth are not connected to you now. You will not remember the time you spend in the hospital or your bicycle accident.

Patrik, someone is coming forward, Cassie said as a beautiful being of white light stepped forward, adorned in necklaces of shells and colored stones.

Cassie, I am Akaleia, she said extending her arms. *Welcome to Lemuria. We have been waiting for you to return to us for a very long time.*

Return? I don't remember, Cassie said. *Your vibrations feel familiar to me though.*

Yes, many thousands of years ago you lived with us in Lemuria. I was your mother in that lifetime, and this, Akaleia said motioning to a smaller being behind her to come forward; *this is your sister, Christina.*

Jack, Connie, and Papa Ed waited together for Cassie to come back to her room from the Radiology Department. It had been several hours since her accident, and test results were still being processed.

"Why is this taking so long?" Connie asked. "Surely we should know results by now."

"Connie," Jack said, "there are a lot of people here waiting to be seen. I think they took Cassie in as soon as they could."

"I know you're worried, and waiting is the hardest part," Ed added. "I am thankful that what we do know looks good."

"Did you text them at home to say we are still waiting, Jack?'

"Yes. They are in waiting mode, too. Phe made some supper for everyone, so they are well taken care of."

"Twirla and Poppy must be exhausted. Poor Poppy, she was so upset. She saw it all," Connie said sadly, trying not to cry.

"Phe said that Twirla and Poppy are planning to go home after supper. I told Phe we would update them too. I think we'll be here for a long while."

In Lemuria Cassie, Akaleia said, *we are always learning.*

Do you have a school? Cassie asked. *I go to school in Pine Cove. My teacher is Miss Douglass.*

Our school is outdoors, and our learning is always one with nature. All of us attend together. No matter what our age, we are all in the same classroom. The elders of Lemuria are our teachers. They are very wise and have existed for all time. They know our origins and history.

They must be very, very old, Cassie said.

Akaleia smiled. *Age is not counted in the same way as it is on Earth. Our lifetimes are thousands of years and counted in vibrational energy. We do not age physically because we are not physical beings.*

Cassie nodded as she moved forward to listen to the elders and be with Christina.

Lemuria has evolved over many lifetimes, they began. *Telos, a land within the embodiment of Mount Shasta, is the home of our Lemurian survivors when the oceans swelled.*

The Elemental Kingdom is a creation of thought, and represents the spiritual forces of the four basic elements of nature. These are Earth, Fire, Water and Air.

I know Archangel Uriel, Cassie messaged Christina. *He is the angel of the Earth.*

Air is the intention of thought. Fire is the intention of desire. Water is the intention of emotions, and Earth sets the intention of stability. Within each of the four elements are nature spirits that assist in work that is needed. The nature spirits in the Elemental Kingdom and on Earth are called gnomes.

We have gnomes in the mines beneath our magic tree! Cassie shouted.

Our newest member, another elder said. *Cassie comes to us in this experience from Earth.*

And what do your gnomes do? The elder teacher asked.

They bring up basanite from under the earth. There are powerful crystals in the rocks, but they haven't been able to do that for a long time.

How did you get your crystal energy to travel here? The elder asked, as all the others turned to hear Cassie's answer.

I am travelling with Patrik. He is my dog. He brings me crystals from the Elemental Kingdom. I use them to send energy to Akaleia too.

I see. The elder continued smiling. *Where is Patrik?*

I am Patrik, a Being of Light answered near Cassie.

You are also known as Archangel Gabriel, the elder clarified. *The half human angel. The strength and communicator of the Divine Creator.*

Yes, Patrik said. *I am asked to be with Cassie to re-establish vibrational energy on Earth for the creation of the highest good.*

Cassie's nurse wheeled her stretcher back to her room in the emergency department and began to reconnect the monitoring equipment. "The doctor will be with you soon," she said to Jack, Connie and Ed, as she transferred the oxygen tubing from the portable canister on the stretcher to the wall unit. She then reconnected the cardiac leads on her chest to the monitor above the bed and checked the images of Cassie's vital signs that appeared on the screen.

"Hi folks," the ED Physician said coming back into the room. "The results of Cassie's Cat Scan show a hairline fracture, a small fracture, to her forehead and also to her nose. There is some swelling as you might expect in this area," he continued gesturing to Cassie's forehead, "but no intracranial bleeding. There is no evidence of bleeding within her brain."

"Oh, thank God," Connie said.

"What happens now, doctor?" Jack asked.

"She needs to be admitted, continued to be monitored, and further observed. She has had a serious injury and, for now, remains unconscious. I have called in other physicians and both the pediatric service and neurology will see her."

"Can we stay with her?" Connie asked.

"One parent can stay in her room upstairs after she is settled. We are waiting on a bed to be available. You can all stay for now, and one of our nurses will be in soon to help facilitate the admission process."

"Thank you," Jack said. "Thank you very much."

Cassie continued to lay motionless on the stretcher as her family stood watch. Her eyes were closed, and her skin was pale. An ice bag was secured to her bruised forehead with a large bandage, and a thin tube laid above her lip to supply oxygen through her nose. An IV bag and tubing was connected to her arm to give her fluids and medications if she needed them.

"I think you two are pretty well set," Ed said. "I'll go back to the house with Phe and Mandy until one of you comes home."

"Will you please update Twirla, too?"

"Yes. I will tell them that everything is stable, and we are waiting for other doctors to evaluate her, a room, and for her to wake up," Ed summarized.

"Thanks, Dad," Jack said. "Connie is going to stay the night here. I'll be home after we get Cassie settled in her room."

"Don't worry, you two. Cassie's in good hands."

"Thank you, and thank Phe too," Connie replied as she reached out and grabbed hold of Cassie's hand.

In a short time, the pediatrician on-call came into the Emergency Department to assess Cassie and write admitting orders. Connie and Jack took a break and went to the cafeteria to get some coffee while he examined Cassie.

"You should eat something, Connie," Jack said as he took a sandwich from the refrigerator case.

"I feel so sick to my stomach," Connie said. "I keep seeing her in the street, and she was so lifeless. And I thought, you know, maybe she was, was not going to ever wake up."

"It was frightening," Jack said reaching out to take her hand, "for all of us."

Patrik, Cassie messaged, *you have many special abilities. Can you help my Mommy to accept what I understand and believe? Can you help her to be happy with me?*

Each of us must create our own happiness. Your mother is afraid that if she is open to believing things outside of herself, she will lose control of the outcomes she wants. She is worried about you, Cassie. She sits with you in the hospital and prays. She truly loves you.

She is often mad at me, Patrik. I am not sure how to respond to her when she is angry.

Anger is an emotion of fear, Cassie. A negative thought which produces other negative thoughts and actions. These have been engrained in her mind and behavior since childhood. Remember, thoughts become things.

Can I send a message to her? Cassie asked.

She is not open to receive the flow of messages.

Can I send a message to Auntie Chloe? She will hear me and understand. She will tell Mommy.

Yes, Patrik agreed. *Let me help you translate your thoughts into energy vibration which will transcend to the earth dimension. First, you must put your thoughts into light language.*

Cassie was moved to an inpatient room on the Pediatric Unit later in the evening. Dr. Howard, the pediatrician, met with Jack and Connie while Cassie was still in the emergency room and discussed his preliminary findings and his plan of care. "The nursing staff will be doing neurological assessments every hour as well as continuous monitoring of all her vital signs from the nurse's station."

"Thank you, doctor," Jack and Connie replied together.

"They will contact me if there are any significant changes," he said reassuringly, "and I will be back in the morning. I have ordered some tests for the morning also, and based on those results and her status, I can discuss next steps."

"Do you know when the neurology consult will be done?" Jack asked.

"Yes. I have already spoken with Dr. Blake, and he will be in to see her tomorrow morning."

Jack shifted in his chair, "What did you say his name is?"

"Dr. Edward Blake. Do you know him?"

"No," Jack said. "We know of an Edmund Blake from this area a long time ago."

"She's in good hands," the doctor said reassuringly. "Time is on our side. Healing takes time. I'll see you in the morning."

"I'm going to head back to the house," Jack said after the nurses had settled Cassie into her hospital room. "Do you want anything before I go?"

"No, I'm good," Connie replied.

"You haven't eaten anything."

"I'm not hungry. I'll be fine."

"Mrs. Murphy, let us know if you want anything," Cassie's nurse spoke up as she checked on Cassie and elevated the head of her bed a little higher. "We have a full kitchen up here."

"Thank you, Debbie, I appreciate that very much."

Jack sat down again and took Connie's hand. "Accidents happen. This is no one's fault, not even Cassie's. We were there for her. We are here for her. She's going to be fine."

Connie began to cry and leaned into Jack. "She looks so still. I keep checking to see if she's breathing."

"I know," Jack comforted. "This will all be behind us in a few days."

Cassie and Christina spent as much time as possible together. They looked alike and often finished each other's thoughts. They walked toward the ocean edge every day and played games in the sand.

Cassie, come closer, Christina said, *the land beings are changing into dolphins.*

How does this happen? Cassie asked. *They are of one form and then turn into another.*

Yes, and you have that power too. We know it as shape shifting.

My Mommy said she would like to work with animals and children to help connect them. She used to ride horses.

Your earth mother has many untapped talents, Cassie. You are just beginning to discover yours.

Cassie smiled and nodded. *Tell me how to help her.*

You have many ways of transmitting energy and communicating to your mother. This can be done by voice, by mind waves, vibrational, and healing energy. I want to teach you more about healing energy. It is the purest form of Love.

Jack drove into his driveway and parked in front of the garage. Cassie's bicycle was laying on the grass next to his workshop with a bent wheel and twisted handlebars. He took a deep breath and walked over to it.

"Jack, are you doing okay?" Mike asked coming up behind him. "I saw you drive in."

"Yeah, Mike. Okay I guess. Cassie is still unconscious, but all her tests look good. They tell us she just needs to wake up."

"That sounds like good news. Your parents, Ed, came over to tell us earlier."

"Thanks," Jack said grasping his shoulder. "Now we just wait."

"We are here for you. Millie already took Ned out for the night, so he's all set. We'll plan on taking him out in the morning too."

"That'd be great. I want to go into the hospital early and meet with her doctor again. The neurologist is coming in tomorrow morning too. You know what his name is?"

"Patrik," Mike guessed.

"Close. Dr. Edward Blake."

"That's a little spooky."

"I thought so too. Connie's going to call if anything changes in the night. I'm going to ask my parents to stay overnight in case I need to go in."

"We are a phone call away Jack. I'll catch up with you tomorrow."

"It's only been a few hours, but this feels like an eternity," Jack said. "I have never felt so helpless."

"It's going to be okay," Mike said reassuringly and giving him a hug. "We have to give it time."

Cassie and Christina sat by the ocean watching the dolphins swim and jump over the waves.

When they shape shift into land animals, Christina said, *they always yearn for their other way of being. It is as if they are existing in two worlds.*

I know when I am at home I also want to be with Patrik. I want to travel with him to the Elemental Kingdom.

In time you will know how to make that transformation yourself. You are learning.

Christina, what do you know about the dragons who inhabit here? I didn't see them, but Patrik said they guided us as we traveled closer to Lemuria.

Dragons are protectors. They are large dominating beings with wings like dinosaur pterodactyls. Their long tails balance them as they fly. Their ultimate purpose is to change environments for the greater good. As they evolved, and our world evolved, they shape shifted. Ultimately, they became what you know on earth as salamanders.

They were hot, and I thought there were colors of orange and red, like fire.

Yes, Christina continued. *They can breathe fire. When they breathe fire, they are protecting us from any negative forces that may be near. Their fire projects outward and away and will not burn you.*

Cassie nodded and paused before she spoke again. *A long time ago, when Patrik was an earth being, there was a fire in the barn on the property where he lived. That is where my family and I live now. I was told the salamanders set it. They were tricked!*

Like the dragons, the salamanders will always act in the highest good, Christina added. *Even if it was not understood at the time, their actions were not to promote harm, but to extinguish it. They were trying to stop the evil that was coming forward.*

Cassie thought for a moment. *I think there is something behind the stone walls in our cellar. I felt them. I told my Daddy not to open the brick, ever.*

Did you feel energy or evil? Do you know?

I believe it was energy. I didn't stay very long to know its full message.

You will need to spend more time there in order to be sure. In time, all is revealed.

"Hi Mom," Jack said coming in the kitchen door, "Dad."

Phe walked over and gave Jack a big hug. "Any other news since you called us from Cassie's room?"

"No, everything still looks good. We just have to wait for her to wake up."

"Dad?" Mandy said running into the kitchen and hugging her father. "I was so worried!"

"I know, Amanda, we were all worried. It's going to be okay."

"I made some hot chocolate for everyone," Phe said bringing over some mugs to the table. "Let's sit and relax a bit."

"Connie is going to call if anything changes tonight," Daddy said. "Can I ask you to stay overnight Mom, in case I need to go in?"

"Of course, Jack!" Phe said. "I'd be happy to stay."

"I saw Mike in the driveway. Mike and Millie will come back in the morning to take Ned out again, so you don't have to do that."

"I'll be back over in the morning, too," Ed said. "Right now, I think we all need to try and get some sleep."

Patrik, Have you and Akaleia finished our work here?

We are very close to finishing. We have been working on translating Light Language into energy that can be used for manifesting, creating the connection bridges.

Do we need that to go home? Cassie asked. *I miss my family.*

You are still in the hospital Cassie. All of this time we have spent in Lemuria has only ben several hours in Earth time. It's nighttime now and your mother is sitting with you in the hospital.

Am I awake?

No, not yet.

When will I wake up?

When we return home, to Earth.

Jack called Connie from the kitchen after Ed had left for the night, and Phe and Mandy went up to bed. "Hi, I just wanted to tell you we are all good here. My mom is staying overnight in case you want me to come back, and so I can come in early in the morning. How's Cassie doing? Any changes?"

"No, huh? Okay. I'll see you in the morning. Hang in there. Call if you want, anytime. I love you too."

Jack walked into his office before going upstairs and patted Ned who was sleeping on his dog bed. "Good boy, Neddie. She'll be home soon. Don't worry."

He proceeded to the front stairs and began to walk up. The house was eerily quiet, and he heard several steps creak under his weight; sounds he hadn't noticed before. "I should fix that," he mentioned to himself as he reached the top of the stairs and turned to the left. Mandy's light was on and he tapped on the door. "Mandy?"

Mandy lay curled up in her bed asleep, with Merton and Elroy under her arm.

"Oh, Mandy," Jack whispered. "So sweet of you."

He turned off Mandy's lamp and walked down the hall into Cassie's room. The moonlight cast it's beam across the floor and illuminated the potting shed dollhouse. "Of course," he said, as he knelt down in front of it.

The figurines were in various places. Mike and Millie were off to the side with Luna and Kai.

Nanny Phe and Poppy stood in the fairy garden with Twirla. Chloe was inside the potting shed sitting at the table with the Jack and Connie dolls. Jack looked around but couldn't find the Patrik and Cassie dolls.

"The tree!" he said leaning over and opening the door in the magic tree. "Ah, Cassie and Patrik. You need to come out now. No more playing around. Time to come out and be seen again."

Jack laughed as he closed the little door and placed them on the other side of the dollhouse by the garden and front doors. Time to wake up you two!"

Akaleia and Christina are waiting for us Cassie. They wish to say goodbye.

I have had a wonderful time here, Patrik, thank you.

You were very important to our work, Cassie, in translating Light Language. You seem to see each symbol as it truly is, a transforming message.

Christina and I did that together in school each day, Cassie replied. *When we used our third eye and opened space for the vibrations to come through, we knew the meaning of the symbols.*

Yes, you taught many others as you worked together on the lessons.

My Daddy has the leather satchel in his office with all of Dr. Blake's Light Language papers.

Akaleia nodded, *Yes, they are very important and must be protected.*

I can write like that too. That is how I write my stories. Did Dr. Blake tell you stories Patrik?

They are not stories Cassie. They are instructions. Dr. Blake has written out the instructions in Light Language to extract crystals from the basanite rock.

Cassie and Patrik, many blessings to you on your travels as you return to Earth, Akaleia messaged them as Christina reached out to embrace Cassie.

Sister of my ethereal light, Christina spoke softly, *may our next meeting be a reuniting in Telos, my city of Lemuria. May you be blessed in all your travels and Light work. Master Adama,* Christina continued, *the High Priest of Telos, offers these words to all of us, "Until we meet, keep practicing the art of true love, which begins with loving yourself dear one."*

Patrik moved forward with Cassie on his back, holding the handle of his mane. They floated into the mist, into the spaces of life energy between the dimensions of existence. The dragons of Lemuria encased them in red and orange flames at the start of their journey, protecting them until they were beyond the Lemurian energy field and safely headed to the Elemental Kingdom.

Cassie, Patrik messaged, *we do not have enough crystal energy to return to earth. Something has happened. The crystal powers have been reduced. We will need to have new energy created.*

My father knows how to create the energy with the crystals in my room. You have to tell him Patrik. He has been able to hear you before.

Jack lay in his bed looking up at the ceiling. He thought about Cassie laying in the street, unconscious, and still unconscious in her hospital bed. He thought about Connie, and the desperate look on her face as they navigated through the Emergency Department waiting for test results and hoping for improvements. And he thought about Cassie's bike, laying crumpled on the ground by the garage door. *I can't sleep,* he said to himself sitting up in bed and turning on the light.

Jack, open the door. Put us in the tree. Put us with a crystal in the tree. Close the door.

"What, what?" Jack said aloud as he began to hear Patrik barking.

161

Jack, open the door. Put us in the tree. Put us with a crystal in the tree. Close the door.

Jack rubbed his eyes and shook his head. This must be a dream, he thought. This whole thing is a bad dream.

Patrik's barking echoed from the hallway, and Jack followed the sound across the hall to Cassie's bedroom. The moonlight still glowed in the room and sparkled on the floor.

Jack, open the door. Put us in the tree. Put us with a crystal in the tree. Close the door.

Jack knelt on the floor and opened the door in the magic tree behind the potting shed doll house.

"Where's the dolls?" he said, picking up the Cassie and Patrik figures. "Come here you two."

"Crystal. Crystal." Jack looked all around the shed and in the classroom and the fireplace.

"Come on, where are you?" he asked getting up and going to Cassie's closet. He turned on the light and knelt down to run his hands over the quilt on the floor. "Where are you?"

Patrik barked again, and again, this time coming from the direction of Cassie's bed, Jack thought.

"Under the pillow," he said walking quickly over to sit on the bed. Jack ran his hand under her pillow but couldn't find anything. He opened the drawer in Cassie's bedside table and lifted out the folded tissue packet inside. "Okay, here we go," he said unwrapping the tissue to reveal a large stone. It felt cold.

Jack got up quickly and went back to his bedroom. He reached into a jar on his bureau, taking out the crystal Cassie had given him at Christmas.

"Cassie, you told me that Patrik would tell me how to use this and I am asking now. It's time for you to wake up. It's time for you, for you both, to come home."

Jack walked back to Cassie's room and remembered the ritual Cassie had shown him with the crystal and the moonlight to send energy to Akaleia. He held the crystal out in the palm of his hand so that the moonlight could shine on it. He watched intently as the stone began to glitter and give the appearance that it was moving. He closed his hands and brought the crystal to his heart.

And then I close my eyes and see a wish, Jack said out loud as he remembered Cassie saying it, *and it happens.*

Jack closed his eyes. "Time to wake up, Cassie. Time to bring Cassie home, Patrik."

Jack felt warmth and tingling in his hands, and when he opened his eyes, the crystal was still glowing.

Patrik's bark got louder and louder. Jack walked back to the potting shed doll house. He placed the crystal inside the tree along with the Cassie and Patrik dolls.

Patrik continued to bark louder and louder.

"Tree of Life, Worlds Unite! Tree of Life, Worlds Unite! Tree of Life, Worlds Unite!" Jack yelled out.

The barking stopped.

"This is it Patrik," Jack said out loud. "I have done all I know how to do. I have done all you have shown me to do. It's up to you now."

Jack went back to his bedroom and got dressed, knowing he wasn't going to get to sleep anyway.

He went downstairs and made a pot of coffee. The clock on the stove showed 3 am.

"Jack," Phe said coming into the kitchen. "Is everything all right?"

"Mom, sorry, I didn't mean to wake you."

"You didn't really. I was sleeping in naps, tossing and turning. You know, thinking."

"Yes. The mind can take you to some really dark places."

"Especially when it concerns people we love. Fear is not a friend."

"What if she doesn't wakeup? Or if she has problems from her head injury?"

"One day at a time, Jack. We will face whatever problems and needs that may arise together. We will also rejoice in her recovery. Cassie is very blessed, and I trust in her angels."

"Do you really believe in all that stuff? Angels and fairies and Patrik?"

"Why would I not? They represent goodness. We should put our faith in everything that brings joy into our lives."

"Cassie, you know, has had some challenges," Jack said. "When this Patrik character showed up, Cassie seemed to open up and come out of her shell. Moving here, having Katie as her teacher, she has grown exponentially this year."

"Parenting is not easy," Phe admitted.

"But I never had any troubles as a kid," Jack said.

Phe broke into peals of laughter. "You always just remember the end result. Not the processes in getting there."

"I had issues? Peter had real issues."

"Hmmm ... let me just say that each of you had moments that required parental involvement."

"Yeah," Jack laughed. "I remember when Dad was crazy mad at me for spending all my money on that junk car because it looked cool."

"Yes, well it wasn't safe to drive you know."

"I think," Jack started to say as his phone rang. "It's Connie."

"Connie, Hi! Is everything all right? She's waking up?"

"Oh Jack!" Phe exclaimed. "Thank God!"

"Okay, I'll be right there. Love you."

Jack went to grab his coat from the hallway. "I'll call you with an update Mom. She's starting to open her eyes and look around. She's saying some things. Connie thinks she's dreaming."

CHAPTER 10

Cracks in the Window

When Jack arrived at Cassie's room in the hospital, she was lying in her bed with her eyes still closed. A large bandage covered her forehead and part of her head, and he could see the corner of an ice bag above her right eye.

"Is she awake yet?" he asked.

"Jack!" Connie exclaimed hugging him close. "I'm so glad you're here! She has some brief moments of moving and mumbling. It seems to happen when the nurses are assessing her or moving her. The nurses say she's starting to wake up, and they have called to update Dr. Howard."

"Okay. That's some progress. You can't understand what she's saying?"

"No, not yet. But the nurses have told me that all her vital signs remain stable and the fact that she is beginning to move her arms and legs is very positive. We have to have more patience I guess."

"And faith," Jack added.

Cassie, your father has added more crystal energy to our travels, and we are continuing to move forward now in the levels of dimensions to reach upper Earth. He heard my barking and my messages. He followed your previous instructions; what you showed him to do in the moonlight to generate crystal energy.

Cassie smiled. *I knew he believed.*

Cassie's doctors came in early to re-examine her and review additional test results with Jack and Connie.

"How does this usually happen?" Connie asked. "The waking up. Is it all at once, or gradual?"

"Once she is awake enough to remain awake," Dr. Howard said, "her ability to communicate and accurately remember can be better evaluated. Cassie has had a significant concussion and injuries. I do believe however, that she is showing positive changes this morning."

Jack and Connie continued to sit quietly at Cassie's bedside. They had updated people on her progress and texted back as they received responses. Jack notified Dan about the accident and was planning on being out of work for several days, or as long as was necessary.

"I'm going to call the school and let them know Cassie is not going to attend this week. I know Katie was aware yesterday; Phe said she had called her and Peter."

"Cassie?" Jack said noticing she had opened her eyes. "Are you awake?"

"Patrik? Is Patrik here?" Cassie spoke softly.

"Cassie!" Connie shouted. "We are so glad you are awake! Let me call the nurse to check you."

"Is Patrik here? Do you hear him, Daddy?"

"I haven't heard him today. I heard him barking last night."

"Cassie, my name is Diane. I am your nurse today. How are you feeling?"

"Good."

"We are very glad to hear that! I need to assess some things and ask you some questions. Is that okay?"

"Yes."

"I am going to shine this little light in your eyes. Good! When I move the light, can you follow it with your eyes?"

"Yes."

"You are doing great, thank you. How well can you see Cassie? Is your vision blurry at all?"

"A little."

"You have a big bandage on your head and some swelling too. That might contribute to some blurriness. Your Mom and Dad are here. I heard you have a sister too. What's her name?"

"Christina."

"No, no. That's not right," Connie interrupted. "It's Mandy. Mandy is your sister."

"Mrs. Murphy, all Cassie's answers are important," Diane replied.

"You know what? Cassie, your Mom and I are going to go get some coffee for a few minutes while the nurse is here with you. Diane, we'll be nearby in the waiting room."

"Thank you, Mr. Murphy. The doctors will be in again soon."

"Jack!" Connie exclaimed coming out of the room. "Who is Christina?"

"I don't know. I'm glad Cassie is awake and starting to talk. Let's get some coffee and wait for the doctors. Everything is going to be okay."

"She's not remembering the right things! What if she doesn't remember?"

"Let's not jump to conclusions, Connie. I think we need to update people that she is awake and starting to talk, because that is a very good thing."

Phe and Ed sat in Jack and Connie's kitchen having breakfast while they waited for Mandy to wake up.

"I told her she could stay home from school today," Phe said. "She needs some extra sleep."

"Hi, Millie," Ed greeted her opening the back door. "Thanks for coming over. Did you get Jack's message?"

"Yes! Cassie's waking up, that's fantastic! All good news."

"I imagine Cassie will be in the hospital for a couple more days," Ed continued. "They'll want to keep an eye on her and do some follow-up tests."

"Agreed. How's Ned this morning? I offered to take him out. I can be available all week, morning and evening. Whatever they need."

"He sleeps all the time Millie," Phe said. "He's very old, poor pet."

"I see Jack trying to take him up the driveway sometimes," Millie nodded. "Ned requires a lot of extra help."

"Ned is at the end of his years," Ed said. "I know it's hard, but the dog really doesn't have a quality of life anymore."

"Well, let's see how far we can go this morning," Millie said walking towards Jack's office.

"He doesn't need a leash anymore that's for sure."

Cassie's doctors, Dr. Howard and Dr. Blake, met with Jack and Connie in the consultation room on the Pediatric Unit following their re-evaluation.

"Cassie has made more improvement in the last few hours, and we expect that to continue. It's been a relatively short period of time since her accident, less than 24 hours, and we anticipate gradual improvements in her memory as well."

"But what about the things she's not remembering correctly? When does she become oriented again to things that are real?"

"Mrs. Murphy, I'm sure it can be unsettling when there is confusion in what Cassie remembers," Dr. Howard advised. "We have to let these things come about slowly. If they remain issues, we can suggest further tests and resources to follow-up."

"Oh, I just thought that if we told her the answers it would help her remember."

"That's really not necessary. We need to let her just talk."

"Do you know long she will be in the hospital, doctor?" Jack asked.

"I think we will need to keep her a few more days. I will be ordering some follow up x-rays, and have the nurses continue to monitor her vital and neurologic signs, though not as frequently. She also needs to get up to a chair, walk independently, eat and drink normally, and do some daily activities. We need to assess if she needs any help with these things when she is home."

"Who is Patrik?" Dr Blake asked. "She seems very concerned about him and wants to make sure he is okay."

Connie and Jack looked at one another. "Patrik is her imaginary dog friend," Jack said. "She often thinks he is real."

"She doesn't remember falling off her bike," Dr. Blake continued, "and she doesn't have a clear concept of time. She thinks a long time has passed and she was away with Patrik. Someplace called Lemuria?"

Connie shifted in her chair, "This has been a fantasy play she has been involved in for a while. We hear stories about Lemuria and its characters at various times."

"Well, she has a great imagination then. I am glad she has had such a good day."

While Cassie was re-emerging into her whole self in the hospital, Patrik came back from Lemuria through the portal in Cassie's closet and laid on her bed. He tried several times to message her but there was no reply. He had overheard conversations in the house and knew Cassie was still in the hospital and regaining her consciousness. But there was no way to connect to her directly.

Cassie I am here for you. I am sending crystal energy to give you strength. I am not able to be with you.

"Mandy, dear, come sit down," Phe said motioning her to the table. "Let me get you some juice to get started and tell you some good news."

Mandy turned to look at her grandmother. "Do we know something more?"

"Yes, dear. Cassie is awake now and talking."

"OH!" Mandy exclaimed. "Is she all right? Can she come home?"

"Not today," Ed added. "But your Mom and Dad will have more information later."

"Are they coming home? Can I go see her?" Mandy asked.

"I think they are going to take turns staying with Cassie as long as she is in the hospital. I expect at some point one of them will be home. You can call them, honey, and ask about visiting," Phe said putting a glass of juice on the table. "What about some breakfast?"

"I can't eat," Mandy said. "I still feel sick."

"It's going to be okay, Mandy," Phe said reaching out and hugging her. "I'll put a few things out on the counter to eat that you can have when you're ready."

"Are you going home?" Mandy asked with a quivering voice.

"Not for now, honey. One of us will always be here with you."

Cassie drifted in and out of sleep all afternoon. She had started to drink fluids and some soup. The nurses removed the bandage from her forehead to reveal a large area of bruising and swelling that extended down through the bridge of her nose and created two black eyes. "This will resolve over a few weeks," Diane said motioning to her face. "It will turn colors as it heals. Dr. Howard has made a referral to a specialist Connie, to follow-up on her nose fractures after she is discharged, as well as an eye doctor.

In between the nurses checks on her, Cassie napped with visions of Lemuria and the time she and Patrik had spent there. She could see Akaleia, and Christina close to her, smiling and speaking in Light Language, and hear the songs Christina had taught her while they played. She remembered the elders and going to school, and the shape shifting dolphins diving into the aquamarine waters. *Patrik,* she messaged, *where are you? Can you come to me?*

Cassie, I am in your bed. I will wait for you here, and continue to send healing thoughts. There is no portal to reach you.

Jack and Connie spent the next few days between the hospital and the house, taking turns to be with Cassie. Neighbors stopped in to say hello and leave premade dinners and baked goods, and offering to help in any way they could.

"Poppy and I made these cookies," Twirla explained as she placed a box on the counter.

"For Cassie," Poppy said. "Cookies always make you feel better!"

Phe continued to come over to be with Mandy whenever needed, and Mark was allowed to bring her back and forth to school each day and come in and visit whenever they both had time.

"He's a very nice boy," Phe had said to Mandy. "I think you two are good for each other."

"Yes, Mandy replied. "I can always talk to him. He understands."

Phe nodded, "Special. Very special. Especially at a time like this. Challenges always bring us closer together."

Cassie came home two days later with very strict rules about activities she could and couldn't do. "I want to go upstairs and see Patrik," Cassie said immediately as she came in the back door.

"Don't run!" Connie exclaimed as Cassie headed for the stairs.

"The doctor is going to re-evaluate her in two weeks," Connie told Phe. "Based on how she's doing other activities can be added after that. She'll be out of school for that time."

"Healing takes time. This was a traumatic experience for a little girl. If you want me to call Katie, I can ask for some papers she could do at home."

"Yes, thank you, I appreciate that. It will give her quiet things to do between times of resting."

"Cassie, Poppy is here," Connie announced Saturday afternoon. "You can go ahead up Poppy. Cassie needs to stay quiet. No jumping around, okay?"

"Yes, Mrs. Murphy."

"Poppy, I'm up here!" Cassie yelled from the landing.

"Cassie, quiet!" Connie yelled out. "You need to stay quiet!"

"Sounds like you're the one who's loud," Chloe said coming down the hall from the kitchen.

"Chloe!" Connie shouted grabbing her sister and bursting into tears. "I was so hoping you could come up."

"It's okay, Connie. It's all behind us now, Cassie is safe."

"I saw her in the street. I can't get that image out of my mind. I thought we had lost her."

"I know. It's going to take some time for that image and those fears to fade."

"Poppy just came. They hadn't seen each other since the accident. Poppy was very brave and scared to death!"

"I bet so. Sounds like that was how everyone felt. Let's make some tea and sit. I have news too."

"Hi Cassie," Poppy said looking at her face. "Does it hurt?"

"It hurts if I touch it. Sometimes my head aches and then Mommy tells me I have to lay down and rest."

"I heard Patrik barking! When you fell off your bike, he was barking really loud. You told me I would hear him with my crystal wish, and I did! Is Patrik here now?'

"He's been here. But he wanted to go to the magic tree now that the snow has melted."

"Can we go down there too?" Poppy asked.

"I asked my Daddy, and he said not until next weekend. He said I would get too excited."

"Can we play in the shed? We could bring our toys out again and set up the school."

"He said not yet. Do you want to play with the dollhouse?'

"I brought you a present to get well," Poppy said pulling a little wrapped box out of her jacket pocket. "My Momma helped me pick these out."

Cassie unwrapped the box to find crystal beads and three more dolls that looked like angels.

"The angels were with you when you had your accident. My Momma said they encircled you and kept you safe. And the little crystals are for your dollhouse. They are just the right size for the gnomes."

"Thank you," Cassie said as she moved over and knelt down by the dollhouse. "Do you want to play school with me here?'

"I want to help the Nanny Phe doll plant the fairy garden again. It's spring!"

"So, what's your news Chloe?' Connie asked as they sat in the kitchen having tea.

"First, tell me all about Cassie. What's the plan for her care?'

"She will see her doctors in two weeks and until then she can do quiet activities. No school. We are to watch her and help her with anything she needs. Truthfully her advances in these past few days have been remarkable. Except her memory."

"What do you mean?"

"She doesn't remember the accident. But she believes she and Patrik were gone for a long time to Lemuria. She recalls all these strange beings. She calls them Akaleia, Christina, the elders; she says they are people she lived with for a while. It's more than just imagination. It's quite the bizarre story."

"Connie, remember when I told you and Jack that Cassie said she and Patrik were planning a trip to Lemuria when they had enough time? These were all thoughts within her subconscious."

"Maybe. I don't know Chloe. I don't know what's real and not real anymore. Poppy says she heard Patrik barking at the time of the accident. Jack says he heard a message from Patrik the first night Cassie was in the hospital. Cassie insists she has another sister named Christina. It seems really crazy to me."

"This has been a very challenging and stressful time Connie. You may just have to step back and let things settle down of their own accord. You might want to ask Cassie some questions when she talks about her travels to elicit more detail."

"Even if I don't believe it?"

"Well, she believes it. You're trying to access her reality."

"Enough of this! There's one reality! Tell me what's happening with you."

Chloe smiled, "I have a new job! I decided not to renew my contract in Boston!"

"Wow, Chloe, great! Where are you going to be working?"

"Here. I am opening a practice in southern Maine. I will have associated privileges at the hospital also."

"Do you think you'll have hospital work?"

"Not really, but I expect to receive referrals."

"You need an office! And some staff! Do you have a plan? Do you have a place to live? Stay here! You can always stay here."

Chloe laughed. "Thank you. That's a lot to respond to at once. I'll just say I'm in process. My contract officially ends in a month, so I have time to relocate. I have already made some professional connections here and I will look at opportunities for office space they have told me about."

"I am so happy about this!" Connie said hugging her sister. "This is answer to prayer!"

"What was it like in the hospital Cassie? Do you remember your accident?"

"No."

"We were riding bikes together," Poppy continued. "You saw Patrik running in the street and tried to get to him before he was hit by a car. You crashed into the mailbox post."

"I don't remember."

"I stayed with you. People came running when I called out for help."

"What did I say?"

"You couldn't talk. I was really scared, and there was blood coming down your face. That's when I heard Patrik barking. I knew he was with you. My crystal wish came true!"

"We went to Lemuria, and I got to meet Akaleia and Christina. Christina is my sister from when I lived there before."

"Is it nice there?"

"It is always summer and shimmering and filled with flowers and beautiful trees. The dolphins can swim in the ocean or shape shift and walk on land. I went to school too! It's very different. Everybody goes together."

"How did you do all that while you were in the hospital?"

"I don't think I was in the hospital really. I think I was with Patrik."

Jack went back to work the next Monday, and Connie stayed home with Cassie. Phe brought over the school papers that she had received from Katie and spent time with Cassie to review them.

"Thank you, Phe, I'm not really the best person to do these with Cassie."

"I am happy to do it! It brings me back to my teaching years. I miss students."

"You and Ed have helped us so much Phe. We couldn't do this without you. Thank you!"

"Let's have a get-together," Jack said to Connie. "We can celebrate Cassie's recovery and Chloe's new business and relocation to Maine. And spring!"

"Yes, it is finally spring," Connie said, "but I think we should wait until after Cassie has had her recheck appointments and she is well enough to be back in school."

"How about if we call people up and ask them if they want to come over that next Saturday? That will be three weeks since her accident, and she has her appointments Monday. It can be a pot-luck thing. Nothing fancy."

"Okay," Connie said.

"Okay? You don't need to have a big list and have everything planned out?"

"Cassie's accident has started to change me. I know I need to live more in the moment. I want to be grateful for the present."

"Whatever you want," Jack said with a kiss.

"Hey, buddy," Mike called out while patting Luna and Kai in the paddock. "How are you all doing?"

"Good Mike, thanks. We are getting back to some normalcy, gratefully. Did you get my text about getting together next weekend?"

"Yes, sounds good for both of us. Do you want to discuss a plan for fixing the windows in the potting shed?"

"Yes, that's on the spring to-do list. Do you have time this weekend?"

"I have time right now. Since we created the windows for the dollhouse, I think I have a good handle on this."

"Come on over. I'll tell Cassie too. She has been waiting for any opportunity for me to open the potting shed again."

Mike laughed, "Better tell Patrik too. You know how these things go."

Mike, Jack, and Cassie walked over to the potting shed together with the sweet smell of new grass growing in the yard. Mike carried a toolbox, and Jack carried a step ladder. "Can Poppy and I play out here now?" Cassie asked.

"Yes. I think you can play in the shed. No going down to the tree yet."

"Patrik's very excited too, Daddy. There's a lot more energy around when the shed is opened."

"Uh, huh," Daddy said lifting the trowel up from behind the spade to open the gate.

Cassie walked through the gate and began to take off her shoes, "Cassie leave your shoes on," Daddy told her.

"I just have to feel the earth energy and then I'll put them back on Daddy. I have a crystal for the gnomes too," she said as Jack and Mike started to walk over to the door.

"Wait Daddy, I have to give them this crystal!" Cassie shouted running over.

Daddy stepped back as Cassie stepped forward.

"Fascinating," Mike said. "I could be a believer."

"Okay, let's get these cords off and open the doors. Wow, it's stale in here. It will be good to let some fresh air in," Daddy said as he lifted one of the gnomes to prop open the door.

"How are you going to open the windows?" Cassie asked.

"The same way we made them for your dollhouse," Daddy said. "They are going to open in the same way."

"Today we are just going to start removing them. We'll have to come out another day to put the new windows in with the pulley system," Mike explained.

Daddy unfolded the ladder and stepped back to let Mike climb up to reach the top of the window.

"I'm going to take the sash off first. It's so old it's probably going to crumble when I start to pry it out."

Cassie walked over to the chalk board and placed her hand on the writing.

"Daddy, did you come out and write a new message?"

"No, what?" Daddy asked as he turned towards the board. "No, I didn't. That's not the message you wrote here last winter Cassie."

"I know. *Ana'a Anamaka,* " Cassie read. "It's Light Language. It means with our heart as one in energy with Mother Nature, from Akaleia."

"Are you making this up?" Daddy asked while Mike handed him pieces of window framing.

"No. I learned it in Lemuria. We speak in Light Language there."

"Cassie has a number of remembrances from when she was unconscious," Daddy explained to Mike. "They revolve around this land called Lemuria."

"I went to school there with the elders who were our teachers," Cassie added.

"There's a lot of wind coming through these cracks in the framing now Jack. It's starting to lift the other pieces off."

"Let's get out of here," Daddy said, as a couple more wooden slats independently fell to the floor.

"No Daddy! Patrik says we have to open the back door," Cassie cried out as she ran to the little door and took hold of the handle.

"No! Cassie, No!

"Jack, the framing is coming off the other window too," Mike said as he came down from the ladder and laid it on the floor. "The wind is picking up more."

"Cassie! Wait!" Daddy yelled as Cassie lifted the handle and swung the door open to the right.

WHOOSH, WHOOSH!! WHOOSH!

Daddy reached out and grabbed Cassie as Mike knelt down on the floor and covered his head with his hands.

The wind coming up from the forest sounded like thunder. It encircled the room and cracked the windows.

"Mike! Are you okay?" Daddy asked as he held Cassie tightly.

"Yes, I think so," Mike said. "I don't understand what happened."

Daddy laughed as he let go of Cassie. "Me either. I give up. What's going on Cassie? What does Patrik say?"

Cassie closed her eyes, "Patrik says you freed the magic. Patrik says the energy vibrations are open again, one with Mother Nature."

"Jack, there is something very powerful going on here," Mike said as he stood up and shook his head. "I assume when these windows were locked up, permanent like this, the people were trying to prevent something from happening. I guess we'll find out now what that was."

"Yeah, Mike," Daddy laughed again. "Let's call it a day. We can put the new windows in another day. Cassie, we need to close the back door again."

"I need to go to the tree, Daddy. I need to make sure it is okay."

"Are you coming, Mike?" Daddy asked as he nodded to Cassie. "Let's get this over with."

Jack, Mike, and Cassie descended the stone steps leading to the magic tree in silence. Spring had regenerated the vegetation on the forest floor and the smell of new earth was prominent.

Cassie moved forward to the tree and placed her hands on the bark.

"It's here," she said. "It's still here."

"What's here?"

"The opening."

"Do you have to do any running around today and chanting?" Daddy asked.

"No Daddy, it's open. Patrik says we opened the door behind the open door. It will stay open now."

Daddy moved forward and placed his hands on the bark. Energy vibrations reverberated down through his arms, his body, and through his legs. He felt the ground move as he knelt down. "Well, there really is something here," he said.

"Let me try," Mike offered as he moved past Cassie.

"Mr. Mike," Cassie said, "you can use your crystal wish if you want."

Mike looked back at Cassie and smiled. "I was saving that for something Millie and I might want together."

"You can use this one," Cassie said pulling out another crystal from her pocket.

Mike took the crystal, put his hands on the tree bark, and closed his eyes. "I wish to feel the vibrations of this tree," he said. Slowly the warmth of energy began to flow through his fingers and up his arms, erupting in his chest and flooding his whole body with crystal energy. "Wow!" he exclaimed stepping back. "Wow!"

Jack was ambivalent as to what to tell Connie about the potting shed experience. It was just like what Mike had said, "unbelievable!," yet it was real. It really did happen, and although Mike and Jack were left speechless, Cassie was unabashed by it all.

"What are you going to tell Millie?" Daddy asked Mike as they all walked back towards the house.

"I'm not sure. I have to think about it for a while. I do plan on telling her, though, if that's what you're asking."

"Yeah, I know," Daddy said. "The cat's out of the bag now."

"What cat?" asked Cassie.

"It's just an expression. There is no cat."

"Why would the cat be in a bag?"

"Cassie," Mike said bending down to her eye level, it would be hard to keep a cat in a bag wouldn't it? They would claw their way out."

"Yes."

"It's like hiding. If the cat is in the bag it's hiding. If it's out of the bag it's in full sight."

"Okay," Cassie said. "Like Patrik. He's out of the bag now too."

"Yes sweetheart. He certainly is."

"Momma! Patrik's out of the bag!" Cassie yelled coming in the back door. "And the tree is all open now. The wind blew and cracked the windows!"

"What? What happened?" Mommy asked as she concentrated on Daddy and wrinkled her forehead.

"Hi Connie," Daddy said following behind Cassie. "Yes, there were a few new developments. I'd like to process them a little bit and then we can sit and talk."

"Is everyone okay? The windows cracked open? You look like you're shaking."

"Well, yes, they did. And Mike is fine, and you can see that we are fine. I just need a few minutes to get my balance back."

"Sure, Jack. When you're ready, but don't leave out anything. Should we be selling this house?"

"No! We can't!" Cassie exclaimed. "This is where Patrik is and where I am supposed to be!"

"It's okay Cassie. We aren't going to sell the house," Daddy said as Mommy stared back at him. "But we need to let a few things calm down, okay?"

"Okay. I'm going to go find Patrik. He'll be really excited!"

Cassie's follow-up appointments on Monday went well. Both doctors were pleased with her recovery and the resolution of the swelling, bruising and her vision. They agreed she could go back to school.

"She can resume normal activities but let's wait another few weeks on bike riding or anything strenuous. You may want to ask her teacher to monitor her recess too."

"She has a dance class, tap and ballet. Is that okay?" Mommy asked.

"No gymnastics. No jumping. Otherwise, dancing would be okay."

"I'll call Katie," Moher said. "That's her teacher."

"Cassie, you need to go slower than you normally would," Dr Blake advised. "If you feel tired or have a headache you should sit down and have a quiet time."

"Okay."

"Connie, we'll printout the visit summary and all the instructions. I won't need to see her again unless there are problems. Dr. Howard will continue to follow-up with you."

"Thank you, Dr. Blake. Jack and I really appreciate all you have done," Connie said as she stood up. "I just want to ask one question though. Did you have any relatives who lived here a few hundred years ago? Our house, where we live, used to be a farm owned by a Dr. Edmund Blake."

"Oh, I haven't heard that name in a long time! That's your house?"

"Well, yes. There are strange things there sometimes."

"Edmund, great, great, great grandfather, was a renowned physician. You should read his medical papers and science papers. They might be insightful to your circumstances."

"Do you know something more?"

"I've never been out there. I couldn't say."

"Thank you. Cassie, let's get going. Thank you again doctor."

"You're very welcome," Dr. Blake said and then hesitated by the door. "Connie, I can tell you that my family sold his farm years many years after his untimely death. They wanted to farm the property, but it never worked out. I would be careful if you are going to dig anything up."

"You mean like talk about it?" Connie asked.

"No. I mean literally. If you are digging something up."

The following days went smoothly as Cassie resumed her school activities and Katie guided her in catching up with any schoolwork she had missed.

"Nanny Phe sat with me so I could do my papers when I came home," Cassie told Katie. "She's just like a teacher!"

"Yes Cassie, she is a really good teacher, and I am glad she could be with you. You are doing really well."

Patrik resumed coming to school several times a week in Cassie's backpack, and except for recess, remained fairly quiet in the classroom. Cassie felt well and was able to resume more activities.

"Patrik, come play with us," Cassie and Poppy called to him as they went outside to play on the playground.

"Let's play tag!" Poppy said, "Patrik, you're it!"

"How's everything going for the party tonight?" Daddy asked Mommy the next weekend.

"Good. People are bringing potluck, and the weather is wonderful, I love April!"

"Yes. Everything is starting to green up. I imagine my mom will be out in a few weeks with Cassie and Poppy to plant the fairy garden again."

"That'll be nice. It was a very pretty garden last year. When are you and Mike planning to finish the new windows in the shed? Cassie and Poppy really want to take all their toys out there again and play school."

"We really do, Daddy, it's not the same playing in my bedroom," Cassie added.

"I think Mike said he was available tomorrow. I'll check with him. Soon, though."

"You haven't been out there since the incident, right?" Mommy asked.

"Yes. I'm sorry I haven't set aside time to talk more about that."

"What about now? We have an hour or so before people arrive. You can help me in the kitchen."

"I always talk better if I'm chopping something," Daddy smiled.

"Of course, you do!" laughed Mommy. "Here. Vegetable platter with a dip."

"Can I help too?" Cassie asked.

"Here, Cassie," Mommy said handing her a large bowl. "It's for a pasta salad. You can stir in the black beans and canned corn."

Daddy proceeded with telling Connie about their experience in the potting shed as he peeled and chopped vegetables. "It was so real at the time, Connie, but now, I am doubting it all."

"Well, with Mike as another witness I think you have very credible company."

"Yes. Maybe I still wish it was just a fantasy. Okay, here's what happened," Daddy continued as he relayed all the events of that afternoon including their time at the magic tree.

"I would like to say I am shocked, but truthfully I am not," Mommy replied. "I didn't tell you the other information Dr. Blake told me at Cassie's appointment."

"What information?"

"It turns out he is related to Dr. Edmund Blake, great grandfather several times removed. He said he's never been out here, and his family sold the property decades after Dr. Blakes death.

They tried to farm it, but they were not successful. When I was leaving, he paused. He said to be careful if we are digging anything up. In fact, he said, don't dig anything up. He meant it literally."

"I'm not planning on digging anything up."

"Just saying what he said. He also said we should look up all of the Edmund Blake papers and research. I think he knows something he's not telling us. He was very serious."

The day of the party everyone arrived in the late afternoon. The dining room table was filled with casserole dishes, platters, and bowls of salads. Ed stood by his "drink station" to once again help with any beverages people asked for. Chloe had officially left her employment in Boston and moved to Maine to begin her new practice. She temporarily rented an apartment in Pine Cove above a store front, and an office space near Millie's vet business in the downtown area.

"I'm very excited to be here!" she told Peter and Katie. "Everyone has been so welcoming. They seem very happy to have more resources for children in the area."

"I second that," Katie said. "Maybe when you have your practice up and running you could reach out to the school system. I am sure they would like to work with you on many types of assistance our children need."

"That's a great idea, thank you. And I look forward to spending more time with you and Peter!"

The fire pit was lit, and everyone was out on the deck to enjoy the fresh air and beautiful sunset.

"I love this time of year," Phe said. "Cassie and Poppy, it's almost time to think about plants for the fairy garden! Are you excited?"

"Poppy has been talking about the fairy garden for several weeks," Twirla said. "I know they enjoyed their time with you very much."

"Oh, Jack and Connie," Phe continued, "we've all been so busy this past month. I forgot to tell you I met with Anna and have a copy of her thesis. It's very interesting."

"You do?" Mommy said excitedly. "That's wonderful!" "How interesting?" asked Daddy.

"Nothing that I think you don't already know," Phe said. "Except for Dr. Blake's other publication. His first publication, "The Vibrational Forces of Nature" was the one Anna had first referenced. The one they said was very controversial. Anna told me the other paper was more difficult to find and created more discord within the science community. It was compared to witchcraft. It is called "The Transformation of Energy Light." He proposed that energy from basanite crystals can be transformed to create matter. He was way before his time."

"My head doctor is Doctor Blake," Cassie announced. "His family used to live here."

"Really? That's incredible," Ed chimed in. "imagine that!"

"That's her neurologist," Mommy clarified. "His name is Edward Blake."

"He said he's never been out here Dad. He said there are some stories passed down through his family though."

"What stories?" I'm getting interested in this," Dan said. "You always said there were strange things going on in the shed."

"He cautioned us not to dig anything up, and we're not," Daddy said.

"That's odd," Mike chimed in. "This was a farm. And we dug up earth to make the fairy garden."

"Maybe you have to find the right spot," Dan offered. "It's not about the whole property."

"Do you know what the current theories are about Light Energy?" Peter said. "There is scientific evidence that particles, elements really, from within the outer universe, are present in our human bodies. There was conversion, a transformation at some point in time."

"I'm ready to believe anything," Mike voiced. "Including Patrik."

"From our Earth below," Cassie spoke up. "The gnomes brought up the basanite for him."

"What?" Daddy exclaimed. "Cassie, why did you say that?"

"I learned it in Lemuria. That's what the elders taught us."

"And did they tell you what to do with it?" Mommy teased. "Are they all-knowing?"

"They said Dr. Blake told us how to do it. The Light Language papers in his satchel. Those are the instructions."

CHAPTER 11

Dreams

Cassie twirled in circles in the yard absorbing the suns vibrant energy. "Go easy Cassie. Slow down," Daddy reminded her, as he stood on the deck drinking coffee and surveying the yard.

"Can we finish the potting shed today?" Cassie panted trying to catch her breath. "Poppy and I really want to play out there."

"Yes. I just have to check with Mike to see when he will be ready."

"Nanny Phe said we could start to do the fairy garden too. She said next weekend because after that it's school vacation."

"I forgot about April vacation. That's always a good time."

"When can I ride my bike again? Has it been a month?"

"Yes, it has been a month, just barely, since you had your follow-up appointments," Daddy said.

"I'm ready. I will wear my helmet."

"Thank you. That is an absolute necessity. I think your Mom would like to wait a little longer though. Maybe over school vacation."

"Poppy is waiting for me, Daddy."

"Well, you can't ride today."

"No, Daddy," Cassie replied. "Poppy isn't riding her bike anymore until I can ride mine."

Daddy smiled, "That's a very generous friend. Poppy is a great friend. I will talk to your Mom about riding over April vacation, okay?"

"Yes."

"And I will also ask Papa Ed how your bike repairs are going. He took your bike into the repair shop for me."

"Did I hurt it?"

"No, the mailbox post did."

"Okay team, I'm ready!" Mike said getting out of his truck with the two new windows leaning up against the tailgate.

"Let's do this!" Daddy said. "I'll grab the ladder. Are you ready, Cassie?"

"I have to call Patrik. I know he wants to come."

"We aren't going down to the tree," Daddy said.

"Okay, I can call him from my closet," Cassie said heading for the back door. "He can come through the portal door."

"The portal door?" Mike asked.

"That's what she calls the door to the eaves that's in her bedroom closet. In the very least, she has a vivid imagination."

"In the very least, she understands things beyond my comprehension," Mike added. "You have to admit Jack, there is more than meets the eye here."

"Let's get the windows and start over to the shed. She'll catch up," Jack said ignoring Mike's comment and walking down the steps.

Cassie could hear Patrik barking in the distance. "*Patrik?*" Cassie called out as she entered her closet. "*Are you in here?*"

Cassie knelt down and put her head through the opened door to the eaves. *Are you coming? Daddy and Mr. Mike are going to put the new windows in the potting shed today.*

I have to come through the tree Cassie, after the windows are in.

Daddy said I can't go down to the tree today.

You don't have to Cassie. If you open the little door in the potting shed, I will come up. Remember, the tree is open now for passage at all times.

Cassie patted the gnomes as she entered the potting shed. "Thank you for sending energy to Lemuria," she said.

Mike was up on a ladder inside the shed handing Daddy pieces of the cracked window and frame he had pried off the walls.

"Cassie, honey," Daddy said, "you can stand over on the other side of the room or sit at the table okay?'

"Is Patrik here?" Mike asked. "Maybe he could help carry these pieces outside."

"Patrik is in the tree," Cassie said. "He said he'll come up after the new windows are in."

"That's a great excuse to avoid work!" Mike said winking at Cassie. "I'll have to remember that!"

Cassie watched as her father and Mike carefully placed a new window into the wall, making sure it was level and fit snuggly. Pulley ropes hung from the middle of the frame to open and close the panes. Before they nailed in the window, Daddy tested the ropes to make sure they opened the window exactly as they had planned.

"It works!" Cassie shouted.

"Come on over, Cassie. Let's see if you will be able to pull on the ropes when you and Poppy are out here."

Cassie nodded to her father and walked over to the wall, reached up and grabbed the ropes. She pulled one way and it shut. She pulled the other way and it opened. "Patrik will like this!" she said enthusiastically.

"Nice job Cassie! Let's get the other window done!" Daddy exclaimed moving the table so Mike could get the ladder across the room. "One more to go."

Cassie moved over to the back wall and lifted the rod from the handle while Jack and Mike installed the second window. *Patrik, when do you want me to open the door?*

When the window is finished.

"What are you doing, Cassie?" Daddy asked.

"I need to open the door for Patrik when you're finished."

"We're not going down to the tree," Daddy said again.

Cassie nodded. "That's okay. We don't need to."

"Here Mike," Daddy said handing him some nails. "Let's button this one up."

Mike finished nailing in the second window and climbed down the ladder. "Looking good buddy!"

"Open Sesame! Open the window!" yelled Cassie.

Mike laughed as he pulled on the rope while Cassie swung the little door in the back of the shed open to the right.

"Patrik's coming up," she reported. "There's a cloud too."

"A cloud of what?" Daddy asked as a white fog filtered onto the floor through the little door.

Mike came down from the ladder and stood in place with daddy staring at the apparition. It covered the floor and began to slowly swirl, lifting upwards in visible vibrating rings.

"It's breathing now," Cassie said. "It's breathing again."

"Cassie, what?" Daddy said reaching out to take her hand.

"Patrik says we are not in any danger."

"I can't believe I'm watching this," Mike said. "In real life, not dreaming."

The rings transformed into fog again and divided in half; each half drifting towards an open window. All at once it twisted into a cord speeding through the window.

WHOOSH!

"What was that? Cassie, what was that?" Daddy asked in a shaky voice as he could hear Patrik wildly barking close by.

"Patrik says to tell you that was Dr. Edmund Blake."

Mike walked outside and laid down on the grass. He closed his eyes and tried to slow his racing heartbeat. His mind was filled with ghostly images. His body was shivering.

"Mike?" Daddy asked coming out of the shed and sitting on the granite doorstep. "Are you breathing?"

"I am taking a moment to literally ground myself," Mike replied without lifting his head. "Was that real? Did that really happen?"

"I now believe all of this is real," Daddy said. "Connie's father was right; we bought a haunted house."

Mike laughed and sat up. "Well at least he or they seem friendly."

"Now that they've been unleashed," Daddy added.

"I heard Patrik barking, too," Mike confessed. "Thank you, Patrik."

"Cassie are we done now? Ask Patrik. Are there any other crazier things?" Daddy asked.

"Patrik says, just don't dig anything up."

"I don't think Cassie and Poppy should be allowed to play out there anymore," Mommy said to them all after Daddy had recounted the events in the potting shed. "That was scary. Are you making this up? Is this a joke?"

"No, not a joke," Daddy said shaking his head. "I think it's all safe now."

"I know you are trying to downplay this," Mommy interrupted him, "and probably leaving some scarier things out, but I saw you and Mike when you walked over here. You were as white as a sheet!"

"That would be as white as a ghost," Daddy laughed. "As white as the ghost of Dr. Edmund Blake."

"Should we be worried?" Mommy asked.

"No, I don't think so. Cassie says that Patrik says there is no danger. I heard Patrik barking again and so did Mike."

Mommy nodded. "Well, Mike's a reliable source."

"You think I'm not a reliable source?"

Mommy laughed, looked at Jack, and laughed again. "You have had your moments."

"I told Mike your father was right. We bought a haunted house."

"Don't say that. He's not right, he's mean."

Daddy took Mommy's hand, "Yes, he is mean, sorry. I think after the apparition floated away it's not haunted anymore. I think Dr. Blake was waiting for Patrik to create these circumstances and engineer his release. I do think it's okay for the girls to play out there."

"I'm not up on ghostly behavior so I can't comment," said Mommy. "I may regret asking this. What does Patrik via Cassie say?"

"Ah, don't dig anything up."

Jack took Ned out in the evening to walk along the driveway, his usual walk.

"Hey neighbor" Millie called out as she was rounding up Luna and Kai for the night. "This has been quite the interesting spring!"

"I know you mean that in the best possible way."

"I actually wish I had been with you and Mike in the potting shed. I would love to have seen the apparition. I would love to have seen your faces! Hearing about it just isn't the same."

"Words cannot accurately describe," Jack said.

"How is Ned doing? Any more changes?"

"Not really. Not since we spoke after Cassie's accident. Thank you again for taking care of him."

"You're welcome again. He's not exhibiting any signs of pain or discomfort?"

"I don't think so. He really just sleeps most of the time. I have to help him stand up and navigate the deck stairs but that's not new. He's just getting older."

"Is he taking the joint medicine I gave you? Do you think that it is helping?"

"He does take it. I don't know if it helps. I am sure it doesn't hurt him. I doubt we'll ever be going further than the driveway again."

"Yes, that's probably true. You know Jack, you know that Ned is very aged and in the last stages of his life."

"Yes, I do know that."

"Well, let me know if there is anything he needs, or you need. Okay?"

"Of course. Thank you, Millie."

"Jack, your dad called earlier," Connie said one night when they talked before bed. "He wants to talk with you this coming weekend about installing an air conditioning system before it gets too hot."

"Thanks. We probably should do that within the next month. It can get hot sometimes by the end of May."

"Is there much to it?" asked Connie. "I am really asking if there's going to be much disruption inside the house."

"My Dad's the expert, so I'm not sure. I believe our existing heating ducts can be used for circulating the air. I know the fan cooling unit is placed outside, and then we have to connect it inside through the cellar. We have to figure out a place."

"How does it connect into the house?" asked Connie.

"Again, my Dad's the expert. I know the wiring will need to connect to the electrical panel in the cellar. I'll call him and we can set up a day for him to come over and explain it all. Do you want to be part of the discussion?"

"No, I just want the air conditioning," Connie smiled. "And no mess."

"It's just a dream," Jack whispered to himself as he tossed and turned in bed trying to wake up. In his mind, he continued to move forward, walking into a mist of endless clouds. Flames began to surround him and pull at him, as the wind howled. He tried to resist and lifted his arms to protect himself. His arms burned. "This is not real," he said shaking his head in the midst of a vast unknown.

"Patrik" he whispered to a vision. "Are you Patrik?'

"This way, come this way."

Jack saw himself standing next to Patrik in a beautiful tropical place illuminated by sparkling sun and waters. "Lemuria?" Is this Lemuria?"

"We are all here, all here" said the voices of the images before him. "Welcome to your place of belonging."

"Why am I here?"

"This is your learning. Remember the flames and let them guide you."

"I want to leave," Jack demanded in his dream. "Let me leave!"

"I am the light of the flame," a voice said coming towards him. "Let me light the path."

"No, NO!" Jack cried out as he began to realize that Connie was talking and gently shaking his shoulder.

"Jack, you're okay. Jack, wake up."

"I'm okay," Jack said as sweat dripped down his forehead. "I'm okay."

"Yes. You are okay. What happened? It sounded like you had a nightmare," Connie said.

"I don't know. It was so real, so surreal," Jack said running his fingers through his hair. "Go back to sleep honey. I'm okay."

"Do you smell something?" Connie asked.

"What? No, I don't smell anything. Let's try and get some sleep, okay?"

"It smelled like perfume, like flowers."

Jack's dream haunted him for several days as he tried to work through the rest of the week. At times his mind drifted, and he visually remembered parts of it. He remembered seeing something he thought was Patrik. His arms hurt but he couldn't remember why.

"Hey Cassie," Daddy asked as they sat on the deck after dinner one night. "Tell me what Patrik looks like, will you?"

"Did you see him Daddy when you heard him barking?"

"No, not then. I was just curious."

"He has long fur and a curly tail. He is as tall as my knees. His neck fur can bunch up and form a handle for me to hold onto when we travel."

"What color is he?"

"Mostly brown colors,"

Daddy nodded and looked out into the yard. "What does Lemuria look like Cassie? When you and Patrik went there."

"Do you believe in Lemuria now Daddy?"

"I'm interested in knowing more."

Cassie smiled, "It is filled with flowers and sunlight. There is an ocean where the dolphins swim, too. Do you want to go there?"

"I don't think so. Unless, I guess, if you were going again I would."

"Patrik says to tell you it looks the same as in your dream, accept you weren't dreaming. He says he brought you."

"How do you know, about my dream? I didn't tell you."

"Patrik told me when he brought you back."

"I don't really remember the dream, but I know it was only a dream. I don't think I saw him."

"He was the cloud too. He has many forms."

The weekend was planned to be busy as April vacation was starting and spring was well underway. Cassie and Poppy had dance class Saturday morning and Nanny Phe was coming over in the afternoon to start clearing and planting some spring bulbs in the fairy garden with them. Papa Ed planned to come over in the afternoon to discuss the installation of the air conditioning system, as well as to bring Cassie's repaired bike back.

"Dad's bringing Cassie's bike back today," Jack told Connie privately after she had returned with Cassie from dance class. "She should be able to ride now."

"Oh, Jack, I don't like this," Connie said. "Is she mature enough to remember to have a helmet on at all times?"

"Yes, that is the question," Jack said. "She has told me several times though, that she will always have it on. I think we need to remember that this was a huge learning experience for her."

"For all of us, as well," Connie said.

"I know it has brought us closer again," Jack said, "as a couple, as a family."

"I feel like I, like I grew in ways I didn't want to. I think the risk of losing those you love brings you clarity. You understand again what's really important."

"You are important," Jack added, "and family is about all of us being together. Those directly related and those we just love."

"Hi Dad, Mom," Jack greeted them. "Thanks for coming out. Poppy and Cassie are already over at the shed Mom. They are so happy to start the garden again. I put some tools and baskets for the weeds out there for you."

"Thank you, Jack. I am so looking forward to this! I brought my own basket too. We'll have to decide if we need more plants. Time for that, it's still a little early," Phe said as she waved bye and headed to towards the potting shed.

"I never see her happier than when she is over here with those girls," Ed said.

Jack nodded, "I really appreciate her time with them, and all she does. All you both do."

"Here's Cassie's bike," Ed said grabbing the bike out of the trunk of his SUV. Just a new tire and a realignment of the handlebars and frame. Good as new."

"Great Dad, thanks. Let me know what I owe you."

"Let's just add it to your tab for now. We can square away when we finish the air conditioning and heating."

"Heating?" Jack asked.

"Depending on what we choose for the air conditioning unit, it may be more cost effective to upgrade the heating at the same time. We'll need to look at both."

"Okay, let's get started," Jack offered. "You're the boss."

Ed laughed, "Thanks Jack. I've waited decades to hear you say that!"

"Hello Poppy and Cassie!" Nanny Phe greeted them inside the potting shed. "Have you started setting up your school again?"

"We have new windows!" Cassie announced. "They open!"

"That's wonderful!" Nanny Phe said. "This will be much better in the summer when the days are hot."

"They released the past," Cassie explained. "The spirits that were locked inside the magic tree."

"I heard a little bit about that, yes," Nanny Phe said. "I assume that was a very good thing."

Cassie nodded, "Yes, because Dr. Blake had been inside the magic tree for hundreds of years. Patrik was very happy they were together again, even for a short time."

"Where did he go? Is Patrik still here?"

"Yes. Patrik is here. Dr. Blake went up, but Patrik can communicate with him now whenever he wants."

"I got to hear Patrik barking!" Poppy exclaimed. "That was my wish and he talked to me!"

"So many good things happening girls. Let's come outside and look at the garden. You can tell me what you think needs to be done. I brought some bulbs we can plant now."

"Will they be flowers soon?" Poppy asked.

"Pretty soon Poppy. These grow fast in spring. Some tulips and daffodils, early summer plants."

"Do we have to dig up a new spot?" Cassie asked.

"Well, I was thinking they might look nice over here by the edge of the shed. What do you think?"

"I'll have to ask Patrik," Cassie said.

"Hello, spring gardeners," Twirla greeted them as she walked into the fairy garden.

"Twirla, how nice to see you. Yes, we are planting some early bulbs. We are trying to determine a good place for them."

"Don't dig anything up," Poppy said to her Mommy.

"Patrik says that if we are within the potting shed fence it is okay to dig."

"This is where someone planted herbs and vegetables a long time ago," Phe added. "I'm sure it's safe."

"Do we need something to ward off unwelcomed spirits?" Twirla asked. "I could donate the doll I brought back from New Orleans. That was its purpose."

"I think that's a great idea!" Phe said. "What do you girls think?"

"Good," Poppy said.

"Patrik says YES!" Cassie shouted.

"I'll be right back," Twirla said. "I think you can start digging."

Ed and Jack looked at the air conditioning plan Ed had created with options to replace the heating unit. "This is a big house, Jack. You want to make sure you adequately cover all the square footage. It will save fuel."

"That sounds logical."

"The system will have several thermostats in various rooms so that they can be set individually. It's cheaper in the long run to replace your heating with one of the newer units. More efficient."

"Where would you put the outside cooling unit?"

"I think over here on the other side of the deck. We can drill through the foundation to connect to the electrical panel."

"We don't have to dig anywhere, do we?"

"No, I don't think so. We need to lay a concrete pad under the unit though, to lift it up off the ground and keep it level. Is digging a problem?"

"Did you hear about the apparition in the potting shed when Mike and I put the windows in?"

"Peter tried to tell me while he was laughing hysterically," Ed chuckled. "It's pretty funny."

"Not if you were there," noted Jack. "It was another warning, from Patrik. Don't dig anything up."

"Okay," Ed said. "We'll try not to dig."

Twirla and Poppy came over the next day so the girls could ride bikes together. Poppy had colored tassels on her handlebars and brought a set for Cassie's bike too.

"Thank you," Cassie said as she waved them in the air. "They sparkle!"

"Your bike got fixed!" exclaimed Poppy as she wheeled her bike closer.

"My Papa Ed had it fixed for me. Do you want to ride now?"

"Helmets girls," Daddy announced.

Poppy and Cassie obediently placed their helmets on as Mommy came out of the house to watch the first ride. "Girls, I want a picture please. This is a special day for all of us!"

"Agreed!" Twirla replied. "We are very grateful for this wonderful day of new beginnings."

"I'll send it to you, Twirla," Mommy said as the girls started riding up the driveway. "That was so special of Poppy to wait for Cassie to ride her bike again."

"She was very upset after the accident as you know," Twirla said. "Once she knew Cassie was going to be okay and they played together again, she was much better."

"They look like they're doing fine. Good job, girls!" Daddy called out to them. "I think our work is done here. This week we should start teaching them about road safety for when they want to go out of the driveway."

"Oh Jack," Mommy said sharply. "Please let me just adjust to this step before we go further!"

Daddy laughed. "A couple of days then. April vacation would be a good time to start."

Connie walked back to the house as Jack and Twirla started to make plans for road safety lessons. "This is just too much for me," she had said excusing herself.

"Hey Connie," Millie waved to her from the fence. "How's things going?"

"I think I'm having flashbacks of Cassie's accident as I watch them ride up the driveway."

"That was an awful day. Very scary. Glad Cassie is okay."

"Yes, me too. In fact, everything turned out fine and healed well."

"It's like a miracle, don't you think?"

"Yes, I do. I think Cassie is very blessed. Twirla says all the angels were surrounding her."

"Twirla would certainly know that!" confirmed Millie. "She's got an 'in' with the angels."

"She tells me she just asks for what she wants, and it happens. Simple, huh?"

"Speaking of what you want, have you given more thought to following up with stables to provide riding lessons for special needs children?"

"Not yet. It's been such a crazy spring."

"Yes it has been, but I think that's behind you now. Time for you to take care of your needs and what's important to you."

"This next week is school vacation. It'll be really busy with both girls home and Mandy starting driver's education."

"Wow! That happened fast!" Millie replied. "The years go by fast."

"She took the classroom course in school and now she has to do the education with a driving instructor. We don't want her to have her license till later in summer, so she'll have plenty of practice time with us."

"I bet you could find some time in the week to pull out the lists you created last fall. You could start to call those stables. Just to plant some seeds, you know?"

Connie nodded. "Why am I procrastinating? I know what's important to me. I've known for a long time."

"We all procrastinate at times, trust me."

"You, Millie? You're pretty busy all the time."

"Yes," Millie agreed. "Both Mike and I have very busy businesses plus the animals. I think that's what is making me feel so tired."

"Change of seasons too," Connie added. "With increases in sunlight each day I seem to get less sleep."

"That's true, yes," Millie said. "I know! Let's go riding this week! There's plenty of time in the evening and the horses would love it! You would love it!"

"Yes. I would love that. Let me check with Jack and I'll get back to you," Connie said. "Have a great rest of the day, Millie. Thank you."

The full moon shone through Jack and Connie's bedroom window, giving a sense of early morning daylight. Jack turned on his side and glanced at the clock on his bedside table one more time.

"Two a.m.," he whispered as he got up and closed the window shade.

"Are you okay?" mumbled Connie.

"Yes, fine. Go back to sleep," Jack said. "I can't sleep. I'll be right back. I'm going downstairs to get a drink."

Jack put on his bathrobe and walked into the hallway. The moonlight shone through Cassie's open door and lit the stairs. Jack reached out, held onto the railing and proceeded downstairs.

The front outdoor lights were on and illuminated the yard where he could see several deer grazing on the fresh green grass. He laughed and turned towards the kitchen. "Deer. At least they are not eating the bushes."

Jack continued to walk down the back hallway guided by the moonlight. He thought he saw something move and turned towards his office door. "Cassie? What are you doing up?"

"Ned," Cassie said. "Patrik told me to come be with Ned and give him comforts."

Jack's throat tightened as he moved slowly forward. "Is Ned okay?"

"He needs my pats, Daddy. He needs your pats too."

Daddy took a deep breath and then sighed. "Let me sit with you."

Cassie sat beside Ned with his head in her lap. "Patrik helped me move him," she said as she caressed Ned's ears.

"Has Ned said anything? Do you think he is comfortable; do you think he is in any pain?"

"No, he is resting before his travels."

"What travels,   honey?"

"Patrik is going to stay with him on his travels."

Daddy sighed and closed his eyes until he could open them and process the situation. Ned lay peacefully with Cassie. His breathing was shallow and irregular. He bent down to sit with them and began to pat Ned's back. "You have been a great dog, Neddy. I have loved you very much; we all have."

"Patrik has loved him too. Ned is his best dog friend."

Daddy laughed as tears came down his cheeks. "Yes, that would be true, I guess."

Ned let out a long breath, and then his breathing became very more intermittent.

"He is saying goodbye," Cassie said as she began to cry. "I am saying goodbye to him too."

"Oh Cassie, you are such a beautiful loving child," Daddy said holding her other hand. "You bring love to everybody."

"Have you said goodbye Daddy? Patrik says it's time to go."

"Oh God, yes. I am saying goodbye."

Jack reached over as he cried and patted Ned's head. He ran his hand down his back for one last time. "Be well Ned. Go with Patrik."

Ned sighed again, once.

"I think he has passed Cassie," Daddy said reaching out to hold his daughter in his arms. "He was a good dog."

"He loved you too, Daddy."

CHAPTER 12

Planting Seeds

"Jack, so sorry to hear about Ned," Mike said, as he and Millie came over later that morning to help Jack bury him.

"Thank you. I need your help."

"Of course," Mike said grasping his friend's shoulder. "We are here for you."

"I'm here too, Jack," Millie said coming up from behind and giving him a hug. "Are you doing okay? He just passed away in his sleep?"

"Yes. I got up in the middle of the night because I couldn't sleep, and Cassie was with him. She said Patrik had told her to come down and give him some comforts."

"That's very beautiful," Millie said. "How beautiful that is."

"I'm here, Daddy," Cassie said coming out of the house and giving him a hug.

"I thought you would want to be here Cassie. We need to pick a spot for Ned to rest in. Do you have any ideas?"

"The magic tree," she said. "We need to bring him there."

"What about up here by the fairy garden," Daddy offered, knowing it was nearby and less complicated than getting to the tree.

"Don't dig anything up," Cassie replied, "not up here."

"We can all work together and make that happen," Mike said. "Millie has a sling stretcher we can use."

"Patrik says he will help us down the stairs. Patrik says he will tell us where we need to bring Ned."

As much as Ned had not been very active and slept most of the time, his presence was missed in the house. There was a new quietness.

"Are you sad, Cassie?" Poppy asked.

"I just miss him. I liked to pat his ears. And he liked Patrik. They played together a lot."

"Is Patrik sad?" Poppy asked.

"Ned is with Patrik. Patrik is helping him travel. They are both happy," said Cassie.

Cassie and Poppy played all the rest of vacation week together. They brought all their stuffed toys and dolls back out to the potting shed, along with teaching supplies: paper, books, pencils, and chalk. They rode bicycles in the driveway and under the instruction of Twirla and Jack, they began to ride in the street.

"Remember to look both ways!" Daddy called out.

"You are all doing so well!" Twirla praised both of them. "Safety first!"

Nanny Phe came over at the end of the week with some early spring plants for the fairy garden. "You all did a wonderful job cleaning up the garden last weekend and planting bulbs," she said. "These plants will bring some early summer blooms and color to our garden!"

"The fairies like that," Cassie noted. "When do the fairies come out again Nanny Phe?"

"Oh, I think they are coming out now. As long as it's not too chilly they will be out."

"Will the other plants come back too?" Poppy asked pointing to some green shoots in the dirt.

"Yes, isn't that the blessing of life? It renews again," Phe said.

"How was your horseback ride with Millie?" Jack asked Connie as she came up the stairs to the deck.

"It was lovely. It was truly lovely. Relaxing. Inspiring."

"I'm glad you took the time do that. You've been talking about doing something with horses for a while, since last fall really."

"Jack, I made some phone calls this week to follow-up with horse stables about giving riding lessons."

"This is good, Connie. And?"

"Next week when the girls are in school, I am going to do a site visit to one that especially has lessons for children. I want to talk to them about giving lessons for children with special needs."

"That's great, really. You'd be perfect!"

"I want to talk with Chloe, too. She's been so busy setting up her new practice that we haven't seen much of her. Katie suggested she reach out to the school and offer to work with troubled students. I think she could recommend some children that would benefit from horse therapy."

" You have some great ideas! What day are you going over?'

"Wednesday. I'm really looking forward to it."

"Me too," Jack said. "New beginnings are good."

"How long does your driver's ed instruction go on for?" Daddy asked Mandy at dinner one night.

"We only have three more weeks!" Mandy said excitedly. "Then I can get my license!"

"Are you going to drive me and Poppy to school?" Cassie asked.

Mommy shook her head. "No, Cassie. You will still take the bus with Poppy."

"Patrik will have to come with us, Mandy," Cassie explained. "He can help you drive!"

"Don't be ridiculous," Mandy snapped back. "I don't want to drive you anywhere."

"In the future when you have your license and are driving," Mommy said looking directly at Mandy, "you will be asked to do certain things for us, and we expect you to do them."

"Before you can get your license, you need to have driving time with your Mom and I first," Daddy said. "We will determine when you can take the test for your license."

"That's not fair!" Mandy shouted. "My instructor says that I am a very good driver and very careful."

"I'm happy to hear that, Amanda. We will still need to see that for ourselves."

"And even after you have your license," Mommy added, "you aren't going to drive whenever you want to. You have to ask for permission to use the car."

"Maybe I'll have my own car," Mandy said smugly. "Papa Ed and Nanny Phe would give me a car."

"No, Mandy, listen to me," Daddy said sternly. "That's not going to happen."

"You are making this much harder than it needs to be!" Mandy shouted. "It didn't take Mark this long to be able to drive."

"Mark was older than you when he got his license," Daddy said. "Do you want to wait until next year to get your license?"

"What? No!"

"Okay then, let's work the plan."

"Cassie, there's dance class today," Mommy said at breakfast. "And this afternoon, Auntie Chloe wants to show us where her new office is!"

"Is Mandy going to go too?" asked Daddy.

"I think Mark has a baseball game today. She asked if I would drop her off at the high school. That'll be okay. It fits with the time we will be meeting Chloe."

"What about picking her up?"

"That's the question I need to get an answer to. She can't call you because you and Ed are starting the air conditioning installation today. She can ask me, but I'm not going to wait around all afternoon till the game is over."

Daddy nodded, "And I don't want her riding with just anybody."

"Yes, agreed. So, we'll see what her plan is."

"Ned came to see me last night," Cassie spoke up across the table. "He wanted to tell me that he is happy."

Mommy lifted her head, "That's pretty unbelievable, don't you think Cassie? Maybe you were just thinking about him. Like a dream."

"No, it was real. He laid on my bed the way he used to when he was a puppy. I patted his ears."

"I'm glad he told you he's happy," Daddy replied.

"Wherever that is," added Mommy.

"Patrik told me that Ned is with Dr. Blake now. He's his new dog."

"That Dr. Blake, he really gets around, you know that?" Daddy smiled.

"Yes. Ned brought me a toy he plays with now too."

"What toy?"

"I can go get it if you want to see it."

"Yes, please do that," Daddy said, as Cassie started for the stairs.

"This should be good. Maybe Phe gave her something to remember Ned by."

"Maybe it's one of Ned's old toys from the basement," Mommy said. "We haven't brought them to the dump yet."

"Here it is," Cassie said reaching her hand out to show the toy, a doll-shaped figure wrapped in twine. "He said it's very special and that I can make a wish with it."

"Did Nanny Phe give you this?" Mommy asked. "It's like a primitive doll."

"No, Ned gave it to me."

"Cassie, Ned has died, remember?" Daddy said gently.

"Yes."

"So, he can't give you things or come sit on your bed."

"Yes, he can. He's like Patrik now."

Ed arrived in a box truck that morning with two other men that used to work for him when he owned his electrical company.

"Jack, you remember Tony and Bill," Ed said as the men shook hands.

"Of course, thank you for coming out."

"No problem," Tony said. "These are my favorite jobs, family jobs."

"I called Peter too, Dad, and he said he'd be over."

"Where's the bulkhead? Let's start unloading the boxes and getting the old furnace out," Ed said.

It took a while to disconnect and dismantle the old system in the basement and bring the pieces up to the driveway. Peter arrived as Mandy was getting into the car with Connie and Cassie to spend time with Chloe.

"Hi Peter! Bye Peter!" Mandy said as Connie and Cassie waved from the car.

"Just in time Peter," Ed greeted him. "Help me wheel this air conditioner unit over past the deck."

"So, Mandy, how are you going to get home?" Mommy asked as she drove into town.

"I don't know yet. I might be able to get a ride with Mark or one of the other kids."

"I'll text you when Cassie and I are headed home. You'll need to come with us if you don't have a plan for a ride that I agree with. I think I might, isn't a good plan by the way."

"Whatever. Yes, I will let you know."

Chloe's new office was on a side street on the bottom floor of an old building that overlooked a saltwater marsh. Mommy parked on the street as Chloe drove up.

"Hi, guys!" Chloe said. "I'm so glad you came. This is my new office! I'm so excited!"

"I really like the location," Mommy said. "Close to town but not on the main street."

"Yes. A little quieter on this side. Come on in, I'll show you around. How are you, Cassie? Did you have a nice vacation?"

"Yes. Poppy and I played school together in the potting shed, and we rode bikes again!"

"That's wonderful! I'm glad you're all better too."

"Nanny Phe came, and we started working on the fairy garden!"

"That was a very busy week for sure," Chloe said opening the front door. "Welcome everyone. This is the waiting room!"

"Oh, Chloe," Mommy spoke softly, "this has history."

The original wooden floors creaked as they walked in. There was a soft smell. "Oil soap," Mommy said.

"I always loved this smell," Chloe added. "It's clean but not chemical."

"It reminds me of saddle soap," Mommy replied. "I have to tell you about my site visit to a stable next week too."

"Come this way," Chloe said moving forward. "I have an office for myself and two consultation rooms."

"Are you going to have a staff person out front? Mommy asked. "Someone to answer phones and greet people?"

"Not right away. I have to build up some clients first."

"I could help you if you want," Mommy offered. "A few hours a week."

"Thank you, that's so sweet," Chloe said. "I may take you up on your offer."

"What's out here?" Cassie asked pointing to the back door.

"That's just a second exit Cassie. You know another way to get out in case of fire."

Cassie shuddered, "There was a fire here one time."

"Here? They didn't mention anything when I rented," Chloe said.

"A very long time ago it was a store," Cassie said, as she ran her hand along the wall to the back door. "They went out this way."

"Yes, I did know that it was a store at one time," Chloe said. "The people who owned the store lived upstairs. I'd love to rent that apartment just for the view! It is also much closer to town."

"How do you know it was a store, Cassie?" asked Mommy.

"They sold the herbal medicines that Dr. Blake made. The bad people tried to burn the store down before they came out and burned down his barn."

After they toured Chloe's office space, they walked down the street together to find a place for lunch.

"How about the 'Lunch and Ladle'? Mommy asked. "They have soup, sandwiches, and salads."

"Connie, tell me about your site visit next week," Chloe said after they were seated in the restaurant.

"It's a stable right here in Pine Cove. Millie recommended them, actually. I'm going to talk with them about giving riding lessons, specifically to special needs children."

"Connie! I am so excited for you! You have thought about this for a long time."

"Yes, I have. And I think the time is right for me to move ahead. It won't be full-time, not at this point."

"I think that will fit in well with everyone's schedule, Connie."

"And I was going to ask you Chloe, if you start working with the school maybe there are children that would benefit from a loving connection with a horse."

"Like you did!" Chloe chimed in.

"Yes, that's true. I think my horse is the reason why I am able to love anything."

Chloe reached her hand out across the table. "Well, you are the person I always loved."

Connie reached for her phone when they were done eating. "Sorry, I need to text Mandy and find out her plans for getting home from the baseball game."

"Mark's game, right?" Chloe said.

"Yes. She wants to get her driver's license now too."

Chloe laughed. "Oh, what fun times!"

"Mommy, I can help you with the horses," Cassie spoke up. "Millie said I am very intuitive, and I know things."

"Millie said that?"

"Yes. The day she took me riding. Before my accident."

"I don't know how this is going to work out yet, Cassie. But thank you for offering."

Mommy's phone beeped. "I have a ride," she read out loud.

"Not enough information," Mommy said as she texted back. "With who?"

"She's not answering me," Mommy said after a of couple minutes.

"Call her then," advised Chloe. "If she doesn't pick up, that's a different story."

Mommy called Mandy and waited while it rang and went into voicemail. "Amanda, I am waiting at the restaurant to find out who you are riding with. Call me back ASAP." Mommy swiped her phone. "Now I'm just getting mad," she said.

"Try the phone again," Chloe said.

"I think she just walked by the window," Cassie announced. "That's Mandy!"

Mommy turned in the booth and gazed at Mandy and a group of teens walking down the main street. "Excuse me," she said. "Stay with Auntie Chloe Cassie. I'll be right back."

Mommy hurried out the front door as Chloe laughed. "Oh, Mandy. Not a smart move. I hope you are taking notes Cassie. What not to do when you are a teenager!"

Mommy, Cassie and Mandy drove into the driveway a while later in silence. "We aren't done yet Mandy," Mommy said as they got out of the car.

"I don't know why you are making such a big deal out of this," Mandy shouted as she slammed the car door. "You embarrassed me."

"Go to your room, Mandy. We'll talk when we both have calmed down."

"Hi Ed," Mommy called out. "How's the installation coming along."

"Good," Ed replied. We have the heating unit all in incase you need it to take the chill off the morning. We have to come back to finish the air conditioner unit."

"Well, we don't need that yet," replied Mommy. "I'm so grateful you've made such progress."

"Can I help?" asked Cassie. "Can I watch?"

"Sure Cassie, come with me," Ed offered. "I'll keep an eye out for her Connie."

Cassie walked past the deck and the outdoor cooling unit that was sitting on the grass. "Is this where it's going to be?" she asked.

"Yes," Papa Ed said. "It's a good place to connect the electric cables through the foundation. See, over here, that's where I started to drill a hole."

"It's a big hole."

"It's a big cable honey."

"Do you have to dig?" Cassie asked.

"No, your dad already warned us."

Cassie nodded. "Good."

Cassie and Ed continued walking around the house to the bulkhead, and then walked down the stairs to the cellar.

"Hold onto the railing Cassie," Ed advised.

Additional lights had been added to the cellar that made it easier to see. "Hi, Daddy," Cassie said grabbing his hand.

"Hi, Cassie! Did you have fun with Auntie Chloe?"

"She has a nice office. It used to be a store and it smelled old."

Daddy laughed. "Like how old?"

"Dr. Blake used to sell his herbal medicines there."

"What?"

"And then there was a fire. They tried to burn the store down before they burned his barn down, our barn down," she said.

The cellar was quiet. Everyone had stopped working and they were looking at Cassie and listening to her story.

"Jack," Peter called out. "Can we dig out these foundation stones so Dad can finish drilling the hole for the cable?"

"Dig! NO!" Cassie yelled.

"Cassie, this isn't like digging in the ground. Let's go over there and take a look at it, okay?"

Daddy and Cassie walked over to the cellar wall. "Right around here," Peter said. "Right, Dad?'

"I measured from the outside corner. So, it should be four feet from here," Ed said walking to the end of the wall.

"Daddy," Cassie said reaching out and putting the palms of her hands on the stone. "Remember? "It's moving."

Daddy looked over at Ed. "Cassie," he said, "let's see if we might be able to move the stone rather than dig it out."

Daddy looked at the stone and realized that it was held in place by the weight of the other stones. "If I pull this out Dad, is the wall going to cave in?"

"It shouldn't, but then again, we know how to fix it if it does," Ed laughed. "The problem is the thickness of the wall. I can't drill through it unless you remove some rock."

"Here, use the crowbar," Peter offered. "I'll do it if you want. I don't think anything's going to jump out."

"Go for it, Peter," Daddy said. "Be my guest."

Peter started to pry the stone out using the blade of the crowbar. "Is this okay, Cassie? Are we doing okay?"

Cassie nodded. "It's not digging."

Peter wedged the crowbar in again and pulled, jarring the rock from its space.

"Be careful," Cassie said. "There's something behind it."

Mandy sat in her room talking with Mark on her phone. "Do you believe my mom?" she complained. "She's having a cow because I wasn't specific enough about how I was getting home."

"What did you tell her."

"I said I had a ride."

"Who did you have ride with? I thought you were going to wait for me, but then after the game we had to stay for a review with the coaches."

"I was with the gang. I figured someone would give me a ride."

Mark laughed. "Well, that may not have worked out for you. You live pretty far out of town."

"I think she was just mad because I didn't pick up my phone when she called me."

"Yeah. I can see that."

216

"They don't trust me to make my own decisions."

"Mandy, have you ever been stranded? You know, you think you have a ride but then you're in the parking lot and you're the only one left?"

"No! Gosh no!"

"One time playing football in 8th grade I told my dad I was getting a ride with someone and wouldn't be on the bus. He knew the people, so he was okay with it. But then, I got asked by another kid if I wanted a ride, and he was more popular, so I said yes to him. When we got to their car, the parents said they weren't going home. I ran back to the parking lot just in time to see the bus pulling out. Then I had to call my Dad to come pick me up. He had to drive and hour to get there."

"Oops, bet he was mad," Mandy replied.

"Mad? That is not the right word. Furious? I think he was just worried because he knew I was alone in the parking lot, and he couldn't get to me."

"What happened then?"

"The more I tried to explain what happened the madder he got," Mark laughed. "I don't think I have ever seen him that mad. I thought he might hit me."

"Did he?"

"No, he doesn't hit, ever, but I think he wanted to. I was grounded for a month including not being able to play sports. That was huge."

"That is huge."

"Just say you're sorry for not letting your mom know the plan. And make sure you have a plan that works next time."

"Okay. Hey, you played well today. It was a good game."

"Mandy, will you go to the Prom with me? I'm sorry I didn't ask sooner, but with Cassie being in the hospital it just didn't seem like the right time."

"Yes! I would love to!"

"I wasn't sure if you were going to ask me."

"There isn't anyone else I would ask," replied Mark.

Mandy blushed and her cheeks got warm. "Great. Just a couple of weeks! Talk later unless I'm not able to."

"Understood. In that case I'll see you in school."

Peter leveraged the crowbar again and pulled the rock out further from the foundation. Daddy grabbed hold of the edges, wiggled it out, and stepped back.

Everyone looked at the wall and waited. "Reach into the hole, Daddy," Cassie said.

Daddy looked at Cassie and inserted his hand into the hole. There was a large space and a package. He grabbed the package and brought it out.

"Cassie, is this what I'm supposed to be looking for?" Daddy asked as he held the leather package tied in a woven string towards her.

"Patrik says we can open it," Cassie said.

"Let me do it," Peter offered.

Daddy handed the package to Peter who held it in both hands and looked it over. "This is very old," he said as he proceeded to untie the string and unwrap the leather.

"It's like the satchel," Peter said. "This is the same leather and twine."

Inside was a doll-like figure. "Primitive," Peter said as he looked at the weave of the strands around the form and the absence of any facial features. "This is old," he said.

Daddy stood silent. "It matches the one Cassie has in her room," he said. "The one she said Ned brought her last night."

"Twirla brought one over when Nanny Phe was in the garden with us," Cassie said. "The doll she brought back from New Orleans. We planted it in the fairy garden to protect it from any evil."

"Does it look like this, Cassie?" Daddy asked.

"They match. Patrik says Dr. Blake made them all. They had special purposes. Now they are being reunited for a purpose too."

"Jack," Mommy said at supper on Wednesday, "I had the site visit today with the horse stable."

"How did it go? What do you think?"

"It was very special. I liked the people. They understood that my interest was with children. That was fine with them because children are their largest client base."

"How are you planning on following up?"

"They are going to call me. Probably with specific client needs. I think we can grow the program from there."

"You can speak to the horses, Mommy. And the horses can speak can to the children," Cassie said..

"Well, I don't know, Cassie," Mommy answered.

"I can show you, Mommy. Luna and Kai speak all the time." "Thank you for the offer, Cassie. Let me think about it."

"That's all very exciting Connie, and I am happy for you," Daddy said. "I think you'll find it very rewarding, and so will the children!"

Twirla came over late one afternoon to retrieve Poppy from the potting shed 'schoolhouse' as they called it, for supper, and to help her finish school papers for the next day.

"Come sit a minute on the deck," Connie asked her. "I'll get some iced tea."

"That sounds wonderful," Twirla replied. "These days seem busier now that spring has arrived."

"Hectic," Connie said. "That's how I feel. Trying to fit everything in."

"How are your plans going with the horse stable?"

"Very good! I'm excited! I really like the people, and the woman I spoke with. Her name is Esperanza, but they call her Zee."

Twirla looked over at Connie, "What a beautiful name. Esperanza means 'Mother of Spirit', horse spirit."

"I didn't know that, but it fits her. She says she speaks to them."

"I can only imagine all the things you will learn."

"I will be starting my first client next week. A child with muscular dystrophy. Can you imagine the emotional connection with the horse? They have beautiful horses there. They also have rescue horses. I think those are the ones that will connect the best with children. They know pain."

"That is wonderful. You are going to make a beautiful difference in their lives."

"Hey, girls," Twirla greeted Cassie and Poppy as they walked over from the potting shed. "Are you all done for the day?"

"Cassie, did you close up the doors?" Mommy asked.

"Yes, just the front door. We didn't open the back door."

"Oh, Patrik wasn't with you?"

"He was in my backpack from school. He went to take a nap."

"Cassie, what's in your hand? Twirla asked. "Some kind of artifact?"

"This is the doll Ned gave me when he laid on my bed. We found one in the cellar too. It matches this one."

Twirla extended her hand, "Can I see it?"

Cassie put the doll in Twirla's hand. "It's very old."

"Yes. Connie, this is the same doll that I found in New Orleans in the cellar of my business. It matches the one I buried in the fairy garden."

"Are you sure, Twirla?"

"Yes, I thought about it for a few months. When the girls were working with Phe in the fairy garden last weekend, I brought it over. It seemed right with Cassie's information about 'don't dig anything up'. It's meant to keep us all safe."

"Mom, we have to go shopping this weekend," Mandy announced at dinner. "I have to have a dress for the prom right away! Mark asked me to the prom. It's May 20th!"

"It's okay, Mandy, we have plenty of time."

"No, we don't! Everybody is buying dresses!"

"I am working at the stables on Saturday," Mommy said, "and they have an open house on Sunday I need to be there. What about the weekend after that?"

"MOM! That's not enough time! What about Auntie Chloe? I could ask her to take me."

"Well, yes, I guess that would be okay. I just thought I would be going with you."

"Mom, I can take photos and text them to you and you can see them."

"That's okay, I guess. I'm sorry I can't go with you."

"I'm going to call Auntie Chloe now. I'll let you know."

"I have been thinking," Cassie said at breakfast with the figure doll in her hand. "I have been thinking that we need to put this doll together with the other doll from the cellar. I want to plant them both in the fairy garden with Twirla's doll."

Daddy continued to eat his toast as he considered his reply. "I guess that's okay. Nothing adverse has happened in the fairy garden so far."

"Maybe we should wait a week or two," said Mommy. "To literally let the dust settle in the cellar."

"Let's ask Nanny Phe what she thinks!" proposed Daddy. "She's the magician with gardens."

Cassie nodded. "Let's ask Twirla too. She's the magician with the angels."

Saturday morning Nanny Phe took Cassie and Poppy to dance class so Connie could get over to the stables. "I'm sorry Phe. With Jack and Ed putting in the air conditioning system today and me working, I didn't have another option."

"That's fine, dear, I am happy to help. I love to watch them dance too. They are so cute together. You go ahead. I'll plan on staying at your house when we get back so the men can finish installation."

"Chloe is picking Mandy up around 10am. They're going to look for prom dresses together."

"That'll be nice. I assume she is going with Mark?"

Mommy laughed. "Is there anyone else?"

"They make a good young couple. He was very supportive to her when Cassie was in the hospital."

"Yes, he is a good friend. Very kind too."

Phe smiled, "Well, look at his parents. The apple doesn't fall far from the tree."

Phe was returning with Cassie and Poppy after dance class, close to lunchtime. "Girls, I was wondering if you would like to go to Petroni's and get pizza or sandwiches for lunch. What do you think?"

"YES!!" they both said.

Phe laughed. "Let's drive over and we can decide what to order. We'll bring some things back for your dad and Papa Ed too. It'll be a nice surprise for them!"

"What's all this?" Daddy asked as the girls and Nanny Phe came into the yard carrying a few pizza boxes and a bag filled with subs."

"Lunch!" yelled Cassie. "And some special drinks too."

"Thank you so much! Go ahead up to the deck, and we'll be right with you," Daddy said. "We're just about finished connecting the unit."

The girls went up to the deck with Nanny Phe and placed the lunch on the table. "Go head and bring your shoe bags up to Cassie's room and wash your hands," Phe said. "After lunch we'll decide what we want to do next."

"Can we go out to the potting shed?" Cassie asked.

"And play school?" said Poppy.

"Can we go to the magic tree? Can we visit Ned's grave and put some plants on it? Can we make it pretty there too?" Cassie requested. "Please?"

"Why, Cassie, what a lovely thought. I'm sure we can do that."

After lunch, Phe and the girls went out to the fairy garden and opened the potting shed doors.

"Cassie and Poppy, we can transplant a few flowers from here to take down to the magic tree.

I can tell you from last year what is here and how tall they'll grow. Do you want to pick out a few?"

Cassie and Poppy started to look through the garden. "This one," Cassie said pointing to a shoot coming up. The fairies liked this one."

"And I think this one had pretty yellow flowers," Poppy remembered. "The bees liked this one."

"Yes, they did!" Phe agreed. "These are wonderful choices. Let me get a basket and a little shovel to move them."

Cassie gasped, "Do you think that's digging? Don't dig anything up!"

Phe put her hand on Cassie's shoulder, "I think that's gardening Cassie. There is not one creature on Earth or heaven or any underground abode, that does not respect gardening as a sacred gesture. I believe it will be fine."

Cassie nodded. "Patrik should be here."

"Please ask him then, dear. We'll wait for you."

Cassie turned towards the potting shed and sent a mind wish to Patrik for his advice, then ran towards the house to catch up with Nanny Phe and Poppy.

"Whoa, Cassie," Daddy said as she ran by. "What's up?"

"I'm waiting for Patrik," she panted. "We are going to plant flowers on Ned's grave."

Daddy looked at his daughter tenderly, "That's such a lovely idea. Patrik will agree with you!"

Jack and Ed accompanied Cassie back over to the potting shed when she returned outside.

"Where's Patrik?" Daddy asked.

"Right here," Cassie said. "He's being quiet. Luna and Kai know he's here though."

Daddy looked over to the paddock where Luna and Kai trotted back and forth by the fence.

"Patrik will have to play with you on the way back," Cassie called out to them. "He can come over then."

Daddy nodded and looked at Papa Ed, "I just go with it, Dad."

Nanny Phe had placed three plants in her basket to take down to the tree. "I put one in for each of you and one for me," she smiled. "Are you coming with us too?" she asked.

"Yes. This is important," answered Daddy as he walked towards the shed. "I'll open the door in the back."

"I haven't been down to the magic tree since we buried Ned," Cassie said. "That was sad."

Poppy reached out and took her hand. "We can be sad together, Cassie."

Daddy went through the back door and stood up. He was surprised how much vegetation had grown up in just a couple weeks.

"It's so lush here!" exclaimed Phe. "I've never been down here before."

"Mom, really? I never knew that. Wait till you see the tree!"

Everyone proceeded down the stone steps and stopped at the base of the tree.

"Oh, my word," Nanny Phe announced, "We are in the presence of greatness."

"I think it's getting taller," Papa Ed said. "I was down here over last summer when we were looking for Cassie in the woods. Everything's bigger."

"This is where Patrik asked us to bury Ned," Cassie explained as she walked to the side of the tree. He said it was okay to dig here because it was between the roots. The roots are arms from all the lifetimes that reached out for him."

"That is a beautiful way to think about it, Cassie." Daddy added. "It was easy to dig here. Patrik had a good plan."

"Girls let's see where these plants fit," Nanny Phe said as she knelt down by Ned's grave.

"Which plants do you want to put where?"

Cassie and Poppy picked out spots to place their plants as Phe tenderly dug spaces for them to rest in. "This will work out just fine," she said. "Dear Ned, sleep well."

"We had great success!" Mandy announced carrying a long plastic bag over her shoulder as she and Chloe came into the kitchen. "Is Mom home yet?"

"She's upstairs getting changed, she'll be down in a minute. Chloe, do you want something to drink?" Daddy asked.

"Seltzer would be great," Chloe replied.

"Did you have a good day, Mandy?'

"I'm going to put my gown on to show her, she'll love it!" Mandy said racing to the stairs. "There's parties after the prom that I want to go to too!" Mandy said.

"Here we go," Daddy said. "Fasten your seat belts everyone. Hang on!"

How was your day, Jack?" asked Chloe.

"We got the air conditioning unit finished and then Cassie, Poppy and Phe planted some flowers on Ned's grave."

"Oh, that is so precious," Chloe replied.

"It was very moving. A nice final closure."

"Mom!" Mandy exclaimed as she ran up the stairs to her bedroom. "Come look at my gown! It's beautiful!"

"It really is pretty," Chloe agreed, "A very good choice."

Phe came back the next morning to help Cassie plant the other two doll figures in the fairy garden. She also brought two fairy statues to place on top of the soil. "These are special reminders for us Cassie. For Ned, for Dr. Blake, for all those who give us influence and understanding of our greater universe."

"I like them," Cassie said. "Patrik does too."

Connie walked Chloe to her car to say goodbye, as Millie was coming across the paddock. "How did it go at the stables?" she asked.

"I'll call you soon, Chloe, thank you for all your help."

"Love you," Chloe said with a hug. "It's a great dress. I had a great time!"

Connie walked over to the fence smiling. "It was a wonderful start. It's been a terrific week. I have at least four clients."

"Excellent! That is such a great addition to the community and benefit for the children."

"I feel that way too. I feel a real sense of purpose."

"Hello, Miss Cassie," Millie called out to her as she came across the yard. "And did you have a good weekend too?"

"Nanny Phe has been planting with us. We planted some flowers for Ned, and we made a place for the two doll figures in the fairy garden."

"The doll figures?" Millie asked.

"Remember when Twirla talked about the doll figure from New Orleans?" Mommy said. "There are two more."

"Oh," Mille said. "Are these all-good things?"

"Yes!" Cassie said. "They are protectors."

"You've all been very busy!"

"Patrik's home too," Cassie added. "He's been helpful with getting the potting shed open again for school. He plays with Luna and Kai too!"

Cassie climbed up on the fence and began patting Luna and Kai. They tossed their heads up and down and shook their manes which sent Cassie into peals of laughter.

"I can hear Luna and Kai," Cassie said. "I know what they're saying."

"Oh, Cassie, you have to stop this nonsense!" Connie said.

"Is Patrik here now?" Millie asked. "Is he playing with Luna and Kai?"

"No, Patrik's down by the tree now."

"They've been very frisky today," Millie said, "I don't know what's gotten into them. Spring I guess."

Cassie giggled and turned to face Millie. "They are telling me a secret," she whispered placing her finger to her lips. "Shh ..."

"Really? What's the secret?" Millie asked.

"They're very excited for your baby! It's a boy and girl!"

Millie is expecting twins!

I hope you enjoy reading my ***Behind the Open Door*** book series!

Sign up to receive a free short story of Patrik, Cassie's invisible dog friend

as he waits hundreds of years for her to come to Maine in ….

Between the Open Doors, The Story of Patrik.

You'll also be the first to hear about new books, characters, and exciting events in Pine Cove, Maine.

Use the link below to sign up. There's no charge or obligation.

https://sallygallotreeves.com/

About the Author

Sally Gallot-Reeves is a spiritual gardener planting seeds of love. Her life's work as a writer, healer, and life path coach is dedicated to promoting the Highest Good for all individuals, animals, and nature kingdoms.

Sally writes in both fiction and non-fiction genre. In her middle grade fiction series Behind the Open Door, she draws from her background in child behavior, psychology, and nursing to create an exciting, imaginative, mystical world in which children who are feeling misunderstood have a safe place to explore their special abilities. The Book of Light emphasizes the importance of appreciating others' differences, and fostering relationships through trust and compassion.

Her nonfiction work, The Soul Garden Pathway Discovery Guide is a self-help workbook journey assisting readers in discovering their life paths; and Between Shifts, a collection of vignettes in poetry drawing inspiration from her years in nursing service. She is also the author of the Soul Garden Pathway website where she pens daily blessings and blogs out into the world to offer hope and insight into life's challenges. www.soulgardenpathway.com

Born in New England, she resides in New Hampshire where she continues her literary work and spiritual life creating sanctuary space for all living things.

You may visit her website and contact her
at www.sallygallotreeves.com
https://www.facebook.com/BehindtheOpenDoorSeries
https://www.instagram.com/sgallotreeves/
https://www.linkedin.com/in/sally-gallot-reeves-b2011413/